# THE
# GOOD
# SISTER

# Chelsea Bolan

HARPER**AVENUE**

*The Good Sister*
Copyright © 2016 by Chelsea Bolan

Published by Harper Avenue, an imprint of HarperCollins Publishers Ltd

First edition

This book is a work of fiction. The characters, incidents, and dialogue are drawn
from the author's imagination and are not to be construed as real. Any resemblance
to actual events or persons, living or dead, is entirely coincidental.

HarperCollins books may be purchased for educational, business,
or sales promotional use through our Special Markets Department.

HarperCollins Publishers Ltd
2 Bloor Street East, 20th Floor
Toronto, Ontario, Canada
M4W 1A8

*www.harpercollins.ca*

Library and Archives Canada Cataloguing in Publication
information is available upon request.

ISBN 978-1-44344-241-1

Printed and bound in the United States of America
RRD 10 9 8 7 6 5 4 3 2 1

*For Tim, Gayl, Emmilee, and Eli*
*In memory of Michèle de Rham*

# PART ONE

Eres la flor azulita
hecha de la luz del cielo
Si tu te encuentras solita
porque no me das consuelo
porque no me das consuelo
eres ingrata prietita

You are the delicate blue flower
made of heaven's light
If you find yourself all alone
why don't you console me
because you don't console me
you are ungrateful, *prietita*

—from "Las Flores," traditional Mexican song

# 1
...

Papá wanted no sign of Gabriela. She wasn't his daughter, he said, never was. He wanted her presence erased, down to her name, which was not to spill through anyone's lips ever again.

It was a lot of work. She had existed for almost fifteen years, and soon it was evident there was very little she hadn't touched, very few things that did not remind us of her. So we spent an entire day clearing out, Papá keeping the fire in the barrel going morning till night, feeding it with Gabriela's things. We burned photos, piles of them—except for the photos Papá couldn't part with, like the ones of the family on the boat to Mazatlán, on the Sea of Cortés. From these we cut out Gabriela, threw her image into the fire.

We burned everything. School work Mamá had saved, baby pictures, all of her books, her clothes and shoes. We burned things that didn't burn properly, glass and metal, plastic and guavas and *dulce de tamarindo*. Plaster hand- and footprints. Videotapes, perfume, a watch, a stuffed bear holding a red heart. We burned ribbons and hair clips, a gold chain with a gold cross. Had Papá thought about it, he would've known it was futile—we'd have to burn everything to rid ourselves of her. We'd have to set fire to the house he had sacrificed so much to build, set fire to it with everything inside, including ourselves.

We burned the dress too, the only thing that seemed to affect Mamá. The entire time she wore her face like a mask while she gathered up remnants, *recuerdos*, and scraps of Gabriela—until Papá told her to get the dress. Her mouth began to twitch, then the corner of her eye. She pretended she did not hear him; she looked intently into the flames, poked at them with a stick.

It was easily the most beautiful dress I'd ever seen. White satin scalloping around the neck and shoulders, tapering down to the waist, billowing out. Tiny, pearl-coloured beads sewn into flowers ran all the way down. There was an accompanying veil that would cover the *quinceañera* in a sheath of white. All was nearly ready for her party, for all to witness her transformation from *niña* to *mujer*. The invitations had been sent, the DJ hired, the decorations and centrepieces made. The shoes had arrived from León for the ritual of the changing of the shoes—and the dress had arrived from Mexico City, sealed in plastic.

It was obvious Mamá didn't want Papá to remember the dress. She had hung it in the back of the armoire, hidden behind my dresses, skirts, and old school uniforms. But Papá wasn't someone who forgot, and after everything else had burned, he turned to her and said, "Get the dress." When she didn't move from the barrel, he said firmly, "María. The dress." She dropped the stick and walked slowly to the house. I followed her in.

Mamá opened the door to the old armoire, shoved my clothes aside, reached to the back, and pulled out the dress that Gabriela was supposed to wear in a little over a month. She laid it on the bed, unzipped the plastic cover slowly, careful not to catch the fabric, and peeled it away. She smoothed her hands over the skirt of the dress before picking it up and holding it tight to her chest. She burrowed her face into it. I thought she might be crying. I almost went to her then, to put my arms around her and tell her some lie. But in a single moment Mamá gathered herself up as she gathered the dress—draped across her arms like some dead girl—and carried it out to the barrel of flames.

After the fire died and the barrel cooled off, Papá scoured the house for anything that might have slipped past him. In Miguel's room he found a drawing Gabriela had made several years before. It was still up on the wall, a seascape with fish smiling just below the surface of the waves. She'd drawn a curtain framing it so it would be like Miguel had a window that looked out over the Sea of Cortés. He didn't want to give it up, I could tell by his face. I held my breath, expecting an argument, *wanting* an argument—but Miguel did not say anything. He only went to the picture, pulled out one tack and then another, taking his time. Papá tapped his foot. Miguel held the drawing for a moment, looking at it one last time before handing it over to Papá, and that was the end of it.

In our room, Papá pointed accusingly at Gabriela's old stuffed burro, but I told him it was mine. He said the walls had to be repainted. They were turquoise, the colour *she* liked most, and that would not do, so they would be painted over in plain white. Miguel and I spent the first few days of the new year painting, saying little to each other, keeping a silent vigil. It took several coats of paint to keep the turquoise from showing through, and between each coat we let the paint dry, watching Gabriela's favourite colour fade until it wasn't there at all.

Just when I could finally put my things back, Papá showed up with a bag of something that looked like dirt and twigs, and dumped it all over the bedroom floor. All I could think about was how I would have to clean this up, all this dirt, get on my hands and knees to scrub it out of the crevices between the tiles. He ushered me out, saying he was giving the room a *cleansing* to get rid of the evil spirits that might have seeped out of my sister's pores. I had to sleep on the couch for several days. "I don't want any trouble with *you*, Guadalupe," he said to me.

It was a pain: normally I would pass through our bedroom to get from the *sala* to the kitchen, but since this was not allowed, I had to go outside through the garden to get to any other part of the house. It was the way Papá had built it. Not much of a bedroom—the two arched doorways had no doors. It doubled as a hallway, everyone passing through our room several times a day. We'd grown used to it, but I often wished we could have had Miguel's room upstairs, the one he'd shared with Eduardo and Luis, before Eduardo got married, and before Luis went away to *el norte*—that we could have a place to go where no one would see us, where we could talk without being overheard, say almost anything.

When it was time, Papá handed me a broom. He nodded toward the room and said it should be safe now—he'd followed the *curandera*'s instructions to the very last. I swept up the dirt and branches, dumped the refuse into the barrel, scrubbed the floor, and tried to piece together our room as it had been before. I put clean sheets on the double bed we'd shared, smoothed it over with the white embroidered bedspread, put the mangy burro on the pillows, then hung the framed print of the Virgen de Guadalupe where it had always been, on the wall above the flowers and prayer candles on a narrow table. I pushed the low, mirrored dresser back against the wall, and on top of it, I placed my lone hairbrush, a stack of rubber bands, and a single bottle of perfume I almost never used. It looked so strange and spare without the hoard of Gabi's perfume bottles and her big jar of hair gel and pile of barrettes—all of those things had been thrown into the fire.

There had been a photograph as well, sealed under glass in a tin frame, of the two of us when we were last in Mexico City. We were just kids. We stood in the Zócalo, our arms around each other, the shadow of Papá on the ground before us, elbows out, taking the picture. Gabriela looked just like me when I was her age: stick-thin with knobby knees. The same needle-straight black hair just past her shoulders, ears that she hadn't quite grown into yet poking out of her hair.

The photo was no longer on the dresser, but I had saved it. I'd opened up the old burro, pulled out some fluff, and stitched the photograph inside. I missed seeing it there—the outline of the frame in the dust was all that was left. I drew my finger over the marks in order to widen them or make them more permanent, but it was a stupid gesture. It would mean nothing when the dust blew in from the desert and covered everything again.

The day Gabriela was sent away was also the day the president devalued the peso and the day Mount Popocatépetl erupted after seventy years of silence. Everything was suddenly worth less than before. The mountain emptied itself of ash, hollowing out; our pockets hollowed out too. And so did I. I became a shell.

That January, I turned nineteen. I let the day come and go. There was nothing to celebrate. What was another year? I could not keep warm those winter nights, not even with my head beneath the blankets. If I slept, I woke trying to kick her over to *her* side of the bed, but she wasn't there.

I lit a candle for her every morning and every night. I kept my vigil, never letting a candle extinguish until it had burned down to nothing on its own. I prayed to the Virgen with everything I had that she keep Gabriela safe, that she let no harm come to her. I crossed myself, knelt on the cold tile floor, clasped my hands together, and whispered: "O Nuestra Señora y Reina Virgen de Guadalupe, for whom I was named, who miraculously appeared to the *indio* Juan Diego; unblemished Guadalupe, I implore your help in all the needs of my family, beg the protection of your maternal heart on my *querida* Gabriela."

I lost the thread of the prayer sometimes, opening my eyes and looking up at the portrait of the Virgen in the big gold frame—her eyes always in shadow, her hands pressed together in perpetual prayer.

There was always a time in the night when everything finally went silent—when most people were sleeping, or pretending to sleep, when the roosters stopped crowing and the dogs stopped barking, when the wind stopped blowing and the palm trees were flat against the dark sky. It was the part of the night when the room would become unbearable and I had to get out. I would walk through the laundry hung on the criss-cross of lines, the sheets and shirts stiff and still as cardboard. The hill was always behind me, nothing but a shadow if there had not been the white cross on top. It glowed in the night; it glowed in the day. Every time I saw it I could not keep from crossing myself.

I would walk to the far end of the yard, check the wall for cockroaches before sitting down, and lean all my weight against it. I'd shiver, even with two sweaters—that winter I shivered even in the heat of the day. Feeling the solid wall against my back, that was when I would allow myself to cry, but quietly. I thought about where my sister might be, when and how I would see her again. Mexico, D.F., was my only guess, the capital city, where Papá was from, where some of our family lived, and where I was born. It was where he met Mamá. It was the place he had fled, leaving behind his old life, his past. That was the only place he could've sent her, into his past, where she did not exist. Back to a time before her.

# 2
...

Raúl Amador knew everyone was laughing at him. He felt it everywhere he went. Not to his face, but after he'd turned around and walked out the door.

*Did you hear about his daughter?*

*I always knew she was no good, the way she strutted in those short skirts.*

*How can such a* mala *come from such a good family?*

*Maybe not as good as we thought—*

Then the laughter—loud, irreverent. Mocking laughter. Mocking *him*, his good name, his family, after all he had done and how hard he had worked. That was what he got for giving up his whole life for them—for working sixteen-hour days all those years, six days a week, for saving them from the city, for building a house for them. For giving them a yard, a garden, an open desert—*entire oceans*, for the love of Christ. What more did they want?

Hadn't he raised his children better than this? Hadn't he taught *her* what it meant to be a young woman?

Now the town laughed at him as they had never laughed before, not even when Luis left for *gringolandia*. As though that were a better place. As though he hadn't had everything he needed right here. Just when things had begun to calm down, when people had begun to respect him again, this, Gabriela—

No, he would not use her name. He wouldn't even think it.

He would show everyone. He would not weaken for a moment. He had done all he could—he had sent her away, he had washed away all traces of her. Soon they would forget—but only if everything carried on as it always had.

If *he* carried on. So he slept without disturbances, woke early, ate everything his wife put on his plate. He laughed at jokes and made some of his own. He smiled brightly at the shopkeepers, the bar staff, the neighbours. He was impeccably dressed and groomed—not a grey hair shone through the dyed black, his moustache perfectly trimmed. He went to work as usual, every day except Sunday, to El Pescado Loco, the bar he owned that had made him so successful. Maybe not as successful as the Muñoz family, who ran a tour company and lived in a great house on the other side of the hill, but successful enough to be addressed as *Don*. To be called *patrón* by those who worked for him.

Maybe it wasn't enough. But when everything else fell apart there was always El Pescado Loco, still standing, still full of *turistas*, still bringing in more money than any other bar in town. It had withstood everything: slumps in the economy, a hurricane, even fire. When the bar next door caught fire, it didn't spread to El Pescado Loco, as if the building had an aura around it as protective as the glow around the Virgen de Guadalupe. He *had* had it blessed, after all.

He had opened the bar on Calle Morelos, the main strip, where locals cruised in their low-riders at night, trolling for gringas or *chiquititas*, calling out *"Ay! Mamacita!"* The street ran in one long, gleaming ribbon from the beachfront hotels to the bars and trinket shops, past the marina to end at the *mercado* where Mexican crafts and *recuerdos* were sold—where his son Miguel worked.

How hard he'd tried to get Miguel to do something else— to work at El Pescado Loco, or to work for himself, to add something more to the Amador name. Raúl had handed him opportunities: he could manage the bar or manage the liquor orders. But as it was, his son worked at a booth under a patch- work of *palapa* and tarp, waiting for *turistas* to wander by or a cruise ship to come in. The market was hardly better than a *tianguis*, the way it looked, slapped up like one of those instant markets on the streets of Mexico City, full of knock-offs. Miguel sold silver jewellery, little animals carved from semi- precious stones, *milagros* large enough to hang on a wall, T-shirts that said, *Whatever happens in Santo Niño stays in Santo Niño.*

When it became clear Miguel wasn't about to leave the *mercado*, Raúl told him to work toward getting his own booth. But Miguel preferred to work under another man—a man he had to call *patrón*. Raúl couldn't understand it. He had laid out everything for his sons, and they'd refused it as though it wasn't good enough for them.

Even Eduardo, his eldest, had disappointed him. True, he managed the best hotel in Santo Niño—five gold stars—but he was still a servant, working under others. And worse was that his wife, Ana, worked while their *hijos* were in school. She cleaned rooms in the hotel closest to the centre of town, La Bougainvillea, built like a hacienda, reeking of old Mexico. It was shameful, Raúl thought, that Ana worked as a maid. It was bound to damage the children, but Eduardo and Ana were both stubborn as a couple of burros and wouldn't listen, as if nothing Raúl said or did was good enough for them.

Certainly El Pescado Loco was good enough—it was an institution. It was undeniably the most popular bar in Santo Niño, the bar that people knew about as far north as Canada. It was the bar with the most stars in the tourist guides, highly recommended for its lively nightlife, dancing, *a place to rub shoulders with the locals*. It was always busy, even in the off-season. Even now, with the peso devalued and the economy slowing, even more *turistas* flocked south because they could get more for their dollar.

El Pescado Loco was impossible to ignore. Raúl had had it painted in the brightest colours he could find, sunset pinks and electric blues and greens, searing reds and oranges. It had been nestled between a surf shop and an *abarrotes* until that owner retired. The old shop reopened as another bar—an inferior one—called Ricardo's Place, which never managed to get more than three stars in the guidebooks.

Raúl remembered when he had first bought the sagging structure. It could hardly be called a building—it was more like a shack, part of it made out of concrete block, another part slapped together out of bamboo and tarp, the rest either open air or barely sheltered beneath a tattered grass *palapa*. It had been a hangout for fishermen after the catches were brought in for the day, where they'd get drunk and tell their tall tales, reeking of fish guts and sweat, their shirts stained with fish blood. Raúl laughed to himself, thinking their stench was probably the reason there was no real roof on the building.

There wasn't even a real floor. The table legs were shoved into the filthy sand to keep the tables from blowing over. Men threw down their lime rinds and ground out cigarettes there. The drunkest men used one corner to piss in, half-heartedly covering their mark with sand. Now and again they'd get a whore in there, usually a *fea* with buckteeth and a body like a can of Modelo. The entire place was uncivilized, a disgrace.

After he bought it, he razed it all. He let people take what they wanted, then put the scraps that had made the fisher-men's bar in the centre of the lot and set them on fire. He took out a bottle of tequila, had a drink, and passed it to the sad fishermen who'd come to witness the end of a segment of their lives. They all got drunk—Raúl too. They sang some old songs of heartbreak, which rose up and faded like smoke.

He'd razed everything but the hardwood bar inside. He didn't know where they could've gotten such a sophisticated piece. True, it was in terrible condition, weathered and salt-bitten. But he could see the beauty that was buried beneath the worn exterior. There were carvings along the sides, flowers, and swirls that were like waves. A *sirena* floated in the centre—a respectable *sirena*. Her long hair covered her breasts and curled around her fishtailed body. He worked on the bar for a long time, sanding it down and staining it, applying varnish until it gleamed like something he'd seen once through the windows of a fancy place in Mexico City.

Raúl built El Pescado Loco just as he had built his own house—out of concrete block, cement, and stucco, with his own two hands. It was a proper building, with huge glass windows and a real roof. A small patio opened out through glass doors on the sunniest side of the building, with a view of the beach on one side and a view of the marina on the other, but the patio itself was set back far enough from the street so beggars, street sellers, or *malcriados* couldn't harass the *turistas*. The floors were tile, not dirt. A *palapa* was built inside, but over the bar for ambience, not as a way to keep out the weather. The locals scoffed at him for building such an extravagant place, for putting on airs. But by then the gringos were already coming in droves during the winter, throwing money all over the place.

*Who's scoffing now?* Raúl thought. Everyone saw now that he was right, that he had been right all along. The locals thought he was some big-shot *chilango* coming to Santo Niño to show off, but really he'd been right. Now everyone was catering to the gringos, even the fishermen, shamelessly advertising fishing excursions, *panga* rides, glass-bottom boat tours.

He was proud of the name he had given his establishment. *Loco* was a word the gringos knew, a word they had already learned before they came down. Everything to them was *loco*: a price, a person, brain tacos, hot afternoon sun in December, no liquor sales on election day. *Pescado* was another matter, but Raúl had chosen it in honour of Santo Niño so that its origins wouldn't be forgotten: the humble start of a fishing village, not a single paved street, hardly a sturdy house. And now look at it. Richer than D.F. It was like the New World all over again, as good as *el norte*—no, better.

Just so it was understood, a fish was painted on the bar's sign, a great big, silly, green fish with an X for each eye, surrounded by bubbles. In one fin, the fish held a bottle—of what was unclear, but Raúl felt it got the message across to the gringos. That was enough to get them inside, and once inside, they would not be able to resist the dance floor, a professional wood floor at that. Not that it mattered much: people danced wherever they pleased, at their tables, on them, sometimes on the varnished circular bar. Raúl let them do whatever they wanted, kept the drinks coming and the music blaring from the speakers. Mostly eighties American rock, but also some Latin pop. He also threw in *rancheras*, *corridos*, some sad, wailing songs, and some salsa and *cumbia*. It seemed to be the perfect mix, keeping *mexicanos* as well as gringos coming to the bar, putting down peso after peso and dollar after dollar. That was the most important thing, to keep the American dollars coming. It was true he didn't like the ways of the gringos, and didn't like the way *mexicanos* acted around them, but he found it impossible to turn away from the money they waved about and slapped down on the tables.

The gringos, at least, were not laughing at him. They didn't know what had happened. They didn't know the girl had gone bad. Or if they did, they couldn't care less.

# 3
...

María Luisa Prieto felt like she was dying. Her energy was gone. Her eyes fell upon things that should not have been interesting: a shadow, a coffee cup. She got herself up in the morning when her husband, Raúl, was home, got herself up and made breakfast, everything he liked: *huevos, frijoles,* and a chunk of pork. She poured him coffee with hot milk, and listened to him talk about what was in the newspaper. None of it mattered to her, though she nodded when he said, "We'll have to be careful with our money, María," or, "Another *turista* robbed at knifepoint by some *malcriados.*" Not that he really looked at her. He'd rustle the newspaper, turn the page, talk to it instead.

When he finally left and she could not hear the rumble of his truck anymore, she set down the broom, the mop, the dish she was washing, or the basket of laundry, whatever she happened to be doing, and went back into the bedroom.

She shut the curtains. She pulled the tightly made bed apart, untucked the perfect corners, and crawled back into the sheets, where she stayed for much of the day. She was very tired. Guadalupe—her Luz—would do the rest.

Her first daughter. She had wanted to name her Luz, for light. Because she *was* light, her *rayito de luz* coming to her through any darkness. But Raúl had been intent on naming her Guadalupe, after the Virgen, so that her name would always guide her down the right path in life. Then Eduardo, Miguel, and Luis began to call her Lucy. But to María Luisa, she was always Luz.

The bedside candles she'd lit flickered shadows around the room. She would lie there with the sheet up to her chin, watching them move. They were like the shadow plays she had seen as a child. In her sleep she could feel the movements in the house around her, and sometimes they entered her dreams: Luz cleaning, or the telenovela, *La Mala*, the one she used to watch religiously, blaring from the kitchen. She could hear the frantic whispering of the forbidden lovers. Miguel coming in to check on her, poking his head through the door, asking her if she needed anything. In dreams and in real life, María Luisa would shake her head.

What could she need? What could she need except for the impossible?

She could hear her two children, the only two she had left, pass in and out of the house.

Once, when she was alone, María Luisa tried to sing, because she remembered the old song "Cielito Lindo," how it told her to sing and not to cry—*that* was the way to lighten a heavy heart. She hummed the chorus until the words found themselves on her lips:

*Ay, ay, ay, ay,*
*Canta y no llores,*
*porque cantando se alegran—cielito lindo—*
*los corazones.*

She thought maybe it *did* work. Singing pushed back tears, could make her heart so light it could leap into that pretty little sky—

*Cielito lindo!*

On to the next verse, she sang:

*Black-eyed morena,*
*eyes black as my luck,*
*look at me, although they—pretty little sky—*
*may bring me death;*
*for death I wait,*
*because never to see them again—pretty little sky—*
*I cannot do.*

She stopped suddenly. She had to stop. She tried not to think of the song again, but the words wove into her thoughts, reminding her of her misery, telling her it was true all along, what she feared: she was dying.

Watching the shadows spread across the wall, or staring at the cross on the hill or at the wet clothes in a pile, María Luisa thought back over everything. She stared at her life, the house, the garden, remembering when they first moved to Santo Niño, when her children were younger, playing in the yard, when the orange trees were just little twigs and the house only a foundation. She remembered how they bathed in buckets and cooked over fires outside, how hard it was after so long in the city. Sometimes she cursed Raúl for bringing them here. Sometimes she thought she would rather go back to D.F., where at least they'd had four walls, running water, and a roof overhead. But she knew here there was hope for something better—even if they had to camp out like vagrants.

There was some consolation in the fact that everyone in the new *colonia* lived this way, having only a parcel of land to live on, and no house yet. There were fires all along the crude dirt road and sheds of *lamina* and scrap wood—even cardboard and newspaper when the money ran out. They were from Mexico City and Zacatecas, Sinaloa and Jalisco, from all over the mainland. They were all in the same place, all on the ground trying to make something of their own in this new world.

They had all built the house together: Eduardo and Luis helped cement its block walls, one by one; Miguel, at five years old, mixed the cement and carried it in buckets to his brothers; even little Luz, a year and a half old, helped build the house, giving María Luisa the strength to live that *campesino* life, making her keep the fire going throughout the morning until lunch. Block after block, they created a life full of possibility. María Luisa's daughter would have chances she herself had not. Luz would be allowed to thrive, to become her own person.

This plot of land on the Baja peninsula was a blank page— they could draw whatever they wanted. Here they could begin again, across the Sea of Cortés, beyond the Sierra Madre.

María Luisa worked extra hard. She did men's work; she did women's work. Thinking that if she worked hard enough, she could make the life she wanted for her children. She made Raúl proud as she went from cooking breakfast to mixing cement in good humour, and she never complained about where they slept—beneath a shelter of tarp and *lamina* that Raúl had slapped up before she and the children arrived. Instead, it was her favourite moment of the day, with her body curled around Luz, her boys breathing all around her on their own flimsy mattresses, and Raúl on the other side of her, keeping her warm.

The house began to take shape and rise; the trees in the garden began to grow. They built the outer walls, and soon after they installed the gate, María Luisa's belly began to swell with Gabriela. It was all beginning to turn out as she had hoped.

After Gabriela was born and they finished the first floor, they could finally sleep in a place with real walls and a solid ceiling. It was free of dust—there were no cracks to let the desert air come through. They bought thick new mattresses and lined the concrete floor with them. The entire family slept together there until the other rooms were finished.

She woke in the night, baby Gabriela between her and

Raúl, the rest of their children scattered about the floor around them, deeply asleep. She was the only one awake. She lay in the dark and listened to the rise and fall of so much breathing, her whole family breathing. She had the odd thought that each one of them was like an organ inside a body, each one essential for the survival of the whole, all sealed up safely within the walls of the room they had built together.

The boys went to school in their blue and white uniforms, came home to play *fútbol* on the road. She remembered one evening in particular, when they had roasted a boar buried underground and made goalposts out of rocks in the road, Raúl dragging the heel of his boot in the dirt to carve out the boundaries of a makeshift *cancha*. They divided into teams: Raúl, Luz, and Luis on one side; María Luisa, Eduardo, Miguel, and Gabriela on the other. Raúl and María Luisa faced off at the centre. They smiled at each other, and María Luisa kicked the ball through to the goal, where Luis caught it with one hand. That match, nobody won or lost, not that she could recall, but they played until they were filthy and sweaty, until the boar was done roasting and they all gathered around to eat it.

As the finished room became a house, as the lime, *ciruela*, and orange trees finally stretched above their heads, providing fruit and shade, as clotheslines multiplied and festooned the yard with laundry like *papel picado*, her children grew. They did not always get along, but it was enough for her to see the small moments in which they bonded. Miguel and Luz came together over prayer or *fútbol*, and Luis took both his younger sisters by the hands and taught them dance steps out in the yard, between the lines of laundry. That was most precious to her: hearing the boom box blaring a *son* or a *cumbia*, looking out the window to see Luis twirling both sisters, the girls looking down at their feet. He'd instruct them in English—*Quick, quick, slow . . . quick, quick, slow*—and sometimes María Luisa would dance along with them in the kitchen.

In her darkened room, María Luisa's bones ached with exhaustion. She was always on the edge of waking and on the edge of sleeping, but never able to be fully in either place. She felt as though she were submerged in water—the clatter of dishes and silverware, the TV or the radio, the world outside, all these sounds dulled and distant.

It was not unpleasant, submerged and sinking like that. The lines that tethered her to her life were on the verge of snapping. It would feel good to let go. She let the candles burn down to nothing, snuff out.

Out of the dark an image would come to her like a buoy in the sea: A white room, sealed and locked, her family inside it, sleeping. The sounds of all of them breathing. She should never have let them out—she should have kept them in that room forever, the house perpetually unfinished. She should have kept Gabriela safe, wrapped her body around her like a wall.

# 4
...

El Pescado Loco was already packed when I arrived, the place full of tank-topped, sunburned *turistas* down from the cold North. Guns N' Roses blared from the speakers: "Paradise City." It was only six o'clock in the evening but people were already on the dance floor, bouncing about drunkenly. There were no more tables left. Many stood around the bar or along the wall, shouting and laughing and watching the dancers, downing Coronas, Sols, and Pacíficos. The bartenders, Sam and Jaime, were spinning around making drinks as fast as they could, barely pausing to greet me when I went behind the bar to put on my apron—black, embroidered with the same *pescado loco* as on the sign outside—and grab a notepad and pen. Isabel was running around like a *loca* herself in pink high heels, her frizzy hair falling out of its pins. I smiled at her as she darted past me with a tray of drinks. She frowned. "You're late!" she said, even though I wasn't.

Turning to the crowd, I nearly ran right into Papá, who was heaving buckets of ice onto the bar, sweat beading along his hairline. "Ah, here you are," he said, pointing to the tables in the far corner. "Those first." He poured the ice into the bins. "And be careful. You know how they are."

*They* meaning the gringos. He said this to me every time I came on shift, as though *they* were dangerous animals, ready to attack. As though I risked my life every time I took one of their orders. Maybe he blamed them for Luis leaving us—as if it wasn't a choice he had made but *they* had stolen him. They could be irritating, but no worse than anyone else.

At the table in the far corner was a group of boys around my age, white boys reddened with sunburn, blond hair bleached even lighter by the sun. I approached the table and smiled. "*Buenas noches*, señores," I said. "What would you like?"

"Bucket of beers," one slurred.

"A bucket of *mexicanas*!" said another, looking me up and down.

I kept my smile. I was used to this one. I responded the way I always did. "For that," I said, "you go out to the street."

They laughed, thinking I was a real sport. I rushed away to the other tables, to the bachelorettes giggling over their piña coladas, to some old retired folks who probably came down the Baja in their *casas*-on-wheels, to the couples from the cruise ships, who wore diamonds, constantly checking their shiny watches so they wouldn't miss the boat. There were whole families, the kids looking embarrassed and bored by their tipsy parents, some teenagers drinking margaritas because no one was going to ask them for ID in Mexico if they had dollars to put down.

I raced to and from the bar, picking up empties, hauling trays heavy with drinks, shouting over the music, and still smiling. Work took my mind off Gabriela, took me away from that house. For a few hours, I could forget everything but the present moment. But soon it was nearly eleven o'clock, time for me to go home. Papá didn't like me to be out late and had been a little stricter after what had happened with Gabriela. He was constantly telling me to *be good*. He attached it to everything these days: "Good night, Guadalupe, *be good*." Or: "*Be good* and help your mamá."

Of course I knew what he was getting at. His words made me queasy, but I never said anything. It was too late. I knew I wasn't good. I wasn't. I prayed to Dios he would never know, though part of me knew it was only a matter of time.

Eleven o'clock. Miguel would be out front soon, waiting in his red truck.

I was delivering a last tray of margarita *especiales* (two for the price of one!) to a group of college boys from San Diego when I saw Antonio Rodríguez walk through the door. I almost dropped the tray, but I steadied myself and set the drinks on the table. He took off his cowboy hat as he entered, revealing matted, greasy hair. His moustache tipped over his upper lip. He wore the same thing he usually did: a western-style shirt tucked into his jeans, held there by a heavy belt, the silver buckle gleaming in the smoky light. He settled down at a table in the back, one that was clearly occupied by someone else who must've been dancing and didn't notice or care. He cast his eyes around the room, perhaps trying to find someone to wait on him, but what he found was me.

In one hand I held the empty tray like a shield. The other was clenched into a fist. I imagined grabbing a bottle of beer from the bar, a shiny gold Corona, placing it on the centre of the tray, and carrying it to him, smiling. I would approach him like Santa Muerte, the beer glowing *sagrada* and holy. I'd say, "Here, Tío, take it." My smile would disarm him. He'd relax, might even think I liked him.

That's when I'd take the bottle of beer by the neck and smash it against the edge of the table and plunge the sharp end into his throat.

Antonio looked away. He wiped the sweat off his brow and settled his eyes somewhere else.

A man at a table to the right of Antonio whistled to get my attention. I turned away, went back to the bar, and dropped off the empty tray. The man whistled again but I was no dog. I combatted everything with prayer. *O Señora, help me . . .* But not even prayer, not even the noise, the shouting, the laughter, the reggae rendition of "La Cucaracha," could prevent Antonio's smooth voice from rising up through the depths of my memory, saying, "How's my favourite girl today?"

Papá was on the other side of the bar. He looked in the direction of the whistler, and seeing Antonio, quickly turned back to the piece of paper he had in his hand. I watched my papá's hands for a moment, his leathery knuckles, hands that were strong enough to build houses and tear them down.

They were shaking, just a little. I went around to where he stood, took off my apron, stuffed it beneath the bar.

"*Chao*, Papá," I said.

He glanced out the window. "Wait, *hija*—Miguel's not here yet."

"I'll wait outside," I said.

He glanced back at Antonio. "Wait over there." He pointed to a spot by the plate glass window, where he could keep an eye on me.

I went to the window to watch the street for Miguel, the bar noise at my back. I realized my whole body was shaking just like Papá's hands. I tried to calm myself. *O Señora, help me* . . . I felt the pressure of eyes on my back, afraid they might be Antonio's. *So turn around*, I told myself. *Turn around and go tell him what you think of him. Shame him in front of everyone.* But I couldn't move.

Outside, *turistas* passed by—happy couples hand in hand, groups of teenagers laughing and slapping one another's backs. Old man Pelón passed by with his bouquet of plastic-sheathed roses to sell to sweethearts. An *india* hobbled by with her two children in tow, each with a basket of *chicle*. A woman perhaps thirty years old pulled a bright green jacket around her shoulders against the chill in the air, then looked right at me. I'd forgotten people could see me there, behind the glass. She looked into my eyes, crossed herself, kissed her fingers, and walked on. It startled me—I didn't know why she had done that, until I realized my hands were pressed together in prayer.

My brother's truck pulled up.

"*Luego!*" I called out to Sam, Jaime, and now Ángel, who'd just come on shift. They all called back to me: "*Pronto!*"— what we always said to one another at the end of my shift, our call and response.

My feet crossed the threshold to the sidewalk; I was free for half a second. I jumped in Miguel's truck and slammed the door hard.

"Lucy," Miguel said, "easy."

"Go," I said. I stared down the street. I wanted to be already beyond the curve and into the darkness past the marina.

Miguel drove slowly, stopping often to let the hordes of *turistas* cross the street; his window was rolled down, his elbow resting there. I shivered and wrapped my arms around myself. "What's up?" he asked, glancing at me. He had Papá's wide mouth and thick, wavy hair, but he had Mamá's piercing black eyes.

I let out a long breath. "He was there. That *pendejo* was *there*. He came in and Papá did *nothing*."

"Who?"

I stared at him a moment, unbelieving. "*Who?*"

"Antonio?"

"Of course. Who do you think?"

"Lucy." He said my name gently, like a lullaby.

I didn't want gentle. I didn't want him to smooth this one over, the way he always did. "I want to kill him," I said.

Miguel turned onto the cobblestone road that would eventually give way to dirt, leading home. "You shouldn't say things like that."

"You *don't*?"

"Don't what?"

"Want to kill him?"

"Well, yeah," he said. "But that's normal. Gabi was my sister."

"*Was?*"

"No sister of mine would do that," he said. "We all know she wasn't the smartest kid, but . . ." He turned down our road: Calle de la Cruz. Over the hill, the sky was black.

"She's still my sister," I said. "She's always my sister, no matter what she did." Miguel said nothing. I looked down at my hands, folded tightly together in my lap.

"Listen," my brother said, pulling the truck to the side of the road. We were home, the tall yellow house peeking out above the walls and the black gate. He turned off the engine. "I don't like Antonio, either. Papá doesn't like him. But men are like this, and Gabi should've known better. She was raised in a good home. We gave her everything." He put his hand on my shoulder, trying to calm me, but I tensed with anger. "We all miss her, Lucy. But Papá is right. He *had* to do it. Gabi did not honour us. She can't be a part of us."

"She's always a part of me," I said.

"Don't let anyone hear you say that." Miguel opened the door. "Or people will think you're a whore too." He got out of the truck. I did not. I sat there smelling the dust burning off plastic, dreading going into our room again. I didn't know where I could go, but I couldn't stand the weight of the house, the silence, the weight of things that nobody would say but that hung above us, thick and corrosive as the air of the capital city.

# 5
. . .

Mexico City had been strangling him. It had been getting harder and harder to live and make ends meet, much less save for any sort of future. Decent jobs were scarce, rents were going up, and with another baby on the way, Antonio Rodríguez would never be able to save enough for a house— or for anything.

When he was a much younger man back in Durango, there had been so much talk about making a fortune in D.F. His father had moved their whole family here to take a better job, and for a while, life *was* better. Antonio found work right away in restoration. He worked long, tedious hours in *el centro histórico* restoring old, crumbling buildings, reinforcing the masonry. It was better pay than anything he could've made back home. But he was tired of living in cramped quarters with his family. He longed for the day he could marry, have his own place. He saved all the money he could, what he didn't give to his mamá or spend in the *cantinas*. There were so many *cantinas*, all kinds, all over the place, and in some of them they fed you pretty well depending on how much you drank, and sometimes a *puta* would walk in, looking for someone to buy her a drink.

He began to give less money to his family. "*Patrón* cut my pay," he said, handing over some bills, keeping the rest.

"Gracias, *hijo*," his mother said. Never questioning him.

Every day, he took the bus to the *pesero*, crammed with commuters, to *el centro* to work on those *chingados* buildings, doctoring them, babying them, applying mortar bandages. *Someone should just raze these things, build new ones*, he thought as he worked, the sun beating down on him, the city air scratching up his lungs.

Not that he was complaining. He was making money, saving for his own place, and the after-work rewards were more than worth it. How many clubs, *cantinas*, cabarets, strip joints, and underground brothels were there in this city?

"Here, Mamá," he said, placing the money in her hand, less than the week before.

"Gracias, *hijo*."

So his younger brothers would have to tighten their belts, eat a little less. They should be getting jobs by now anyway—even Ana was working, pouring coffee in a diner—and Papá's new job should be bringing in twice as much as before. Plus, he ate most meals in the *cantina* for free, so they should have more food than usual. Why was it all up to him to support everyone anyway?

His mother never questioned him, but he could feel her judgment.

Every day he was tied to a plank swing and hoisted up the face of a building, a bucket of mortar tied to him, tools in his belt. As he worked, he would keep one eye open for women passing by. One girl in particular. One beautiful girl with black wavy hair, in her school uniform, all white and navy blue, white blouse unbuttoned at the collar, knees he'd like to touch. On her way to school every morning, a good girl—a virgin, he was sure. He didn't whistle at her like he whistled at other women. He didn't cry out, *"Ay, mamacita, qué buena! Dame un beso!"* He silently watched her go by, bit his lip.

He couldn't get the girl out of his head, couldn't drown her out with *pulque* or tequila in the *cantinas*, or lose her in the *chichis* of women in the dance bars.

Her name was Cristina, and she wouldn't give in to him. It made him more crazy for her. He promised her castles. He would build her one like the one in Chapultepec, he said. He promised her jewellery and clothes from the United States. She'd raise an eyebrow at him and say, "We'll see, *chico*." Calling *him* "boy." Offering him her cheek to kiss, a glimpse down her shirt.

In the end, though, she *did* give in, and he'd married her. All her toughness fell away when he presented her with a ring with a tiny, glittering gem. *Women are weak*, he thought. *All it takes is something that sparkles, real or fake.*

Life was coming together. Antonio was on his way—a deposit paid on an apartment in a decent neighbourhood, a wife, his dreams within reach.

But then the earthquake came and knocked down a good chunk of Mexico City and Antonio's life. The buildings he had been working on collapsed, as if God had heard his complaint and agreed. Antonio's new apartment building shook and went down too, taking with it all the money he'd put into it.

Life went on in this way, and exactly in this way: his future continually robbed from him. As soon as he was back on his feet, the city rose up and knocked him down again. As soon as he was able to get a decent apartment for him and Cristina and their recently born son, prices went up. He lost his job. He had to pay back a loan. Cristina was pregnant again.

Years later, he still hadn't become rich, hadn't achieved anything. He still worked in construction and restoration, but had nothing to show for his hard work. He found himself longing for his old, dried-up *pueblo*, singing some of the old songs now and again. Longing for space and freedom—their tiny rental house was already cramped with three boys in two rooms, with a wife who'd grown fat and couldn't keep up with the cleaning. He found it more and more difficult to go home after working a long day of constructing houses for other people. Sometimes he pretended he was building his own home, putting up walls for so many rooms, but by the end of the day the pretending began to chip off.

He couldn't bear the thought of going home. After work he resumed his old life, went back to the days before he ever laid eyes on Cristina. Maybe he should've let her pass by.

He went out to the *cantinas*, the clubs, sometimes made his way to a curtained-off backroom with a *puta*. Many nights he came home just before dawn. He'd find his wife, tight-lipped, with circles beneath her eyes, and again with a swollen belly, making breakfast—so unlike the girl he had fallen in love with. She'd slam the pans around but say nothing to him. She'd burn his tortillas on purpose and toss them on the table.

He didn't deserve that, and she certainly didn't deserve the money he left for her every day, but it was his duty as a father and as a husband. So he took the cash out of his pockets and laid it on the table. He hoped it would shame her, the fact that he gave her his hard-earned money even when she treated him this way. He'd scoop up the egg in his burnt tortilla without complaint and chew slowly. Then he'd leave for work to build more houses, to break his back for a few pesos—

*He* was the one who did the work; why shouldn't he deserve some diversion, some sort of reward for his hard days?

Antonio had considered everything. He even thought of going up to *el norte*. He knew a man who could set him up with a job and everything in El Paso. There was a fee, of course, and if he could only save enough, be good and not go out so much—but it was more than that, he knew. There was always something they needed, a bill they were behind on, or the kids needed shoes or some damn thing.

Then came a call from Eduardo Amador Prieto, his brother-in-law. It surprised him, because he hadn't heard from Eduardo himself in a long time. It was always Ana who called, if anyone called him at all, to see how he was doing. His brother-in-law's voice threw him—it had some authority to it, and at first he thought it was his *patrón*.

"*Cómo?*" Antonio wasn't sure he'd heard correctly.

"*Hermano?*"

*Hermano.* Had Eduardo ever called him that before? He wasn't sure. Only his younger brother called him *hermano* anymore. Even Ana called him Antonio.

They'd begun talking more in recent years, Antonio and Ana. She'd made an effort to call and remember birthdays, keep in touch with his wife and kids. Before now, they'd never really gotten along. Throughout their childhood, she was headstrong, defiant, and never did what he told her to do. She never respected him or any of her brothers. She always made a point of giving their mamá more of her earnings than he did. She ran off with Eduardo to spite them all, to show them she had her own ideas about life. And Eduardo took her selfishly, without thinking about how Ana's departure would affect her family.

But here was Eduardo on the telephone, telling Antonio that Santo Niño was a better place to live, a new world— talking like a glossy tourist brochure. There was work; there was money. There was a parcel for sale down the road from their lot, where he and Ana had built their own house.

Ana and Cristina had apparently been talking to each other, because Eduardo knew too many details about his family's difficulties—many more than he himself had mentioned to Ana over the phone. Eduardo expressed worry about Antonio's boys, growing up without room to breathe, amid so many dangers of the city. "Come on out," Eduardo said. "I'll loan you the money for your ticket. See if you like it."

He was surprised, sure. But it was also about time. When had they ever thrown him a bone? Aside from the occasional package Ana sent, they'd never given Antonio's family a single scrap, even though *they* only had two kids, owned their house, and had money to spare.

Antonio had it in his mind at first to refuse it. He'd opened his mouth to say, *No, thanks,* hermano, *we're just fine without your charity.* But he looked around at his life, the cramped rooms, how tired and old Cristina looked. How tired *he* was. There was no future.

And Cristina had urged him to go. She told him to take the loan, to set aside any differences he and Eduardo had. It was worth it, to think of what they could build, and how it would change their lives.

When the day came, Antonio embraced his boys, told them to care for their mother. "It's time for you to be men now," he told them. He kissed his wife goodbye, put his hand on her belly. Promised her the world Eduardo had spoken of, the one from the brochure. Promised he would make a fortune, build them a house, and send for them as soon as he could. He picked up the small cardboard box he had packed with a few changes of clothes, and soon found himself at the Aeropuerto Internacional Benito Juárez, boarding a plane for the first time in his life.

# 6
...

Not long after they had moved to Santo Niño, while Raúl Amador was building the second storey of his house, he thought he saw something gleaming on the top of the hill. He set down his brick trowel and wiped the sweat from his brow. The gleam was still there, something white, something like a cross, but he couldn't be sure. He called to his wife, who was mixing more cement down below: "María! Look!" But by the time she looked up, and when he looked again, the gleam on the hill was gone. There was only a raggedy cloud disappearing in the heat.

He kept looking up to the top of the hill after that, wondering what it had been, wondering if he would see it again. Sometimes, when he closed his eyes to sleep at the end of a hard day, he would see it behind his eyelids: a white light gleaming on the shadowy hill of his exhaustion.

Then he realized it was a sign, a sign from Dios Himself, telling him, and only him—something.

But what? He thought of the *indio* Juan Diego, how he was walking one day when the Virgen de Guadalupe appeared to him. Her first appearance wavered like a mirage, her skin dark as a shadow, a *morena* herself. An *india*. Her whole body was haloed by a light so stunning it outshone the sun, her *rebozo* as blue-black as the night sky, and her voice—the story went—her voice as close as his own thoughts.

The Virgen told Juan Diego in this voice to build her a cathedral on the spot where she appeared, a cathedral in her name.

*A cathedral?* Raúl thought, shaking his head. But this was nothing like that.

He spent days thinking about the light on the hill, each time exaggerating it a bit more in his mind, the gleam becoming a light to compete with the sun. Maybe he saw arms outstretched. Maybe he smelled roses.

Raúl told his neighbours the story: A flash of light caught his eye. Everything went still. There was a sound like bells . . .

*A cross appeared on the hill, a cross made of light . . . Then disappeared into cloud.*

His neighbours glanced up at the hill with admiration, but the cross of light never appeared again. The more Raúl recounted the event, the more he understood. He knew what he had to do.

Everyone on the unnamed street came together one Sunday after Mass to build a cross of wood, painting it white. It was as big as the one Jesús had to carry, big enough to be seen for miles. They hauled it up the steep hill thorned with cactus, brambles, and scorpions. It took several men to carry the heavy white cross; others hauled shovels, buckets of cement, and paint for touch-ups.

As they neared the top, their arms and legs scratched and bleeding, Raúl waited for the miraculous to happen. He knew it would—a *milagro*, an appearance of the Virgen herself, or a field of roses at the crown of the hill. Maybe Jesucristo would alight on the cross. But at the top, as they dug the hole and poured the cement, nothing happened. They created a scaffold out of their bodies to prop up the cross until the cement held, and nothing happened. They retouched the scrapes on the cross with white paint—and still nothing.

There were no roses or anything else to indicate that something holy had happened. There was nothing but a ratty blue blanket blotched with white paint, spent cans of beer, lime rinds, candy wrappers, and chip bags.

# 7
## ...

I was a little late. I was busy saying prayers. I lit another candle, got on my knees, and prayed to the Virgen—for Gabriela, but also to keep Antonio away. I didn't know what I'd do if I saw him again. I was afraid that maybe I *would* kill him, or at least try to. I knew I should feel ashamed at those thoughts, but I didn't. I was worse than anyone knew, far from anything my name suggested: *O unblemished Guadalupe, sin manchas* . . .

Not that he didn't deserve it. Though Gabi never confided in me about exactly what had happened between her and Antonio, I knew he'd hurt her because of the way she acted. The confused look that came over her face, the sudden tears, how she couldn't sleep. I asked her to tell me what had happened, but she'd only shake her head. Once, just before Papá sent her away, she opened her mouth as if she was finally going to tell me, but nothing came out, no sound, no message, no matter how hard I listened.

I caught a *pesero* to *el centro*, then ran the rest of the way to El Pescado Loco, rushed through the door, threw on my apron. When I turned around, I ran smack into Isabel. She was wearing purple lipstick, thick eyeliner, and a low-cut black shirt. "Watch it, *chica*," she said. "You're late again. Your papá's looking for you."

And there he was, coming toward me. "Guadalupe," he said, slightly out of breath. "Where have you been? I need your English." He pointed to a table with a man sitting by himself, a *norteamericano* by the look of him. "He keeps trying to tell me something. Find out what he wants."

Papá always sent me to wait on tables he couldn't understand. When I wasn't there, he sent other bar staff to translate, since everyone knew some English—but no one's English was worse than Papá's. When he didn't understand something, he'd venture, "Beer? Margarita?" More often than not, those words worked.

It was because of my older brother Luis that my English was any good at all. It had been one of my worst subjects at school, but he sat with me every evening working out the equations of words. Luis had always been good at English, and he got better when he began to work at the bar and have American girlfriends. They taught him well. He always said to me that there was a whole world out there, not just Mexico, not just *español*.

The *norteamericano* wore a plain white T-shirt and a pair of khaki shorts. He had a face that reminded me of an *águila* or a hawk, partly because of his beak-like nose. His hair was dark, nearly as black as mine, but it was curly and stuck up all over the place. "Sir?"

He looked up from a notebook. His eyes were a very pale blue.

"Can I help you, sir? My father, his English is no good."

The man laughed. "Not for lack of trying," he said. "I know you're busy, so I'll make this quick. I'm writing an article about the effects of the devaluation of the peso, particularly on the economy of Santo Niño—"

I stopped him. "Wait—about *what*?"

"*Discúlpeme*," he said. "*La . . . devaluación del peso y sus efectos?*"

"I understand," I said. "Go on."

"Basically, I'm interviewing some of the business owners around here, and I'd like to interview the owner of El Pescado Loco. That's your father, right? Raúl Amador?"

"Yes," I confirmed. "That's my father."

He scrawled something in his notebook. "Unfortunately, I'm not able to communicate very well with him. Usually I can get around in Spanish, but he doesn't seem to understand my accent, or maybe it's my vocabulary? Anyway, could you ask if I could interview him?"

"I can ask him."

"Tomorrow morning?" he asked. "And could you be here too? Otherwise, I doubt we'll get very far."

"I can," I said, "if he wants to do the interview."

"Understood." He handed me a business card, which I glanced at before putting into my apron pocket. He was a reporter from the *San Francisco Times*.

He extended his hand. "Paul O'Connell."

I shook his hand. "Lucy Amador."

"*Mucho gusto*," he said, writing my name down in his notebook.

"Why are you writing that?" It was beginning to unnerve me, how he wrote everything in that little book, like he was watching and judging.

"So I don't forget," he said. "I'm terrible with names."

I felt a hand on my shoulder—it was Papá. "What does he want?" he asked me. When I told him, Papá's face lit up.

"*Sí, claro*," he said to me, then repeated it to Paul in a much louder voice.

# 8
· · ·

When Antonio Rodríguez first arrived at Ana and Eduardo's door, he noticed that Ana looked him over cautiously. He had not seen his younger sister in years, not since she had run off with Eduardo. There was something different about her. Perhaps her eyes were darker, or maybe it was the lines around her eyes and mouth, a mouth that frowned at him. Maybe it was the glasses—she'd never worn glasses before. He didn't know what it was. Finally, she addressed him, "Antonio," extended her hand, and invited him inside.

"How are Cristina and the boys?" she asked, taking his hat.

"Fine, just fine," he said.

Dinner was waiting. Ana and Eduardo's two children, a boy and a girl, both around the age of six or seven, were trying to get a look at their uncle, but their curiosity was overcome by shyness and they took to hiding behind their mamá. The inside of their house was swept and clean, nothing out of place. They had four rooms, with the option to build a second floor if they needed, if there were more children. The metal rebar stuck out from the rooftop, just in case. Unfinished stairs led to the roof, where Ana hung out the clothes to dry. *She's a good woman after all*, Antonio found himself thinking, eating the chicken *colorado* she had made, looking around the impeccably clean house. He remembered how she was before— maybe *that's* what was different—how headstrong she'd been, like a wild horse. But now she did not argue; she served him and treated him kindly, and she obeyed Eduardo's every word.

After Eduardo had married her, Antonio thought that he should warn him, even if Eduardo had gotten what he deserved. "My sister is very difficult. She's going to give you nothing but trouble and grief." And Antonio had been right, at least for the first year. He'd heard from his parents that the newlyweds argued and argued, even after the birth of their first child. But somehow that had stopped. Antonio marvelled at Eduardo. And their children, so well behaved and clean—so unlike his own.

How was any of this possible? He'd never seen a household that was so calm. Maybe Mexico City scrambled brains, and that's why Antonio and his wife argued so much, why their life felt like chaos.

He looked at his sister across the table. She was wiping her son's mouth with a paper napkin. "Ana," he said. She looked at him, and he tried to find her eyes through the glare off her glasses. He felt the need to tell her something, compliment her in some way, let her know that he approved of the changes in her. She'd finally learned, even if it had taken far too long. "You're a good woman," was all he could say. She looked at him curiously, as if he'd said a very strange thing.

Eduardo agreed with him. "She certainly is. There's no one better than Ana." Yet Antonio found it odd that after supper it was Eduardo who cleared the table while Ana took the children into the *sala* and sat them down on the couch with their schoolwork. "Why don't you read to your *tío*?" she said to the kids, then she went to the kitchen. They opened their books but just stared at him, as if paralyzed by fear. He smiled at them until his sister returned with glasses of brandy and a plate of cookies, set everything on the little table, and sat across from him. He raised his glass. "*Salúd*, Ana! To family."

"To family," she said, and clinked her glass against his.

"I know you've been struggling over there," Eduardo said to Antonio the following morning, as they walked the perimeter of the lot. "Ana and I were talking about how much better it could be for you all if you just had the chance to start over here."

*Struggling?* Well, maybe that was true. But he couldn't help but feel a surge of anger. Sure, he'd told Ana over the phone that times could be better, but he had never gone into great detail. It made him wonder yet again just how much his wife had been telling Ana behind his back. Complaining, in the way that women do. It was humiliating that people thought he couldn't take care of his own family, that high and mighty Eduardo could just swoop in and take care of everything, and rub it in Antonio's face.

He didn't have the money to put down on the lot, and by the time he saved enough money, it would be gone, bought by someone else. It was a prime lot at a good price. Eduardo knew this, and was offering to put up the down payment, which Antonio could pay back in instalments. Until he paid back the down payment, the land would be owned by Eduardo. It was humiliating, but as he walked the lot, something inside him began to ease. The thought of it: his own piece of land, room to breathe.

Antonio mulled the offer over, swallowed his anger. It was worth his pride, he decided, the chance to have his own place. He ran his fingers over his moustache, nodded, and said, "Okay, *hermano*."

He stayed with his sister and brother-in-law at first, though as the weeks went on, he was only there for meals. He was busy. In that time, he found work in construction, building a hotel, began paying back Eduardo, and spent the rest of his time on his new plot of land. There were only a few houses here and there, and the rest was desert, with cacti as tall as he was. He put up a fence around his plot right away, put in the wooden posts, and unspooled the wire. He needed to mark it, to know it was his. He felt a strange, irrational fear that the land would be taken from him as swiftly as it had come to him, as if the desert would absorb the lot back into itself. He spent a good amount of time walking around his property, checking the fence. Only then would he allow himself to imagine and dream, to begin planning. Where exactly would he build the house? How many rooms, and how tall? If he built it high enough, he might be able to see the sea.

•••

One Sunday, the first of many, Raúl invited Antonio to his house beneath the hill with the cross. It was wonderful to relax for once, to sit out in the garden, looking up at the big two-storey house that was painted a sunny yellow, drinking Modelo in cans served by Raúl's two beautiful, long-legged daughters. Raúl had a house like the one Antonio wanted to build. Sitting there, suddenly everything he had thought he would never have was within his reach. A veranda on the top floor—why not? A few citrus trees, maybe a pen for chickens, a couple of cages for fighting roosters. He'd gone to the cockfights as one who bet, a player, but what would it be like to be the owner of a prized fighter?

"Here, Tío, take it." It was Gabriela, calling him *tío* in her sweet voice. The girls called him uncle though he was really their brother-in-law—the age difference granted him the title. Gabriela cracked open the can of Modelo for him, squeezed the lime, and even took a salt shaker from her pocket and salted the top of the can.

"Gracias, *angelita*," he said. She *was* like his own little angel for the moment she stood by him, her smile wide, before she skipped back into the house. He watched her disappear through the doorway to the kitchen, where María Luisa was cooking chicken, the delicious smell of it drifting out of the house, making his stomach growl.

"Antonio," Raúl said to him in a voice that meant business. He'd taken off his Sunday Mass clothes and put on shorts and a too-small, faded T-shirt that said Guns N' Roses on it. It was the only day of the week he dressed like this.

"*Don*," Antonio said.

"My good son Eduardo invited you here because of your family's problems in D.F.?"

"Problems? Well, sir, it's not easy, but—" Antonio felt his throat tighten.

"It's not your fault. You can do everything right and work hard and nothing happens. It's the city. It eats up all your hard work."

Antonio nodded, gulped down some beer. "A good, hard-working man can barely get up on his feet," he said.

"Exactly," Raúl said. "I can tell you a lifetime of stories about that . . ."

And Raúl *did* go on to tell him of his hard childhood, his life of struggle as an orphan, how he had finally made something of himself with the help of strangers, and on and on, but Antonio wasn't fully listening. He was watching Gabriela as she came out into the yard and pulled white sheets out of the washer, hanging them on the line, laughing at something Guadalupe had said.

"I was able to open my own shop," he heard Raúl say. "But still, with a family . . ."

"Yes, sir," Antonio said. "My children are suffering. My wife is suffering. I break my back every single day, and nothing I do helps their suffering. And now a baby is on the way." He took a dramatic swig of beer. "But you give me inspiration. I hope to one day be like you, Don Raúl." He saw Raúl's face soften. "And you weren't too proud to accept help when you needed it. That's something I need to learn." He looked down at the mouth of his beer can, the salt stuck around the edges.

"I was a lot like you when I was your age," Raúl said, looking out at the cross on the top of the hill.

Soon anything Antonio needed came to him. He needed a truck, and a truck was arranged by Don Raúl Amador. He needed timber and *lamina* to build a temporary structure to live in, and Raúl put him in contact with the right people, got him discounts. When he was short of money, Raúl loaned him some. Sooner than he had imagined, there were bags of powdered cement and piles of sand and concrete blocks—the makings of his very own house.

Antonio spent most of his evenings in the nightclubs and bars where men and women mixed, where the gringos and the locals danced together. He hadn't been in Santo Niño very long when he realized it might truly be the paradise Eduardo had told him about. Here the gringas sought *him* out, made him dance with them, tried to talk to him in their funny Spanish. But mostly they didn't need to talk. All they needed was to press up against each other, sway to whatever music.

His first was a blonde from Los Angeles. She dragged him onto the dance floor, grabbed his hands and put them on her body. He wasn't sure at first, wondering if she was a whore, wondering if he could afford it. In D.F., the white girls, and especially the blondes, were more expensive and typically out of his range. He didn't drop his hands, though, and when she asked him for his name, he knew she was drunk, the way she slurred the words. She wasn't a *puta*, she was just a gringa. She let his rough fingers climb up the front of her shirt right there on the dance floor, not caring who saw them. Soon after, she led him across the beach back to her hotel. That was when Antonio realized he could get anything he wanted, and he could get it for free.

# 9
...

When Papá and I got to El Pescado Loco the next morning, the sun was just beginning to stream through the windows. It was a different place entirely in the daytime, quiet, contemplative, full of light. Jaime showed up shortly after we arrived to scrub down the bar, hang the clean glasses, and wash the windows. I made some coffee, poured a cup for Papá, then one for myself, and sat down beside him at the bar.

That morning Mamá didn't get up at all. Usually, she was up before I was, making Papá breakfast, pretending that all was well, that she was the good wife she'd always been. After he left she'd go straight back to bed, shut herself in. But this morning she stayed in bed, telling Papá she had a bad stomach; she didn't even try.

"Can you believe it?" Papá was saying to Jaime, who was polishing the bar. "A big American paper wants to write about us!" He blew on his coffee.

"It's about all of Santo Niño, Papá," I said quietly.

"He didn't ask all of Santo Niño—he wants to interview *us*! El Pescado Loco will be even more famous! Six gold stars!" He nudged me with his elbow as though we were in on some private joke.

Outside the window, women were scrubbing the flagstone sidewalks with brooms and soapy water. They did this morning and evening, even though dust was always in the air, waiting for a place to settle. A water delivery truck rumbled by. Just after it passed, I saw the reporter, Paul, across the street, checking for traffic before crossing.

Papá saw him too. "Guadalupe, how do you say *bienvenido* again?"

"Welcome," I said.

Papá muttered the word over and over. He smoothed his hair and ran a finger over his bushy moustache. He checked to make sure his shirt was tucked in. Just as Paul walked through the door, Papá slid off the bar stool and put on the biggest smile I'd ever seen on him. "Wallcome, señor." He beamed, holding out his hand.

Paul thanked him and shook his hand. "*Buenos días*, señor," he said. He looked at me. "Good morning, Lucy," he said.

"Good morning. This is my father, Don Raúl Amador, and that is Jaime García Pérez." Paul and Jaime shook hands.

As we settled around a table, Isabel burst through the door. "So sorry!" She'd left her hair loose and slightly wet—it fell in a frenzy just past her shoulders. She squeezed between me and Papá. Her perfume washed over the table. "Nice to meet you!" she said to Paul.

"Nice to meet you too. Let's get started." He pulled a small tape recorder, a notebook, and a pen from his black bag.

"You have no drink!" Isabel said, horrified. "You people have such bad manners," she said to us in Spanish. "Lucy, get him something."

"Would you like some coffee?" I asked Paul.

Isabel nudged me and whispered, "Coffee! What's he going to think? At least put some brandy in it."

"Isabel," Papá said, putting his hand on her shoulder. She calmed down and began to study her fingernails.

"Coffee would be great," Paul said to me. "Leave out the brandy, though."

I went to the bar to get him a cup. He waited until I returned, pushed a button on his recorder, then explained that he wanted to get a sense of how the devaluation of the peso had affected us. Paul asked his questions to me, and I translated them for Papá.

Papá just waved his hand in dismissal. "That," he said, "doesn't bother *us*. We are going as strong as ever." He cleared his throat. "And we always will. I own the building, the land. The banks can't take it."

That was the only question he answered quickly. For every other question, Papá took a long time contemplating his answer, then he'd compose himself and begin, "Well, señor, you see . . . " in a stuffy, self-important tone. He'd veer from the question asked, take a road that led back to himself and his humble beginnings. I translated everything as best I could.

Paul: "How many years have you had the business?"

Papá: "Well, señor, you see, it's been many years since I came here as a much younger man to start my business . . ."

And Papá launched into his Story: how he had been orphaned at the age of ten and was eventually taken in by a family who owned a restaurant and taught him the value of hard work in the face of hard times—

"Papá," I interrupted, "you're going too fast. I can't keep up—"

—he lived in the city for a long time—how he loved the city when times were good and he had money to spend, so full of energy and movement; before he met María Luisa, he was out dancing every night until five in the morning— he could dance the *son* and the rumba, the cha-cha-cha like no other—

"Papá," I said again. I craned around Isabel, trying to get him to see me, to bring him back to where we were.

He stopped talking, looking around the room as though trying to place himself. He broke out of his Story and looked directly at Paul. "I came here for a better life for my family," he said. "Everything I do is for them. In Santo Niño, there is more for them. More of a future. We make our own economy—and the cheaper the peso, the more tourists come—so there is no loss. It's always like that here." He cleared his throat. "Here I can have a good business, make money, own land, give my children more opportunities."

I didn't say anything for a minute. I held Papá's words in my mouth. I didn't know how to begin to translate them. How could he say such a thing when he had just thrown his daughter out of the house? Finally, I said, "I came here for my family. Everything I do is for them—"

"The man," Isabel interjected, "good man. *Un buen hombre.* He give people the *segundo—Cómo se dice?*" She looked at me. "*Tiro?*"

"Shot," I said. "He gives everyone a second shot."

"Second shot," Isabel repeated. "*Dile el cuento del Ángel.*"

"She wants me to tell you about Ángel," I said to Paul.

"Sure," he said, tapping his pen against the notepad.

"He's a boy Papá hired. He's a little—well, rough. He used to be in gangs. He's had a hard life. He has no papá, and his mamá is a prostitute. He cleans up the bar. My father wanted to help him."

"See?" Isabel said. "A good man."

With that, the interview was over. I cast my eyes down to the table, at the scratches across the wood. They made a map of lines that didn't make sense and didn't lead anywhere.

Paul returned his tape recorder and notebook to his black bag and pulled out a camera. He asked if he could take some photos, which caused Papá to puff up his chest and Isabel to pull a lipstick from her purse, checking herself in the mirror of her compact. Even I smoothed the hair that had loosened from my braid behind my ears.

"How about here?" Paul said, motioning toward the bar.

We sat on bar stools, Papá in the middle, Isabel and I on either side of him. Jaime was behind the bar, behind us. Paul took a long time with the camera, looking into the eye of it, moving dials and levers.

After a few pictures, Papá said to Paul, "*Usted y yo, amigo,*" doing all kinds of pointing to make sure that Paul understood.

"Sure," he said. "Would you mind, Lucy?"

Before I could answer, he handed me the camera. It was heavy in my hands, much larger and fancier than the little camera Papá had, the one he'd used to take the photo of Gabriela and me in the Zócalo. This camera had a longer lens, like the ones some of the *turistas* brought, with levers and dials and all kinds of numbers in red, white, and green. I held it stupidly in my hands. "I don't know how," I said.

"It just looks complicated," he said. He showed me how to focus the lens and read the light meter, how to adjust the shutter, which button to push. All these new words baffled me. It was a new language, and all these numbers and dials were like trying to solve some sort of equation. "Take your time," Paul said. Papá was growing impatient, I could tell by his heavy sighs.

Paul took his hands off the camera, letting it go into my own hands. I adjusted dials, checked the light, not sure I was doing anything right. I said, "I think I have it," even though I was sure I did not.

Papá and Paul stood by the bar, Papá's arm around his shoulders, like they were old friends. I almost laughed at such a thing—Papá having a gringo friend. He used to punish Luis for having gringo friends.

Isabel said, "Me too!" and squeezed between the two men. I held the camera to my eye. I adjusted the lens, putting them all in focus, then out of focus again, seeing Papá in a smear, his features blotted. And Isabel blending into him in a blur of colour. I kept it out of focus like that for a while. When I turned the lens, suddenly everything was clear, precise. The glasses glistening above the bar like a chandelier. The lines in Papá's face, Paul's eyes taking on a tinge of sadness. Isabel with a secret in her smile. There was something in all of them I hadn't seen before. I didn't know what it was. Something I could see through the camera that I couldn't with just my bare eyes.

I pressed the button, and it was over. I handed the camera back to Paul, feeling a little disoriented.

"Did it make sense?" he asked.

"I think so," I said. "I wonder what it will look like." I wondered if having the photograph to stare at for as long as I wanted would help me understand what I had seen.

"I'll send you a copy," he said, "and I'll send you a copy of the article. Here, write down your address." He took out his notebook again.

As I wrote it down, where we lived on Calle de la Cruz, Papá slapped Paul on the back. "You're welcome here anytime. When you come to Santo Niño, you come here. Okay?"

I wondered if Paul knew this was just for show. He handed my father a business card. "Thank you. And the same if you ever come to San Francisco."

Isabel stood on her toes to reach Paul's cheek. She left a purple lip print where she kissed him. "Bye!" she said. "Come back!"

Paul said he would, then he turned to me. "Actually, could I hire you for a couple of hours to translate for my last interview? I'm not confident that I'll be understood very well," he said.

"What's he saying?" Papá asked when I didn't immediately translate. I told him, and Papá ran his fingers over his moustache. I knew what he was thinking. He couldn't trust a gringo alone with me, but more than that, he wouldn't be able to bear what people might think or say if anyone saw me, and so soon after Gabriela.

He shook his head. He spoke loudly and slowly, I supposed for Paul's benefit. "Guadalupe has a lot of work to do today. My son Miguel might be able to help you, though. His English is good. Guadalupe, tell him where to find Miguel."

I explained, drawing a map to the artisan *mercado* in his notebook, an X marking the spot where Miguel's booth was. "If you get lost," I said, "ask for Miguel Amador Prieto. Everyone knows him."

"Right," he said, studying the map. "The market. I've been there."

"You'd better go, Guadalupe," Papá said. "Your mamá is probably wondering where you are." He paused, smoothing his moustache again. "Tell her not to worry about *comida* today—Isabel and I have to get the books in order."

I nodded, thinking about Mamá. I knew she wasn't wondering where I was, nor would she be worried about *comida*. I moved toward the door.

"It was nice meeting you," Paul said to me, extending his hand. But I was already out of reach, and it would've been awkward to go back.

• • •

I walked down the flagstone sidewalk, nodding at the washerwomen as they scrubbed. I walked through their soapy water, tracking my dirt. It was already warm; the women sweated in the sun. I did not. Somehow I still carried that chill within me. I turned off Calle Morelos and took a shortcut through the plaza, then took the road shaded by mango trees. Around the bend, the trees gave way to low desert plants, and I could see the hill we lived beneath, dry and faded, the cross washed out into the sky. I thought about the camera the whole way, wondering what all of *this* would look like through the camera's eye: the hard green mangoes, the sky, the garbage in the ditch. What would it reveal? I thought about what I had seen through the camera, trying to recall the image again. Paul looking straight ahead, Isabel's sly half-smile, Papá's arm around her shoulders.

Then I remembered how, when Isabel arrived, Papá had put his hand on her shoulder and she'd quieted down. I stopped walking. I began to see images from the past couple of years like a stack of snapshots flipping by me: how Isabel always sat close to Papá, her arm against his, the knowing looks they gave each other, all those times they had to *get the books in order*, all those times Papá was late or didn't come home at all.

*How could I never have seen it before?*

A cold wind whipped in from the sea, stirring up dust. I felt sick to my stomach. I looked at our hill with the cross in the distance, leaning against the sky. I wanted it to rage the way Mount Popocatépetl was raging right now, ash plumes and mud flowing down the sides like blood. But the hill was silent, calm.

I stood still for a moment, knowing I'd have to go home eventually. That was the hardest part: I would have to go home with no one to talk to about this, or anything. Gabi was gone; the house would be empty and quiet, Mamá in bed. But there was still Luis, up in his niche in *el norte*. If only I could get a hold of him. I'd already written him a letter after Gabi was sent away, telling him what had happened, asking if he'd heard from her. I'd tried to call him a few times as well, but each time I'd only gotten one of his roommates. I walked the dirt roads to the super-mini near our house. I looked both ways and, seeing no one, walked across the street to the pay phone around the back and slipped a card into it. We didn't have a telephone at home, but even if we did, I wouldn't have wanted Mamá to hear what I had to say. I dialed Luis's number in San Diego. I listened to it ring across so many lines, all the way to *el norte*.

A click sounded—a connection was made. My heart began to pound in the cage of my chest. "Hello?" I said quickly. "*Bueno?* Hello? I need to talk with Luis, please." No answer.

After a moment, I heard a voice on the other end of the line. "Hello? Luis?" The voice ran over my own—it was an answering machine that had picked up, not a real person. It wasn't even Luis's recorded voice, but one of his room-mates, telling me in both English and Spanish that nobody was home.

# 10
## ...

Luis was always dancing. No matter what happened, no matter what rules Papá imposed upon him, no matter how many girls went away with other men, or went back home after their vacations, never to return, he could always dance. Even when Papá fired him from El Pescado Loco, he took the day as an opportunity to work out his steps for an upcoming competition.

Luis was the only one who would really disobey Papá. Papá would say, "I don't want you hanging out with gringos," and Luis would go make three new gringo friends just to spite him. Or, "I want you home by midnight," and Luis would come home at dawn. He took the beatings Papá gave him, took them as a punching bag would, showing nothing. Never breaking or giving in, and never fighting back, as though that would be stooping to Papá's level.

He never obeyed and never seemed to be affected by anything Papá did to punish him. When he was fired from

El Pescado Loco, the next day Luis went to Ricardo's Place and instantly got a job waiting tables and DJing on the weekends. Then there were the dance competitions he frequently won, bringing in a little extra money, not to mention *chicas* and admiration.

Papá said he had fired him because of the gringos. Luis talked to them too much, danced with the gringas, made them laugh just a little too hard, and—worst of all—he made friends with them, often going out with them after work, going on snorkelling trips with them, hanging out on the beach like he was a *turista* himself.

*Flojo*, Papá said. Lazy. "He'll never amount to anything the way he spends all his money and throws away his days. People will think I never taught him anything."

It was just that Luis loved talking to the gringos, all of them, from Canada and the United States, from Germany, France, and England, asking about their lives, what it was like where they lived. He talked to them at their tables, bringing drinks and asking questions, and more often than not he was invited somewhere with them, out to dinner or on a boat trip. He taught them how to dance; he taught them Spanish words. They gave him English words he'd never learned in school, and new words altogether, in French or Italian or German. Invitations were extended to him from all over the world—he could've gone to live anywhere.

But he had fallen in love with a girl from San Diego, a *turista* down with her parents, an Alta Californian.

Papá forbade Luis to leave, but he was a grown man, the same age then as I am now—nineteen. Though he couldn't be sure the relationship would work out—and it didn't—he was planning to leave us for *el norte*, to leave Lower California behind and begin again in Upper California.

I remember hearing a yelp, like a dog had been kicked. I woke, leaving Gabriela in bed. She hadn't heard a thing and continued snoring softly. By the time I reached the kitchen door I could hear the dull thuds of punches, yelling. I ran out into the yard to see Papá and Luis falling to the dirt. In the dark it was hard to see what was going on, but I knew it was serious. I was ready to run out there, put my body in the way of Papá and Luis. I was afraid Papá would kill him. Papá's yelling didn't sound like him at all, but like an animal had taken possession of him, wore his body like a coat. The sky began to lighten—a deep blue easing into the black—and I saw Luis sitting on Papá, punching *him*. That's why Papá was yelling the way he was. They both got on their feet again, Papá landing some punches, Luis taking those as he always did but this time hitting back. Both had blood streaming from their noses, dripping onto their shirts. Then Papá had him—he'd caught Luis's head beneath his arm, locking it there.

Mamá grabbed me, dragged me indoors. She ordered me back to bed, but by that time it was daylight, and though she locked the doors, she couldn't keep me from the windows. I saw Papá slam Luis against the wall. I held my breath and waited for the inevitable blow. But all he did was look my brother in the eye for several long seconds before he let go.

Later that same day, Luis left home.

# 11
...

I turned down Calle de la Cruz and saw our fifteen-year-old neighbour, Carlos Salvador Nieto, in the middle of an imaginary *fútbol* match, weaving the ball past an invisible opponent. He nudged the ball along, then kicked it hard against the side of the wall that enclosed his family's property.

He and Gabriela used to watch for each other out their windows. She always had her eyes on the furniture store his family ran out of their house for any sign of Carlos. They'd pass notes to each other—in fact, for a while I was the one who passed the notes, until Mamá caught me. I stood there, watching him play, trying to imagine what he must think of what had happened.

When Carlos saw me, he kicked the ball up into his arms. "*Buenas*, Lucy," he said.

"*Buenas*," I said, walking past him to my gate, but he followed me. "What is it?"

He shifted from foot to foot. "*Oye*, Lucy. I—" He reached into the pocket of his baggy shorts and pulled out a stack of envelopes, Gabriela's name written on them in what must've been his best cursive handwriting. "Can you get these to her?"

I looked at the envelopes and shook my head. "I'm sorry, Carlos. I can't."

"*Favor*, Lucy." He pushed the envelopes toward me. "They're really important."

I didn't know how to tell him I didn't know where she was. So I took them and said, "I'll see what I can do."

I didn't know what I was supposed to do with the letters. In my room, I dug through the armoire and pulled out a box of shoes—direct from León—I had never had any occasion to wear because the occasion was to be Gabriela's *quince años*. I placed the envelopes beneath the shoes and closed the lid, burying the box beneath the other shoes at the bottom of the armoire.

The door to Mamá's room was still closed. I creaked it open, saw that the lump in the bed was breathing, and closed it again. There was work for me to do: dirty dishes were heaped in the sink, the garbage was overflowing, the floor was in need of mopping, and a pile of dirty laundry was waiting for me by the washer outside. I did it all. I couldn't stop thinking about Papá and Isabel as I opened the washer, threw our dirty clothes in. I went to the big plastic water barrel and filled a bucket to pour into the washer, but I was so distracted I splashed water all over my feet.

I collected the clothes that were baked stiff on the line, pulled them down and threw them over my shoulders, feeling their roughness. I began to yank them off the line, not bothering to unpin them, just pulling—until I ripped one of Papá's good shirts. I cursed, threw the pins on the ground. I told myself to be more careful, but really I wanted to rip everything down, line and all, throw it all into the dirt. I wanted to go inside and smash all the dishes against the walls until the shards covered the entire house.

I was shaking. I went to the portrait of the Virgen de Guadalupe. I lit another candle, clasped my hands together, and sank to the floor. I didn't know what to say. Finally, I closed my eyes and whispered, "Help me, Señora."

I could not find in myself the place of silence I needed. I kept hearing the outside world: a water salesman calling from the street through a bullhorn, *"A-gui-ta!"*; a child crying next door; kids playing *fútbol* down the street. Roosters crowed, dogs barked, and I could not find any words to send as a prayer to the Virgen. I could not gain control of the thoughts in my head, all the things that needed petitioning.

If I couldn't speak, maybe the Virgen would still understand. I looked at her. She was barely visible. The glass reflected everything in the room, reflected light glaring in from the open window. I stood up, looking more closely at the portrait, my own face on the surface now. The Virgen, like a drowned queen, was down at the bottom, her face completely in shadow.

Mid-afternoon I circled the harbour, walking on the dock beside the moored sailboats and yachts. The smell of oil and gasoline was in the air, fish and salt. *Turistas* wore straw hats,

drinking and laughing on some of the boats. A group boarded
a catamaran—a salsa-dancing, snorkelling booze cruise. The
guys who ran the boat called everyone *amigo, amiga*. I walked
toward the artisan market ahead, the lunch I'd made for
Miguel in my hand. I had to talk to somebody, and since it
could not be Luis, it would have to be Miguel.

I stepped from the dock into the cool shade of the tents,
weaved my way through the tables of merchandise. Jewellery,
mostly—Mexican silver, semi-precious stones. But there
were also seashell wind chimes, T-shirts, black velvet wall
hangings, beach towels, and clay turtles with wobbly heads.
There were pottery bowls and papier mâché fruit. Bottles of
pure vanilla. People who ran the booths greeted me. "*Ey!*
Lucy!" I waved at them, smiling as though all was right with
the world.

Finally, I made it to the booth where Miguel worked.
He was in the middle of a sale, so I hung back and leaned
against a post. He was trying to convince a *norteamericana* to
buy a silver necklace, saying to her, "For you, amiga, special
price."

"That's what you all say," the woman laughed.

I couldn't take my eyes off her—nobody could. She was
taller than anyone there. Miguel looked ridiculous beside
her. She had on a pair of high-heeled sandals. She wasn't
afraid to be so tall, to stand out. She wore a sheer lime green
dress over her bikini. Her golden hair was twisted high into
a knot. Everyone in the market who could see had his eye
on her; the ones toward the back were taking turns sneaking
glimpses of her.

I could tell Miguel was taken. "No, really," he said. "You're my amiga. But okay. I give it to you for $140."

She shook her head, smiling. "I thought I was your amiga! You'd rip off a friend like that?"

Miguel laughed. "Okay, you're right. One twenty."

They went on like that for a while, everyone wondering how low Miguel would go. In the end, she wore him down to a mere forty-five dollars. I knew what things were worth. He wouldn't be making any money on this transaction, and after he paid his cut to the *patrón*, he would lose money.

He didn't seem bothered by any of it. In fact, he seemed happy. He beamed at the woman, boxing up the necklace. She was like a *sirena*, singing to young men, luring them. They couldn't help themselves; they did her bidding. Miguel handed over the necklace, and she bent down to give him a quick peck on the cheek. Then she was gone.

Miguel was still smiling when I approached. "Hi, Lucy," he said. He looked at the bag in my hand. "I already ate. I didn't ask you to bring lunch, did I?"

"No," I said. I set the bag down behind the table of merchandise. "Someone else can eat it."

"What's going on?"

"I need to talk to you," I said, pointing toward the parking lot.

"Sure." He whistled to the kid in the neighbouring booth. "Watch my booth, okay?"

We walked through the parked cars, stopping on one of the concrete islands. "What's up?" he asked, squinting in the sun.

"It's Papá," I said. "I think he's . . . he's . . ." I didn't know how to say it.

"He's *what*?"

"Sleeping with Isabel," I blurted. I looked into my brother's face, noticing the creases around his eyes, lines a much older man would have, not someone who was twenty-three. But nothing shifted in his face when I told him the news. He didn't even blink.

"Lucy," he said, putting a hand on my shoulder. "That's been going on a while now."

"You mean you knew."

"Of course I know," he said. "Everyone knows. I'm surprised *you* didn't know. I mean, Papá's always had someone on the side."

I wanted to spit on him.

"Come on, now, Lucy," he said, trying to comfort me. "It's not the end of the world."

"What do you mean, *everyone knows*? *I* didn't know. Does Mamá?"

Miguel nodded. "It's just the way Papá *is*. Before Isabel, it was Sandi, and before her it was Julia. And after Isabel, it'll be someone else."

"And this is okay with you?" I almost shouted it.

Miguel looked around. "Keep your voice down. It doesn't matter if I think it's okay or not—it's just the way it is."

I rubbed my hands over my face and looked up into the sky, the burnt-up blue, the pelicans flapping, the vultures circling.

"Come on, Lucy, you're not a baby." Miguel mopped the

sweat from his brow. "This is how things *are*. A lot of men do the same thing. It's not just Papá."

I said nothing, keeping my eyes on the sky. I couldn't look at him.

He sighed. "It's hot. Let's go back."

I didn't move. From the concrete island, I watched the birds rise up and over everything. Miguel began to walk across the pavement, then stopped. "Lucy. Come on," he said. But I was not going to. I was going to stand there until I burned black in the sun.

"Miguel! Miguel!" A boy was running toward us. "Miguel!" he called. "There's a gringo here looking for you!"

In the shadows of the tents, I could see Paul chatting with the kid who was watching Miguel's booth. He pointed toward the parking lot, and Paul turned in my direction. He smiled and waved. I stepped off the island and walked back.

By the time I got there, Paul had explained to Miguel why he was there. I added some minor details. Paul pulled an envelope out of his bag and handed it to me. It had my name on it. "I wasn't expecting to see you," he said, "but I'm glad I can give these to you in person."

I opened the flap and pulled out the picture I'd taken that morning of everyone at El Pescado Loco. I stared at it, amazed. I could see every line on my father's face as if his story were mapped there; I could see a loneliness in Isabel's, even beneath her smile and bright colours. Papá's hand on Paul's shoulder, nearly clinging. The light through the windows gracing everyone. The glasses glowed over them all, hundreds of tiny halos.

"How did you get it so fast?" I asked. "I just took this."

Over my shoulder, Miguel said, "*You* took that? Wow— nice, Lucy."

"There's a one-hour photo shop," Paul said. "You know it?" I shook my head. "Just near the entrance to the marina. I'd finished up the roll and didn't want to make you wait. I could tell you were anxious to see the photo. What do you think?"

In my hands, the photo was trembling.

"I don't know what I think," I said. But I knew it meant something.

The three of us walked out to Paul's rental car, a white Volkswagen bug, typical of all the rental cars here. I squeezed into the back seat; Miguel sat up front.

Papá had said I couldn't translate for Paul, but he didn't say I couldn't go with Miguel. And Miguel did not say no. Still, I felt like I was betraying Papá. But I kept thinking about Gabi and I kept thinking about Isabel, about Mamá alone and sick in bed, and I saw all the ways he had betrayed *us*.

As Paul pulled out of the parking lot, Miguel asked him, "Do you know where you're going?"

Paul turned right. "No. Not really. I still haven't got this place down yet. And nobody seems to know street names."

"We don't need to know street names because we know all the streets," Miguel said.

"That makes it hard for foreigners like me." We were driving around the marina now, merging onto Calle Morelos. "I ask people and they say, 'Oh, go toward the mountain with the white cross on top, then take the road that goes to the hill that looks like a hat.'"

Miguel laughed. "Everyone always says go to the mountain with the cross. Everyone can find that. That's why we get so many lost tourists in our barrio."

We were passing by El Pescado Loco now, and though I told myself I didn't care what Papá thought, I turned away from the window just in case, not wanting to be seen.

"You probably saw me driving around more than once." Paul stopped at a red *Pare* sign and glanced down at a map.

"What are you looking for?" Miguel asked.

"The Hotel Santo Niño," he said.

Miguel sat straight up, alarmed. I did the same thing.

Paul continued on, oblivious. "It says it's on Cortés, but then there's no road to get to Cortés." The car behind us honked. Paul waved in the rear-view mirror and drove straight.

"Why do you want to go there?" Miguel asked. "It's a no-good place."

Paul glanced at Miguel, then at me, trying to read us. "I'm interested in *all* aspects of this town's economy," he said, "legitimate and underground. That includes the so-called dark sides. I want to talk to the people there."

Miguel shook his head. "Why? I can tell you everything you need to know. It's a place for drunks and *putas*."

"*Putas*," Paul repeated.

"You know—what's it in English—"

"Prostitutes," Paul said.

"Yes, prostitutes. But not so nice." Paul laughed, but he was the only one. Panic was rising up into my chest and throat. *A no-good place*, I thought over and over. *A place for drunks and* putas.

Paul stopped at the only traffic signal in the whole town of Santo Niño.

I kept thinking that Miguel would tell him no, that we weren't going, but Miguel directed him left. "If you're looking for women, amigo, this is not the place."

"No," Paul said, "I'm not looking for women—it's not like that. But I do want to talk to them."

Miguel glanced at him. "Are you Canadian or something?"

"You're about the seventh person to ask me that," Paul said. "People think I'm either Canadian or Swiss. But no, I'm not. I'm from California."

"You're not like other *californios*," Miguel said.

"You mean I'm not from Los Angeles," Paul said, swerving to avoid a gigantic pothole.

"Turn right," Miguel said. Paul turned down a deeply rutted dirt road.

Then we saw it, the dingy, three-storey hotel dead-ending the road. It had been pink once, but the paint was flaking off, the building turning the same shade of brown as the dust. There were two sad palm trees framing the entrance, a greasy glass door with stick-on reflective coating. The Vacancy sign flickered in the window. Paul pulled off to the side of the road and parked.

There was nothing there besides the hotel, not really, other than the lean-to with overturned buckets in the yard. There were a couple of shacks made of *lamina* and newspaper, and there was a partially built structure on the other side of the street that looked like it hadn't been worked on in quite some time. There were piles of sand, blocks, and broken bags of cement meant for a building someone had never built. Dogs were nosing in the ditch. A man stood near the hotel, in the shade of a scraggly palm, staring right at us.

"Are you sure about this, amigo?" Miguel said.

Paul nodded. "It won't take long."

Miguel glanced back at me. "This isn't a good place for Lucy," he said. "She shouldn't go in."

I didn't know what would be better: going in or sitting alone in the car, a rental at that. I wouldn't have my brother, and if anyone saw—

"It doesn't look like a good place for *anyone*," Paul said. "But we sure as hell aren't going to leave her in the car." Paul gestured in the direction of the man beneath the palm tree.

Miguel looked at me, then at the man. Neither option was any good. Paul watched us. I knew he didn't understand. Not really. He understood there was something at stake, but he thought it was safety. It was more. The responsibility was pinned on me now, what was left of our name.

"Stick close to me, Lucy, okay?" Miguel said.

I nodded.

"Ready?" Paul asked.

"Yes," I said.

We stepped out of the car, Paul and Miguel on either side of me, and walked toward the entrance. The dogs pricked up their ears, pulling their heads from whatever they were eating. Hesitating, watching, they eventually put their noses back to the ground, allowing us to walk by. The man stared at me, never pulling his eyes away.

It was the *way* he stared, watching me as we walked to the door, leering, looking me up and down like Antonio sometimes did when he drank too many beers. But it was worse.

Inside, the lobby was dark and grim, stale with cigarette smoke, lit by the blue light of a TV up in the corner of the room. The reception was terrible, showing only ghosts of images with lines running through them, the sound fuzzing in and out. There was music and laughter coming from a room with a red-curtained entrance.

We made our way to the front desk. I was trying to hide behind Miguel, which made the man behind the desk laugh. He was an older man in a stained white T-shirt, with grey stubble on his face. "Need a room, eh?" the old man said, still laughing. But Paul explained who we were and why we were there, Miguel translating, and the man sat up a little straighter, putting on the button-down shirt that was draped on the chair behind him.

I heard only bits of the conversation. Paul asked about the business, the same kinds of questions he had asked us. I could hear the old man saying, "Business can only increase . . . This is the number one hotel for budget travellers . . . " as though it were coming from a radio. "We offer clean rooms, and even some . . . eh . . . *entertainment*." Now and again, I felt Miguel looking at me. At first I thought it was out of concern, but then he'd nudge me and ask me for words he didn't know or had forgotten. "Hey, what's the word again for *divertido*?"

"Fun," I said flatly. "You know that." I realized how into

the translating he was, focusing solely on words, trying to do a good job, forgetting where we were.

Paul took the camera out of his black bag, asked if he could take photographs. I thought the old man would say no, but he puffed himself up with a kind of pride, checked his shirt for wrinkles, smoothed his hair. He tried on smiles, then opted for no smile at all. Who was this man? No matter how he presented himself, the camera would show something else. I stared at the lens, Paul's finger on the button. He'd already focused in on the man, then he took the picture, took another.

The old man allowed Paul to take more pictures of the hotel, and said he was more than welcome to get to know everyone and have a drink. "On the house, amigo."

I inched behind Paul as he took photographs of the lobby, wondering what he was seeing. I tried to imagine what the sofa and TV would look like through the lens, and whether there was any beauty at all to be found if you framed the room a certain way. Or maybe there was more ugliness. Either way, I wanted to know.

Paul turned around and looked right at me, surprising me. I had forgotten I was a part of this scene, this room. I had forgotten I was following so closely.

He held out the camera to me. "Do you want to take some pictures?"

I nodded and held out my hands, and he placed the camera into them. I felt its coolness, its weight.

With my eye to the viewfinder, I felt relieved, like I was in my own place, like the camera was my own room. Removed from this hotel just enough. For a while I did not press the button, only looked. I looked at the lobby in pieces, framed it in rectangles, blurred some of it out, and focused some of it in. I looked at the man, who was still beaming on the other side of the desk, saw that he was an old man who'd been disappointed by life. Or so it seemed to me, behind the glass of the lens.

And behind the glass were also curtains, and through a part in the curtains I could see a bar, thick ribbons of smoke tangling in the red lights, men dancing with women in tiny dresses, hands all over their bodies.

I took pictures through the part, of the prostitutes and their swaying drunks. All it took was a flick of their fingers to get a man out to the dance floor. I took pictures of a man and a woman at the bar, pressed close to each other, side by side, sipping shots; of men slipping cash between breasts; of kissing; of those engaged in conversation. I took pictures of Paul and Miguel at the bar, talking to people there, fitting into the scene as men, as if they were clients.

A young man in a suit was talking to a girl. She was a *morena* with dark, smooth skin; she still had baby fat around her cheeks that no amount of makeup could mask. Her hair was long and black, left loose, falling to her waist. She smiled and laughed, tossing her head back dramatically. The man sometimes toyed with the gold cross around her neck, stroking his finger along the chain.

I backed away. I stopped taking pictures and backed out of sight against the wall, thinking of Gabriela and the gold cross, the one that appeared around her neck one day, the one we had burned in the barrel.

# 12
...

Antonio Rodríguez had been calling his wife less and less. He was tired of listening to her cry—and she cried every time he called. He sent money every week but couldn't bring himself to call every week as he had promised. It was always one thing or another, he told her. He'd been so busy working all the time and making a fortune and building the house. But nothing he said would make her stop crying.

"*Ah, mi cielo*," he'd say. "Don't cry. *Canta!* I'm over here building our future!"

She would talk about the baby pushing at her, the pain that made her stay in bed, the boys getting into all kinds of trouble, how prices were going up every single week, the cost of food nearly doubling in some markets since Antonio had gone away. And they had gotten notice of a rent increase that they couldn't afford.

"Don't worry, *mi vida*, I'll send more money!" he'd say.

But she'd cry, "Antonio, I don't care about money. *No me importa.* Come home!"

*Not care about money?* That's all she had complained about for years, how he didn't give her enough money. And hadn't she encouraged him to come out here in the first place? But he bit his tongue.

She went on, complaining about everything she had just complained about all over again. The baby was due in less than two weeks, and what was she going to do?

"*Ah, mi cielo!* I'll call my mamá—she'll come help you."

That made her cry harder, her sobbing echoing through the line.

"Your very own house, *cielo!* Your very own. It's coming along quickly now. Soon I can send for you."

But really he hadn't gotten very far on the house. He had finally figured out where on the lot he wanted to build it. He had just begun clearing cacti and shrubs. He couldn't decide on a floor plan, though, and drew things out only to change them the next day. He discussed it often with Eduardo and Raúl, trying to decide. He talked to the architects that Raúl invited one Sunday after Mass. They showed him all kinds of plans, but nothing was quite right.

He didn't tell Cristina this. He told her the first floor was almost finished, hoping that would cheer her up. She didn't stop crying. Crying like La Llorona, the weeping woman, flooding all of Mexico City with her tears.

After he had hung up the phone, he got into his truck and drove to the Amador house to spend the rest of Sunday with them. Her crying had made him angry, riling him up until he was cursing her under his breath, calling her an *ingrata*, a *pendeja*, a *quejona*. She'd never even thanked him for the money. She'd never thanked him for anything.

As soon as the cross on the hill was visible to him, he felt better. He could find everything by this cross, following whatever roads brought him nearer to it, and soon he recognized the super-mini on the corner, the furniture store, the Amador house behind the wall and the black gate.

He glanced at himself in the rear-view mirror, smoothing out his moustache with his fingers. He grabbed the plastic bag with the *regalitos*. He brought little gifts with him every Sunday for the girls. This time he had a tiny picture of Jesucristo in a bottle cap for Guadalupe, and for Gabriela, some *dulce de tamarindo* and a stuffed bear holding a red satin heart.

Gabriela ran out to greet him. "How's my favourite girl today?" he said as he always did. She beamed at him, leading him through the gate after the customary handshake and kiss on the cheek, her hand small and soft in his, pulling him to where her papá and her brother Eduardo sat in the shade beneath the orange trees, drinking beer. And almost immediately he received many claps on the back from them, and a beer appeared in his hand.

He handed out the gifts. "For you, Guadalupe," he said, handing her a tiny paper bag. "And for *la hermosita* Gabriela," giving her the stuffed bear and the *dulce*.

Guadalupe always thanked him solemnly, out of duty, but Gabriela appreciated any little thing he brought her, throwing her arms around him with a "Gracias, Tío!" He hugged her too, liking the feel of her against him. He never held her for too long, just enough to inhale her scent and to hear her laughter in his ear.

# 13
* * *

The crowd at El Pescado Loco was exceptionally boisterous. Most people were already drunk from a day of hot sun and beach and beer, or simply caught up in the enthusiasm of others, dancing stupidly to American rock or trying to get their hips moving when a salsa song came on. *Norteamericanos* pulled Mexican women onto the floor for these songs, unaware of how ridiculous they looked, the *mexicanas* just going along with it, blinking their dark eyes at them in mock admiration.

I was strangely fascinated by these people from the North. How loose their morals were, how they did not care what anyone thought, women still in their bikinis with dresses barely covering them, letting *groserías* fall from their mouths, not even thinking about what they were saying. They drank until they were bleary-eyed and swaggering, the women drinking just as much as the men. Couples would disband, husbands allowing their wives to press up against anyone under the guise of dancing, the husbands doing the same. And everyone always laughing. I couldn't understand it, often wondered if this was what America was like, wondered if this is what Luis saw every day all around him in his barrio in San Diego.

At some point, I'd grown used to it. But that night I found myself staring again. Staring at all the men and women groping each other on the dance floor, touching each other in ways that reminded me of what I had seen at the Hotel Santo Niño. I tried to push through as I always did, my tray of drinks and notepad in hand, pushing through the oblivious crowd.

Then there was Isabel, on some sort of rampage, worse than usual. She scowled at me, telling me to work faster. Couldn't I see that it was busy? I kept my face even and said nothing, pushed past her.

"Answer me when I talk to you!" she called after me. I handed over my mixed drink orders to Jaime, grabbing the beers myself. I was trying not to think, but I kept seeing Isabel and my father together. I shook my head hard to get the image away from me. I felt a hand on my arm.

"Everything okay, Lucy?" It was Ángel. The boy unnerved me, the tear inked at the corner of his eye, the teeth crooked in his mouth. Still, he had always been kind to me, had gone out of his way to be kind, particularly since Gabi had been sent away. Papá made him wear long-sleeved shirts to hide his tattoos, but you could still see the vague outline of them through his white sleeves. Besides, they were all over his hands.

I smiled at him. "I'm fine, Ángel."

"You sure?"

"I'm just tired."

"If you ever—" He stopped, trying to work out what he wanted to say. "If you want to talk . . ."

I nodded. I did want to talk to someone, but not him. "Thank you, Ángel."

He half-smiled, like he wanted to say something more, before slipping away with the bag of trash.

Isabel slammed her tray on the bar. "Just standing around now?"

"Waiting for drinks," I said, not looking at her.

"Waiting, waiting, always waiting," she said, throwing her orders at Jaime.

Jaime put the margaritas and daiquiris on my tray. I picked it up, unable to keep my arms from shaking.

"Don't drop it now," Isabel said.

All night I tried to keep everything steady, but I was unnerved. I found myself thinking of Antonio, almost wanting him to walk through the door again so I could put that broken bottle through his throat. I imagined waiting at his *lamina* shack when he came home drunk and putting a knife in his stomach. Or maybe it wouldn't be me at all, but someone would jump him on a dark side street, rob him, slice his throat. It was wrong to think these things, but I couldn't stop myself.

To my surprise, Paul walked through the door. I hadn't thought I would see him again—we'd said goodbye, *chao*, adios. I thought he was already on the plane back to San Francisco. He carried that same black bag. He was looking around the crowded room.

I set down my tray and went to greet him. "I can get you a place at the bar," I said.

He shook his head. "I'm not staying long. I was actually looking for you."

Isabel passed by with a full tray, giving Paul a huge smile that showed all her teeth. I took out my notepad, pretending I was about to take an order. "Why?" I asked.

"I want to talk to you about something. Do you have a minute?"

"It's really busy," I said, jotting something on my notepad. Though I was acting like a waitress, I felt like Paul, taking down notes for a story.

Paul seemed to be looking around for a place to sit and talk, and I was looking around for Papá. But more people were crowding around us, the dance floor expanding beyond the parquet to the tiles. "You have to tell me here," I said. "I'm sorry I don't have—"

"I understand," he said. "This place is insane!"

I laughed. I was used to it, but for a moment, I saw it as Paul must have.

"I want to tell you something," he said, leaning in to me so I could hear him over the noise. "You have a real talent for photography. Look at what you've done." He handed me an envelope with the photos I'd taken at the Hotel Santo Niño. I looked at the top one, which was edged on one side with red curtain, opening to a man and woman leaning in close, talking, with smoke woven above them in a way I'd never seen smoke look before. I glanced through the rest—the lobby, the disappointed old man—feeling something oddly like joy rise up in my chest. I put them back into the envelope and handed it back to Paul. He shook his head. "Those copies are for you." I thanked him and put the envelope into my apron pocket.

"They are much better than anything I took, and I wanted to ask you if we could use them in the paper."

"Of course," I said, trying to be calm, but I felt flustered. I just wanted Paul to go. I saw Isabel looking at me from across the room, so I nodded to no one in particular and held up a finger to Paul, went to the bar, and grabbed him a bottle of Pacífico. I put it in his hand even as he shook his head and said no thanks.

"Please," I said, "I have to look like I'm working."

He laughed, put a ten-peso note into my hand, sipped the beer. "Okay, I'm sorry. I'll be quick. I think photography could be a good thing for you. I mean, your photos, without any training, are great. And I see that you have a—I don't know what it is, but something changes in you when you have that camera."

I thought about that a minute. "Something happens," I began, "when I look through the camera, you're right. It's like I see the world without ..." I couldn't figure out what it was. I took the envelope back out and looked at the first photo again. What made this different from what I saw with my own eyes? It was a client and a prostitute. A man and woman. Two human beings. ". . . without judging it," I said.

He dug into his bag and pulled out the camera. He held it out to me. "Take it," he said. "I want to give this to you."

"Oh, no," I said, shaking my head. "I can't." I glanced around to see if anyone was watching. The bar was crowded with colour and movement and noise. Faces were everywhere, but I couldn't find any that were pointed at me. I couldn't find Isabel, or Papá.

"Take it for payment, then. For the photos." He unravelled the strap and tried to slip it over my head.

I backed away. "I'm sorry," I said. "I really can't take it." The ten-peso note was still in my hand. "Let me get your change."

But I didn't move. I looked down to the notepad again, but my eyes drifted back to the camera in his hands. I wished I could keep it, wished I could say yes. He didn't understand what it would mean, what people would think if he gave me such a gift and I accepted it.

I looked at it again, the numbers along the lens, the buttons, the word *Canon* written on it. Canon, like a weapon. I wanted to see through it again, wanted to see what it would show me. But it was more than wanting.

I reached for it. It was warm from Paul's hands. I put the strap over my shoulder, tucked the camera under my arm. "Thank you," I said. "Thank you very much." I kept my eyes cast down, blinking them dry. Finally, I could look at him.

"Use it," he said. He checked his watch. "Now I really have to go. Take good care, Lucy."

"Goodbye," I said. I took the beer bottle from him, and we shook hands.

Then he left, out the door and into the night. Back to *el norte*.

Isabel was on me, following me behind the bar, where I hid the camera, wrapped in Pescado Loco aprons, tucked into a cabinet. "What'd you do for him?" she said, one of her eyebrows arched so high it disappeared into her frizzy bangs.

"Excuse me?"

"You know what I'm talking about."

"No, I don't," I said, trying to get past her. She blocked my way.

"*Imagínate!* Your papá thinks you're such a *good* girl—"

"Get out of my way, Isabel."

"Don't worry, *santísima*," she said, winking. "Your secret's safe with me."

"I have no secrets," I said, pushing past her and into the crowd, her laughter right behind me.

# 14
# • • •

Ángel went outside to take out the trash. He stuffed the bags
into the barrels behind a little gate built into the wall of the
building, then he leaned against the wall to smoke a cigarette.

It was a loud night; people were screaming drunk. He
hated them, wanted to follow them down dark roads, make
them afraid. How easy it was for them. To drink until you
could not remember anything, not who you were, not what
you did, not where you lived. He wanted to be them.

He had wanted to make everything better, to take care of
his mamá like a proper *hijo* should. He wanted to work hard
enough so she could give up selling herself to men. He paid
for everything, gave her some spending money, told her not
to bring home men anymore. She put her hand to his cheek
and promised him they could begin again. She would stop
bringing home men if he would stop running in gangs. They
would earn their money cleanly. If they were going to do

things right, they would have to do things right all the way.

Promises eroded quickly. The extra money Ángel gave her went to booze, and she did nothing to keep the tiny house in order. Then she was out of money and booze and went to the corner to pick up clients.

They fought for days after that, screaming and throwing things. There was no hope for life to be different because the wrong way was the only way both of them knew. Still, he was angry. He didn't come home. He spent all the money he earned, which was worth less and less every day now, since the suits in D.F. decided that's how it would be. What was the point of working a legit job if they stole the money right out of your pockets? What was the point of anything?

He could never drink enough to block out his life. He thought of the easy money he could just take, but tried to shut these thoughts out. He was reluctant to break his promise to his mamá, if only to prove he was a man who meant what he said, even if she couldn't remember what he'd said in the first place.

# 15
...

The candle from the super-mini had burned down to nothing. I lit a new one and prayed. This time I did not get down on my knees. I wondered if the prayer would still work if I did not kneel. I wasn't sure of the rules, only of what I had always done. I decided I would face things—the Virgen, Dios, all the saints—on my own two feet.

"O Señora," I began, but stopped. I did not want to say anything out loud, not even in a whisper. Instead I silently prayed for Gabriela, for myself, begging the Virgen to protect us both. To forgive me for my evil thoughts and my feelings of hate, for wanting to kill. To never let my papá find out about me, how I was just as bad as Gabriela. I was honest with her about that, never passing the blame onto anyone else, but accepting that it was I who had led Ramón down the dark stretch of beach after the graduation party. I did not stop him when he touched me, and when he asked, "Is this okay?" I said yes.

• • •

Before Gabi was sent away, I would stay up long after everyone else was asleep and take my sister's books, notebook, and whatever homework she hadn't managed to do, and I would sit on the floor and finish it for her. She could usually complete a few equations and several sentences, but those dissolved into butterflies, or hearts with *Carlos* written inside them. The subject of her sentences always seemed to be Carlos: *His eyes are dark as chocolate. His hair smells like candy. We will get married when he saves enough money. We will move to Puerto Vallarta.*

I flipped through these sorts of pages until I came to that day's work, begun with her name and the date at the top in perfect penmanship. Often several problems had even been completed correctly. There was the usual heart at the bottom of the page with clouds and birds, an arrow shot through the middle. I was used to seeing such things. I went on to complete the rest of her math problems. Then, out of the corner of my eye, I saw that something was different. In her fanciest cursive handwriting, the name *Antonio* curled inside the heart.

I thought back to all the Sundays when Antonio had been at our house, how uncomfortable I felt in his presence. I didn't like the way he looked at me. His eyes lingered on my legs, and after he'd had a few beers, his eyes moved wherever they wanted. I didn't like the way he kissed me on the cheek in greeting, or his smooth words. I didn't want to accept his gifts, but I had to take the cheap trinkets and thank him. I had been so busy keeping my distance from him that I hadn't paid enough attention to how he looked at Gabriela. It was all coming to me now: how he hugged her a little too much, how he stroked her cheek, how Gabriela was restless all Sunday until he finally showed up.

I flipped back to previous pages, inspecting other doodles and hearts, realizing that his name was everywhere. At one point, I saw *Carlos* crossed out and replaced with *Antonio*. There were pencilled doves holding ribbons with his name. There were clouds with rainbows that ended in his name.

I tore one of these pages out, crumpled it up into a hard little ball, and threw it at Gabriela's head. She stirred but did not wake. I jumped on the bed and shook her until she woke. "Gabi," I whispered harshly. "Gabi!"

Her eyes fluttered open. "What, Lucy? I'm asleep." She let them close again.

"I don't care," I said. I uncrumpled the paper and held it in front of her eyes. "What is this?"

"Stop it!"

"What is it?"

"I don't know. I can't see it," she said crossly. "Leave me alone." She turned over, pulling the blankets over her head.

I tore the blankets off. I sat on Gabriela and pressed the paper to her face. "Antonio?" I said, trying to keep my voice to a whisper. "Are you stupid? Are you *loquita*?"

She writhed beneath me. "Leave me alone!" she said. "It's none of your business." She tried to shove me off, but I was stronger.

"Stay away from him, Gabi. He's no good."

"You're just jealous." Gabriela's eyes flashed in the candlelight.

"You know he's got a wife and *hijos*? Gabi?"

"You're so naive," she said, sighing.

"You think this is a joke?" I grabbed both of her arms as she tried to shove me off again. I pinned them against the pillow.

"Let go of me."

I squeezed tighter. "Stay away from him. Whatever he's told you—"

"Let go!"

"Promise me," I said.

"No!"

"I'm showing Mamá and Papá."

"Don't you dare." She was trying to twist out of my grasp.

"I'm telling them."

"I'll kill you," she spat, wresting an arm free and swinging at me, hitting me square in the face. I was so surprised, I screamed as I fell off the bed, crashing into the Virgen's altar. The thin table toppled, the lit candles and the jar of flowers crashed to the tile floor, the water soaking me and extinguishing the flames.

When I looked up again, Mamá and Papá were in the doorway. "What's going on?" Papá said.

"We thought someone broke in!" Mamá said, her face full of fear. "What's wrong with you girls?"

I began picking up the pieces of glass from the floor, placing them carefully in the palm of my hand. I felt Gabriela glaring at me. I didn't know how to say it. "It's Gabi," I began. "Gabi . . . she . . ."

But when I looked at her, seeing her fierce dark eyes hating me, I couldn't stand it. "She . . . kept pulling the blankets off me. She wouldn't stop," I said. "And I'm so cold. I'm freezing, and she doesn't even care!"

My eyes were filling with tears, so when I looked back to the floor, everything was blurred, the red carnations and the shattered glass, the water seeping into the crevices between the tiles.

Someone knocked on the gate. I unclasped my hands, left the Virgen's altar, and went outside, opening the little door in the gate. It was Carlos, fist raised to knock again, a plastic bag in the other hand. "Carlos," I said, surprised. "How are you?"

"*Buenas*, Lucy. Can you get these to her?" He held up the bag. I could see my sister's name showing through the cloudy plastic, ghost-like.

"More letters?" I asked.

He nodded. I imagined him, a fifteen-year-old boy, sitting at the kitchen table late at night when everyone else was asleep, writing letter after letter. Still thinking of her. Regretting breaking up with her and losing her to Antonio. Heartbroken, as I was, in her absence.

"I'll do my best," I said, taking the bag from him.

He hesitated, working up the courage to say something. "Lucy? Has there been . . ." He looked at his feet. "Has there been anything for me?"

"I'm sorry, Carlos," I said. "Not yet. I'll tell you when I hear anything."

"Sure." He turned abruptly, crossing the road to his house, leaving me with the bag of letters hanging from my fingers, feeling like I had done something terribly wrong.

• • •

I couldn't part with the camera. I even slept with it at night, kept it under the blankets with Gabi's old stuffed burro. Somehow its cold metal and plastic against my arm comforted me. With my tip money I bought more film at the one-hour photo shop that Paul had told me about and took pictures of everything: dirt roads, half-built structures, graffiti on walls, wooden doors, taco carts. I took pictures of trash in the gutter, a dead dog I came across, a phone booth with the receiver off the hook.

The photos I'd taken at the Hotel Santo Niño, I kept under my mattress. The one I'd taken at El Pescado Loco, I propped up on the dresser until I thought better of it—afraid Mamá might see it and feel even worse at the sight of Isabel— so I put that one under the mattress too.

At home, when no one was around—except Mamá in her room—I took pictures of the house. I began in our bedroom: the altar, the Virgen, my hairbrush on the dresser. I worked my way through the rest of the place. Navigating by the lens of the camera, I peered into cupboards and drawers. In the kitchen, there were Mamá's old school books shoved into the cabinet by the stove, against the dried-up beans, the *masa*, and the bag of rice. I took pictures of the *sala*, the bathroom, Papá's hair and moustache dye beside his cup and razor, the door to the room *de mis padres*, then into the room where Mamá lay, the lines deepening around her mouth and eyes, her normally impeccably dyed hair growing in grey. Her eyelids were still and waxy. I lowered the camera without pressing the button, suddenly afraid. I sat on the bed, brushing loose hair out of her face. I put my ear to her mouth, then her chest—she was still breathing.

I lay down, curling my body around hers, wanting her constant scent of cinnamon and soap to comfort me as it had when I was little. But she didn't smell like her normal self— the sweat on her skin was sour. I shook her by the shoulder, gently at first, then harder. "Mamá," I said, "wake up." I slapped her—not hard but enough to make her eyelids twitch, then flutter open. Her dark eyes were full of confusion. "Gabi?"

"No, Mami," I said.

She inched herself up. She rubbed her hands over her face, then stared at me. "Luz," she said.

I checked the clock. "*La Mala*'s on," I said.

She shook her head. "I'm tired, *hija*."

"Come on, Mami. It's your favourite. Let's go watch it." I wanted to drag her out of bed, make her stand up, slap her again, but harder this time, harder than she sometimes slapped me and Gabi. But she looked so frail and pathetic sitting up in the bed like that, I left her there. I went into the kitchen, turned on the TV that sat on top of the fridge, and caught the last few minutes of *La Mala*—I would have to wait until tomorrow to see what the fiancé would do when he found out.

As the days went on, as Mount Popocatépetl kept spewing up ash, unsated and angry, and as we neared the date of Gabriela's fifteenth birthday in early February, I felt lonelier and emptier. I checked for mail through the slot in our gate, wondering if Carlos's instincts were right, that Gabriela might write to us. I tried to reach my brother Luis in San

Diego every chance I could. I needed to talk to someone. Not long ago, I had two close friends to talk to. One had been Ramón, but he'd broken up our short-lived relationship and left for *el norte* a month after high school. The other, Elisa, my best friend since seventh grade, had stopped coming by the house after Gabi was sent away, and she was never home when I went by—at least, that's what I was told. Her mother finally politely suggested that I stop trying.

I'd even considered talking to Eduardo or Ana, but I couldn't do it. Eduardo had rarely been there for me, and he was the reason Antonio was here at all. Sometimes I tried talking to Miguel, but it was useless—he didn't understand.

Luis would. I was sure of it. I remembered how he had taught me and Gabi to dance in the yard, how he'd wipe away Gabi's tears when her classmates called her *tonta* or *burra*. I remembered his fights with Papá. And I knew he loved me. So why hadn't he written? Why hadn't he come down here and beat Papá for what he had done?

Sometimes when I called, one of his roommates answered, but most times I got the same recorded message. I never left one myself. I didn't know what I would say; I would've felt ridiculous talking to a machine.

I went out early in the morning to the phone around the corner from the super-mini. I put the card in, and as I began to dial the number, I heard women bantering with each other and laughing. I turned; they crossed the street. The few people who were out stared at them—it was impossible not to. They were hardly wearing anything at all. One of them wore a T-shirt belted around her waist like a dress, reaching just past her hips. You could see her underwear. Two others had on short skirts and tube tops, and one woman, the only one whose dark hair wasn't bleached to a brassy, tangled orange, wore a shirt so sheer I could see her breasts. I must've stared too long because she zeroed in on me. I quickly turned, facing the phone. I could feel her approach, the heat on my back. She called to me—"*Querida!*"—but I didn't respond. Then she was at my ear. I jumped when she spoke. "Be an angel," she said, "and give us your phone card. We have to make some calls."

I glanced at the others who stood a few feet behind us, showing their legs to all the women coming to the super-mini, blowing kisses at all the men, who couldn't help blushing. The phone was ringing, the line from here to Luis. I shook my head. "I'm making a phone call."

The prostitute only drew closer to me. My hands began to sweat, the receiver slipped. "When you're done, then," she said, holding out her hand, expecting that I would hand over the phone card any second.

"Get away from me," I said, regretting it immediately.

She put her arm around my waist. "Oh! *Querida!* Don't be that way! You know I still love you!" She wagged her tongue at me. The other ones laughed, spurring her on. "And now you go calling your boyfriend! Such a good girl! Never mind all the fun we had!"

My face was hot. I could feel people looking. I shoved her away. She laughed, ran her finger down my cheek. "Such a pretty little thing," she said. I slapped her hand away. The other prostitutes were closing in, wanting to play the game.

I heard the familiar clicking on the other end of the line, knew the message was coming. I was about to hang up when I heard "Hello?" For a minute I didn't say anything. "Hello? Who is this?"

It was my brother's voice. "Luis! It's you!"

"Lucy?"

The prostitute in the sheer shirt began moaning. "Oh, Luis!" she cried out. "Oh! I can't take it!" The others circled around me, moaning as well, yelling and laughing along.

"What's going on over there?"

"There are all these women here—these *putas*—I need to talk to you. It's so crazy here. Papá—"

"It *sounds* crazy, Lucy. I can barely hear you—"

"*Dios mío!* Did you hear what she called me?" The woman pretended to weep. "A . . . a *puta!*"

"Luis—nothing makes sense—didn't you get my letter about Gabi? And I—and Papá's—"

The others laughed, calling to each other: "*Puta!* No, you're a *puta!* No, you!"

"What about Gabi? I can't hear you. Where *are* you?"

"You don't know how that *hurts* me," the prostitute said into the phone.

"I'm at the super-mini—" I had tears in my eyes. I kicked at the woman, but she wouldn't stop taunting me. "Papá and Isabel—"

"Who's Isabel? I can't *hear* you, Lucy."

I began to explain, but the phone card ran out.

I threw the spent card at the woman and ran back home, relieved to see our black gate, to shut myself behind it.

But inside wasn't much better. There was the garden: lines of laundry, orange trees, the *ciruela* tree by the back wall. There was the house, and inside the house was emptiness. There was Mamá sleeping in her dark room, ignoring everything around her, ignoring me. At that moment I thought it sounded good— to do the same thing, go into my room and block the doorways with heavy wool serapes, make it thick with darkness.

A knock at the gate stopped me in the yard. "Who's there?" I said.

"*Correo*," a man's voice said. "Express delivery."

I unlatched the gate and accepted the small package he held out. It was addressed to me from San Francisco, California, USA.

I went to Mamá's room and opened the door a crack. She had the pillow clutched in one hand. I could hear her breathing.

I took the package into my room. Before opening it I looked at my name, written in thick black pen. Inside were newspaper clippings, a white envelope, and a piece of heavy stationery. I unfolded the stationery and saw it was a letter to me. Paul had terrible handwriting, so it took me a while to read it.

*Dear Lucy,*

*Thanks for all your help. Many people here were impressed with your photographs and wished we could publish more, but there wasn't enough space. Enclosed is payment for what was published. I know I said the camera was payment, but the newspaper is paying you as a contractor. Please consider the camera a gift.*

*Please extend my sincere thanks to your father and your brother as well for helping me. You are all very kind, and it is very much appreciated.*

*Sending you best wishes from the North,*
*Paul*

The white envelope had American dollars inside and a receipt—payment for the photographs. I unfolded the newspaper clippings, two pages' worth. Paul's article. In the photograph Paul had taken, my own face looked out at me from the news page, betraying nothing of the loss I felt without Gabriela, which was strange to me. I looked like everything was fine. There were photos of the artisan market, the owners of a super-mini in *el centro*, the man on Calle Morelos with the taco cart. On the other page were three photos from the Hotel Santo Niño: the couple at the bar, and the girl with the gold cross, laughing the way Gabi laughed, with her whole self, her head thrown back. In the last photo, a row of prostitutes sat on bar stools, some looking bored, waiting for dance partners, perhaps. And to my horror, alongside these images were the words *Photos by Lucy Amador*. My chest tightened. My name. Alongside images of *putas*.

I tore up the article. I tore it up into tiny pieces and went to a candle burning on the altar for the Virgen de Guadalupe and fed the paper into it, the black smoke twisting up and dissolving. But there was too much paper to burn, and ashes scattered all over the room. I took the rest of the article outside and set it aflame, dropped it into the barrel where we had burned Gabriela's things.

I kept Paul's letter, though, folding it into the envelope with the money. I slipped it behind the Virgen's portrait, wedging the envelope beneath the nails that held the backing to the frame.

At El Pescado Loco, Isabel wouldn't let up on me. She was always ready with some smug comment or another. I pretended it was nothing, that she didn't bother me. Not even when she said, "Another gringo boyfriend already?" if I smiled at a customer, or "How's the *good* girl today?" I let her comments slide off me, but really I was afraid. I knew that truth didn't matter here. It would be easy for Isabel to tell Papá some lie, tell a few people in town, and the rumours would quickly catch to full flame.

That night Isabel was like a *mosca*, constantly buzzing around me, somehow always ending up in the same area I was in. Then, at the bar, she came up behind me and said, "You know, that's how Ángel's mamá does it—"

I clenched my jaw. "Shut your filthy mouth, Isabel," I said. I loaded up my tray with drinks and lifted the tray carefully onto one arm.

Isabel raised an eyebrow. "I'd be careful if I were you, Santa Guadalupe. You'll end up just like your sister—or, if you're lucky," she winked, "at the Hotel Santo Niño. I heard you already know the place pretty well."

I hurled the tray of drinks. Isabel screamed, throwing her hands over her face. Glasses smashed into shards on the floor all around us. One smacked her right on the breastbone, piña colada soaking her blouse, oozing all over the floor and on the table behind her.

As loud as it was in the bar, it was impossible to ignore us. People stared at first, not sure what to make of it. But nothing can shock a gringo, and it didn't take more than a second for them to egg us on. "Cat fight!" a man screamed, jumping up on his chair. Others did the same, jumping and shouting at us: "Piña colada wrestling!" "I put five hundred on the young one!" Ángel dropped the trash; Jaime and Sam were on us so fast that Isabel couldn't go after me as she was about to, her hands rolled into fists. Isabel socked Jaime in the eye and mouth, but he stood his ground in front of me, pushing me back to the farthest part of the bar, holding me there so I couldn't move. Sam was having a harder time with Isabel, trying to pull her away with her arms flailing the way they were. But with Ángel's help, he was able to get her on the other side of the bar. "*Pinche puta!*" Isabel screamed.

Jaime had lodged me so tightly between himself and the bar that I could barely breathe. I wouldn't have tried to go after her anyhow. I was too shocked by what I had just done.

"Aw, come on!" someone shouted. "Let 'em fight!"

I rested my forehead against Jaime's back and closed my eyes. It wasn't long before I heard Papá's voice, booming above the other voices, the shouts, the music. Then he had me by the wrist, dragging me through the bar and through the office door.

"Look at me."

I looked up from my hands folded in my lap. It was automatic—when Papá said that, I did it.

But *he* couldn't look at *me*. He was trying with some difficulty to keep his anger under control. He pressed his lips together, clenched and unclenched his hands, breathed in deeply through his nose. All around us were shelves of boxes, most full of liquor bottles. His desk was piled with papers, pens, and pencils; at the corner of the desk sat an altered family picture. It was ridiculous. When Luis left, he cut Luis out of the picture. But after Gabi was cut out, there was a conspicuous hole in the middle, so he filled it with Luis again, but from a different photo that didn't really fit this one. Luis's face floated on the surface like the cut-out that it was. Papá reasoned, I guess, that Luis's crime was lesser, or maybe it was just to make the picture look whole again. I didn't know why he even bothered to have a picture at all. Soon it could be me, cut out from beneath Miguel's arm, and soon there would be more holes than there were people.

Papá paced the tiny room. I felt constricted with all the boxes and the dust, and Papá's growing anger. Finally, he was able to say something. "What's wrong with you, Guadalupe?" He was trying not to yell. I could hear the sounds of the bar from behind the door, the usual noise, as though nothing had happened. "Answer me."

I couldn't think of how I would begin.

So he went on. "No daughter of mine acts that way. You understand?" He jabbed his pointer finger into the air. "Not for *any* reason." His voice got louder. "And not in public, and especially *not* in my bar."

"But *I* would," I said quietly, trying to keep my voice from shaking.

He stopped pacing, turned to look at me full on. I thought he would lose his temper. Before he could say or do anything, I went on: "I would do such a thing for *you*, Papá, for your name and your honour. *Our* name. I will not let her spread lies; I will not let her call me a *puta*—"

Papá put his hands on his hips. He narrowed his eyes. "Now why would she say that?"

I lost control of myself then, tears spilling down my face. I knew I had lost. I knew he wouldn't believe anything I said. She wasn't even family, and he would believe her over me.

Papá shook his head in exasperation. "There must be a reason why Isabel said that," he said.

I couldn't stop crying. "She hates me," I blurted, sounding like a child. "She's never liked me, not since you started—you and her . . ." But I couldn't say it.

"Get out of here," he said, pointing at the door. "If you're not going to tell me what's going on, then get out! I'll find out anyway! If you're going to sit here and lie to me—your own papá—" He threw his hands up in the air. "Go straight home, and wait for me there. Understand?"

I nodded. I wiped my face with my hands and walked as calmly as I could out the office door, through the bar that had now gone back to how it normally was, the incident forgotten. I couldn't see Isabel anywhere. I stepped out into the fading light, the sun low in the sky now. For the length of Morelos, I walked. By the time I reached the corner, I was running.

# 16
...

Raúl Amador stood in his office a while longer, trying to control himself, wondering what to do about Guadalupe. He couldn't have any more trouble, no matter what. He breathed in deeply, let the breath go, then went out in search of Isabel.

The music was too loud and there were too many people. The gringos were ridiculous, he thought, the way they danced, not caring what they looked like. Then he saw her, emerging from the ladies' room, the front of her red blouse damp.

He motioned for her to come to him. She followed him into the office. As soon as he shut the door, she burst into tears, throwing her arms around him. "Oh, Raúl!" she cried. "My clothes are *ruined*!"

"Shh," Raúl said, stroking her hair. "It's all right."

She pulled away, dabbing at her eyes with a wad of toilet paper in her hand. "It was so awful—*she's* so awful—"

"Isabel," he said, "tell me what happened."

"Oh . . . Raúl . . . it's . . ." She sat down, stretching out her legs before crossing them. She kept her eyes cast down.

"It's *what?*" He was growing impatient now.

"It's terrible. I don't know how to tell you. But Guadalupe—"

Raúl got down on his knees and grabbed Isabel by the shoulders. "Tell me."

She dabbed at her eyes. "Guadalupe was . . . *with* that gringo reporter. People saw them walk into the Hotel Santo Niño together—"

"*What?*" Raúl squeezed her shoulders harder.

"It's true," she went on. "At first I didn't believe it—you know how people can talk—but then I asked her about it, and, well—" She pointed to her wet blouse, then buried her face in her hands. Raúl let go of her.

Raúl kicked his desk as hard as he could. It moved a little but did nothing to calm him. He clenched his fists and tried to get his breathing under control.

"Oh, Raúl," Isabel said softly. "I'm so sorry." She walked over to him. She put her arms around him, trying to hold him steady. She kissed his neck. "*Pobrecito*," she whispered, kissing him again. He relaxed for a moment, closing his eyes.

Then he pushed her away from him. "*Déjame.*"

"*Querido*," she said, reaching out to him. Raúl grabbed her hands, then shoved her against the shelves of liquor. "Raúl," she said, "it's *me*. Calm down, it's just me."

"Listen to me," he said slowly. "You keep your mouth shut. If you speak of this to anyone—"

"Raúl," she said, trying to twist out of his grasp.

"Do you understand me? You'll say nothing to no one about Guadalupe—understand?"

"I understand," she said, "but let go!"

"I can replace you in a second, Isabel. Do you understand?"

"*Por Dios*, Raúl, yes! I won't tell anyone! Just let go!"

He released her and stormed out the door into the bar. He squeezed past some gringos dancing, then shoved through the others, feeling disgusted. When he got outside, the sun had already set, and it was nearly dark save for the thin pink line over the hill. He almost ran to his truck parked off the main road by the plaza. He roared down the roads, not sure of what he was doing or where he wanted to go. He couldn't think straight; all he knew was that Guadalupe was his everything now. A single daughter gone bad was one thing, but two—that was too much. There would be nothing he could do to redeem himself, not even if he threw her out. People knew that too many bad seeds meant rotten fruit.

He was headed toward home, but as the hill with the cross came into view, he wasn't sure he was ready yet. For the first time in his life, he didn't know the right thing to do. He stopped before he reached Calle de la Cruz and spun the truck around. He circled back around town, driving down streets he hadn't driven in a very long time. He parked a few blocks away, then found himself walking down the darkening road toward the Hotel Santo Niño.

# 17
### •••

By the time I reached the gate, I knew what I was going to do. It went from a crazy, fleeting idea to the only option I had left.

I didn't have much time, didn't even shut the gate. I barrelled through the garden and into the kitchen, where I nearly ran Miguel over. He was on his way out for the evening, dressed in black and doused in cologne, his hair gelled back. "Hey! Watch it!" he said.

"I'm leaving." I darted past him and into my room, pulling open the doors to the armoire.

"*What?*" He followed me in. "What are you talking about? Leaving where?" No doubt he was thinking I was being a baby again, throwing a tantrum over nothing. I dug through the armoire, pulling clothes off hangers and throwing them onto the bed. Miguel grabbed my arm. "Lucy, what's going on?"

I looked into my brother's eyes and told him what Isabel had said to me, what had happened at the bar, and what lies she was likely telling Papá right this minute. Slowly, he released my arm. "But, Lucy," he said, "I was with you. I can tell him the truth."

But it was more than that. It wasn't just Papá Miguel would have to convince, it was the whole town. He should have known by now it wasn't so simple, should have understood something about how life was for me.

I shook my head. "It doesn't matter. I'm going to find Gabi. Do you know where she is?"

"No," he said, shaking his head. "Lucy, you can't go. I'm your older brother, and I'm telling you no."

"*Do you know where?*" I repeated. I threw my things into a backpack. Peeling the bedspread from the pillows, I grabbed the camera, wrapping it in a T-shirt and placing it into the backpack. I found the two spent rolls of film in a drawer and dropped them into the backpack as well. I reached behind the Virgen's portrait for the envelope I'd hidden. I went to the kitchen, took down the jar with all the money, dumped it across the counter. There were thousands of pesos there, and I took about half.

Miguel shadowed me, telling me I didn't have permission to go, but he watched me take the money without trying to stop me.

"You're going to leave us all here like this?" he said.

I divided up the money, put some in my shoe, some in my front pocket.

"*Tonta*," he said, suddenly changing his tone, "you're going to get robbed."

"Is she in Mexico City?" I put the rest of the money back into the jar.

"Quit being stupid," he said.

"Do you know or don't you?"

I expected he would argue with me, but I must've gotten through to him. This time he answered me. "Papá wouldn't say. But I'm pretty sure he'd send her somewhere he knows."

"That would be D.F.," I said.

I wasn't sure I knew Papá anymore, what he was capable of, what he would or wouldn't do. My heart said he wouldn't just throw her on a bus to anywhere. He would send her to someone. We had relatives in D.F.

"*What?*" I said.

Miguel was looking at my pocket, where the wad of money was outlined in the fabric. "*Oye, tonta,*" he said, "you're not going to last a second in D.F."

"I *know* the city," I said. "I'm *from* there. I'm a *chilanga, pendejo.*"

"You *don't* know!" he yelled. I was so surprised I stopped what I was doing and stared at him. He looked away.

"*Hijos,*" she said. It was her voice, her own voice, without being coaxed. She stood in the doorway to her bedroom, her long hair a greying, matted mess, her housedress rumpled. Her eyes blinked against the light of the kitchen. "*Por favor,*" she said, "don't fight. I hate fighting."

I wanted to scream in her face, tell her a thing or two about fighting. That maybe if *she* had fought at all, even a little—

"Lucy's leaving," Miguel said simply, his head down.

Mamá was silent. As I walked back to my room, she said, "You know I can't do without you, Luz."

"You'll have to," I said, then softened. "I'm sorry."

I finished packing my backpack, listening for Papá's truck. I had to be gone before he arrived. I didn't want to give him the honour of throwing me out. I would throw myself out.

Mamá came into the room and took my backpack. I pulled it away from her.

"Give it to me, *hija*," she said, holding out her hand.

"I won't," I said.

"Your clothes," she said, still reaching. "You just shoved them in there. Let me fold them right."

I was sure it was a trick. Since when did she fold? I was eyeing Gabriela's old stuffed burro on the bed, wondering if I had room for it.

"And the money," she continued. "They'll pick it from your pocket in half a second."

"I don't have time," I said. "I have to go now."

But Mamá lunged for the backpack, and I wasn't ready for it. I didn't think she could move that fast.

Miguel held out his hand. "Give me the money."

I shook my head, but he was quick. He slipped his hand into my pocket and pulled out the bills before I knew what was happening. "You see?" he said. "And I'm not even a pickpocket."

I sat on the bed, wondering what I was doing. Where did I think I was going? Maybe Miguel was right—I was over-reacting. Papá would come home, and Miguel would explain what had happened at the Hotel Santo Niño. I might be allowed to stay. But how could I stay with my sister gone? And who would find Gabi?

Miguel took the money to Mamá, who, to my complete astonishment, was folding all my clothes, just like she said. When she was done, she sat down with a needle and thread, and cut a swatch of fabric from the housedress she was wearing. She sewed the fabric to the inner seam of a pair of my pants, then sewed the money inside. She held the pants out to me. "Put these on," she said.

I glanced around my room, giving it one last look. I wasn't sure if I would see it again. I picked up the burro and held it to my face, breathing in its old, dusty smell—one of the last things of Gabriela. Then I remembered. I plucked at the seam of the burro, made a hole large enough to fit my finger, and tore open the belly. Yellowed stuffing spilled when I pulled the photograph out, curled and bent, but intact. There we were, Gabriela and I in the Zócalo, smiling into the hot Mexico City afternoon, and our papá's shadow. I looked around for something to put it in. I had tossed the original frame into the fire.

Mamá was in the doorway, her eyes full of tears. She had braided her hair. "*Véte, hija.* Miguel will drive you to the boat," she said. "Write to me."

"Yes, Mamá," I said, looking from her to the portrait of the Virgen de Guadalupe beside her.

I took the picture off the wall, pried up the backing. The photo slipped easily between the Virgen and the glass. After tamping the cardboard down, I hung the picture back up. Gabriela and I smiled out of the watery glass of the Virgen's portrait, right at the edge of her *rebozo*. Then I struck a match and lit my last candle.

# PART TWO

| | |
|---|---|
| *Contemplando yo las flores* | Contemplating the flowers |
| *contemplaba una por una* | I contemplated them one by one |
| *preciosas por sus colores* | precious because of their colours |
| *hermosas como la luna* | beautiful as the moon |
| *ay negra de mis amores* | *ay* black one of my loves |
| *pero como tú ninguna* | but like you no other |
| | |
| *Voy a cortar una flor* | I'm going to cut a flower |
| *pa' ponerla en mi sombrero* | to put in my hat |
| | |
| *Voy a cortar una flor* | I'm going to cut a flower |
| *pa' ponerla en mi sombrero* | to put in my hat |

—from "Las Flores," traditional Mexican song

# 18
· · ·

Sunlight hit Raúl directly in the face. He cringed and rolled over, his head throbbing. When he opened his eyes, he realized he was not at home.

He saw long, dark hair tangled on the pillow, the curve of her back where the sheet had slipped off. He could not remember her face at first, but it came to him in pieces, as did the night, coming back to him in shards. He remembered the smoky light, the bottle of whisky, the dancing, then her face before his, only inches away. He hadn't seen her before then. Her lips were painted red, her eyes blackened with pencil, but he could still tell she was younger than the others, the way her face had not found its shape yet. It was still a girl's face.

He remembered she had kissed him, then pulled away, laughing. His lips had burned. He could see the rest of her then, saw that her body, anyway, had found itself. Her breasts were full, her hips and legs shapely. She hoisted herself onto the bar stool next to him; her short skirt rose up even more on her thighs. She leaned on the bar in such a way that he could see down her blouse, just enough, and he knew she meant it like that. She had a gold cross around her neck, which she touched playfully now and again. She attracted him and frightened him at the same time. It reminded him of someone, but his head was a blur by then.

He poured a shot of whisky for her, trying to be a gentleman, but she shook her head. It had been so long since he'd been there, and he'd forgotten that the girls never drank. He told the bartender to bring her whatever she wanted, which, as always, was a glass of water, tinted with something to make it look like a drink. She drank it in little sips, making it a point to look at him each time she sipped from the straw.

She leaned in and kissed him again. He put his hand to her face, then her shoulder. She was very soft. He poured himself more whisky, drank it down. He was sweating. The music wailed in his head.

Raúl pulled the rest of the sheet off her; she stirred. His hands shook. He felt clammy and a little sick. He thought he should leave this room, get out of this place. Why had he come here? This was a place for desperate men. Men who *had* to pay. Yet, there she was, naked beside him, and he wanted to touch her again, wanted to stay with her forever in that dirty, stuffy room.

He brushed the rest of her hair across her shoulder, exposing the nape of her neck. He hooked his finger around the thin gold chain, moving his finger along it. She turned toward him, a smile already on her face, tossing her hair back in the way she'd rehearsed. He knew it was fake, but still.

Her eye makeup was smeared; a trace of red lined her lips. "That was some night," she whispered to him, arching her back in a mock stretch, pretending to yawn, but really it was so he could see her, her delicate body in the strip of sunlight.

Raúl grabbed the bottle from the nightstand, took a long draw from it. She propped herself up on her elbow, watching him with another practised look. He set the bottle down, empty. He hated himself for it, but he reached for her.

# 19
• • •

I woke at dawn. I felt the change in the light around me, the boat shifting. I opened my eyes to see an orange line at the edge of the water. My whole body was stiff and sore from being slumped in a chair all night, shivering in the damp sea air. Other passengers were snoring, curled up in awkward positions; some had given up and were sprawled out on the floor. I pried myself out of the chair, walked out of the salon and onto the deck.

There it was: over the Sea of Cortés an arc, red-orange, igniting the thin swaths of cloud around it, igniting the water, turning the waves into flames. The sun was rising quickly, half of it already up, and we were sailing into it. The boat kept straight ahead. I could see nothing but water. No land yet.

I'd made this trip before. The last time was with the whole family—even Luis was there, before he set off to *el norte*. Eduardo and Ana had their first child with them, just a baby. It was the time Papá took our photo on the boat and in the Zócalo. Mamá was laughing. Eduardo was light of spirit—he and Ana were not arguing. It was the last time we had all been together. In every photo we were smiling or laughing, Luis putting bunny ears on us with his fingers. But the more I thought about it, the more the memory began to crack. I knew that photographs could lie as well as they tell the truth. We were not all happy. There were problems as there always were, Papá and Luis exchanging only a few terse words. Ana silent. But there was something about being on that boat, about moving across a large body of water with no land in sight, that released something in all of us. Almost like we could forget, for a moment, who we were and how we were supposed to be, all of it lost in the boat's wake.

Someone tapped me on the shoulder.

It was a *turista* with a sunburned, peeling nose. He held out a camera with one hand, and in the other he had a little book, from which he read: "*Puede usted tomar una foto, por favor?*" He pointed to a Mexican man who was leaning on the railing.

I took the camera. "*Sí, claro,*" I said, waiting for them to arrange themselves. They put their arms around each other and smiled wide. They were trying to create a perfect memory. So I waited a while more, pretending to fidget with the camera, though it was an easy snapshot type like the one Papá had. Not so they would grow irritated and impatient, but just so they would let down their guard a little, relax their faces just enough to reveal who they might really be. I snapped the picture.

I gave the camera back. They smiled, thanking me. Then they were gone, and I went to the railing, looking ahead. Soon it came into view: the rocks, the lighthouse high on a cliff. We were almost there: Mazatlán. I turned to look back the way I had come. I don't know what I expected, but of course there was nothing but the expansiveness of the sea.

# 20
...

María Luisa did not sleep all night. After Luz had left, she sat up in the kitchen. When the sun began to rise, she switched on the radio, turning it up as loud as it would go. But that wasn't enough. The silence in the house was heavy with everyone gone, so she turned on the TV too. The noise of the news twined with the songs on the radio. She didn't care who it disturbed. She wanted the noise, the chattering voices. Like when the children were younger, when Luz had just been born and they were living in that tiny house in Tepeyac, Mexico City, so tiny that all the children had to fit into one room, and the room was so small that all it could fit were beds. Their neighbourhood had been loud, full of delivery trucks and the rush of traffic. She remembered how she couldn't stand it. But now she longed for it.

She missed how close they had been, packed into that little house. When things got to be too much, she'd send the boys outside to play *fútbol* in the street. They were close to her and depended on her when Raúl worked his long days across the city. And Luz was the closest of all, just born, tied into a *rebozo* across her chest. María Luisa couldn't part with her first girl, as if afraid to lose her. At lunchtime, the boys would be back from school, punching each other at the table, arguing and yelling so that Lucy woke from the noise and added her own. María Luisa could feel her *hija's* lungs working, throbbing against her chest. She could *scream*. It bothered Raúl and woke up the neighbours at night, but María Luisa was secretly proud of her *hija's* ability, whispering in her ear, "Scream! Scream!"

Now everyone was gone. Raúl had still not come home. Another child was far away. Miguel was still here, but for how long? He would have to carry it all now. Raúl would be harder on him, maybe even as hard as he had been on Luis.

She didn't know what she could do about her family falling apart even as she tried to keep it together. She picked up the broom and began to sweep, the broom leading her to her daughters' room, to the armoire where she'd tried to hide the dress.

Gabriela's dress had arrived one afternoon in November. María Luisa took it out of the plastic and ran her hands over it, smoothing it across her daughters' bed. She couldn't wait for Gabriela to come home from school and put it on.

María Luisa had never had a dress like this, not even on her wedding day. They had been so poor then. All she could afford was something white, paying a woman down the street to make it, sewing gauze fabric around the skirt to make it seem fancier than it actually was. She'd never had a *quince años* party, never had the luxury of a celebration to mark the transformation from girl to woman. She'd never had the rite of the changing of the shoes, having her girls' shoes removed and her feet slipped into the shoes of a woman. She had simply had to *be* a woman, travelling alone from her *pueblo* in Oaxaca to the capital. There, she was to stay with her aunt and uncle, find work, and send money back to her younger brothers and sisters.

And she did. She did what she had to and luck had been on her side, she realized now. It could've been so much worse. But in D.F. she had watched the kids at the public school near where she lived, their uniforms and books setting them apart, and she wished that her life could be different, that she could be a student. Eventually, she realized she *could* study, as long as she kept working—she could do both. She went to school for the morning classes, cleaned in the afternoons and evenings. After work, she studied, sometimes reading until dawn. It was hard, but she did it. She kept going to school, even after she married Raúl Amador. But soon there was Eduardito, heavy in her belly, and it all became too much to do.

It was the most beautiful dress she'd ever seen, more beautiful than Luz's when she turned fifteen. *Life will be different for them*, she thought. She might've even said it aloud.

Gabriela was suddenly at her side, as if her thoughts had conjured her. María Luisa hadn't even noticed her coming into the room. Her face was flushed from the heat, her knees scraped from falling down too much. María Luisa put her arm around her daughter. "Here it is, *m'ija*," she said.

"It's *beautiful!*" Gabriela sang out. "It's so beautiful!"

"As beautiful as the girl who's going to wear it," María Luisa said. "Try it on." She ushered Gabriela into her own bedroom, shutting the door behind them. Her daughter took off her school clothes and let María Luisa help her into the dress.

The fabric made such a nice swishing sound, like water, like waves coming to shore. María Luisa zipped up the back. How white the satin was, how elegant. She pressed the veil to the crown of Gabriela's head, and they peered into the full-length mirror together. María Luisa put a hand to her mouth, astonished by the woman in the glass.

When María Luisa was done sweeping up the dust in her daughters' bedroom, she set the broom against the wall, took all the linens off the bed and remade it, tucking the sheets tightly beneath the mattress, smoothing the white bedspread over everything. Clothes that Luz had rejected were piled on the chair. María Luisa picked them up, one by one, the button-downs and the T-shirts, the pants and skirts, shook them out, and hung them back up in the armoire.

At the bottom of the armoire was a wreck of shoes jarred from their boxes. She got down on her knees and began sorting through them, opening lids, shoving as many loose shoes as she could into boxes to save them from the dust.

In one box she found a stack of plain white envelopes with Gabriela's name on them. She held one up to the light. Nothing showed through, so she opened it.

Querida *Gabriela,*

*I hope you don't think I'm angry with you, and that's why you're not writing back. I'm not.*

*Nobody understands. Everyone, my parents, sisters, and even my best friend, tell me to forget you. But that's like telling me to forget eating or fútbol. It's totally crazy.*

*I want to hear what happened in your own words. Everyone says they know what happened but I want to hear it from you.*

*Don't be afraid. I'm a man and can take whatever you tell me, even if it's that you don't love me. Please write to me.*

*Yours always,*
*Carlos*

She sat on the floor, thinking about all the times she had slapped Gabriela because of the neighbour boy, all the times she had forbidden her to see him or even speak of him. María Luisa had given Carlos a talking-to, telling him to leave her daughter alone. How many times had she yanked Gabriela away from the window where she watched him, dragging her back to her room and dumping her school books onto the bed? She had only wanted Gabriela to have a life of her own, and thought that studying was the way to that life.

*What if she had let them be?* Perhaps Gabriela would still be here.

She shook her head. It was no good to think that way.

She carried the box of letters to her room and slid it beneath the bed.

# 21
...

Raúl paid the girl and walked out of the Hotel Santo Niño right about the hour of siesta—or when it should've been. Nobody in Santo Niño really observed siesta because the gringos didn't, and no gringo wanted to wander around a closed-up town. There was money to be made, so everything stayed open throughout the afternoon.

In other parts of Mexico, siesta would be the perfect time to sneak out of a shady hotel unnoticed, but in Santo Niño this was when the day picked up steam, when gringos had forgotten their hangovers and were out in the sun, roasting themselves on the beach or touring the town. Even on the dirt road that the Hotel Santo Niño dead-ended, he could see *turistas* who had wandered from the town centre, exploring, perhaps searching for the *real* part of town.

Raúl hadn't even gotten down the steps when he encountered a gringo with a camera snapping pictures—taking pictures of *him* walking out of the hotel. He screwed up his hand into a fist, threatening him. The gringo stepped back, edging the ditch, saying something in English that Raúl couldn't understand.

"Go fuck your mother," Raúl growled. The gringo was in the ditch now, backing toward a barbed-wire fence. Raúl liked the fear that crept into the man's face. "Fuck your mother and take a picture of that!"

Raúl drove the long way home, circling around town toward the white cross they had dragged up the hill so many years ago. Soon he was on his street, the street that was hardly more than a dirt path with no name when he had come here. Empty desert all around it was divided up by posts and plastic bags. He had picked these lots because he wanted them to be protected, nestled at the base of the hill, to shelter them from the brutal winds that blew in from the sea and stirred up sand-storms. He remembered when he had planted the mango and orange trees, the lime and *ciruela* around where he later built the house. He had planted them before the foundation was poured, before he'd seen the vision of light on the top of the hill.

*They were nothing but saplings*, he thought, parking the truck on the street. And now look at them: the mango was so tall they couldn't reach the fruit near the top anymore, not even with the pole.

As he walked through the gate, he looked up at the house he had built with his own two hands. He could hear the radio blaring, the TV, the chaos of sounds making his head throb. He decided finally, before he walked through the door, what he would do, and what he would say to her.

In the dark, cool kitchen, he found his wife chopping up vegetables, half-watching the TV. It was another telenovela. A woman and a man were arguing about something, the woman giving him a hard slap across the face.

María looked up at him, pausing only momentarily in her chopping. She did not smile or greet him.

"María," Raúl said. His mouth was suddenly very dry. He tried to swallow but couldn't. She wasn't looking at him anymore. She kept chopping, the radio blaring some sad song, the woman in the telenovela storming out of the room, leaving the man all alone.

Raúl turned away from her and went to the doorway of Guadalupe's room, saw the bed made up pristinely as usual. He walked through the room to the *sala*. It was dark and quiet. Turning back, he could see the altar Guadalupe had made for the Virgen, a candle lit. *It's going to take more than that*, he thought. His daughter was not there.

He went back to his wife in the kitchen. "Where's Guadalupe?" He had to almost shout to make himself heard over the noise.

"She left," María said, her eyes on the telenovela.

"What do you mean, *she left*? Where did she go?" He walked to the counter that divided the kitchen like a bar and faced her, surprised that he was a little unsteady on his legs.

María shrugged, set down the knife. "I don't know."

"What do you mean, *you don't know*? You're her mamá! You *have* to know!"

She lifted the cutting board and the tomatoes slid into a

bowl. "I mean I don't know," she said evenly. "Luz came home frantic, packed her bag, and left."

"She didn't say anything?" Raúl was infuriated that nothing seemed to move her. His wife simply picked up the knife again and began chopping an onion. He reached across the counter and seized her by the shoulders. "Did she say where she was going?"

"Why would she?"

He squeezed her shoulders harder. "Do you know what she did?"

"I know what lies were told. That isn't what happened, though."

"Then why did she run?" he said. "If it was all lies! Why did she run?"

"You were going to throw her out anyway," María Luisa said, "just like you did Gabi—"

"Don't you ever," Raúl said between clenched teeth, "mention her in my house again." He was inches from her face. She stared back at him with her fierce, black *india* eyes.

She pointed the knife at him. "If we lose Miguel . . ."

Raúl backed away.

"If we lose Miguel because of you . . ." She jabbed the knife in the air between them as she spoke. She dropped the knife back onto the cutting board, into the onion.

Raúl ran into Guadalupe's room, flung open the doors to the armoire, and pulled out her clothes. He wasn't sure exactly what he was doing, but there had to be something, some clue she had left, something that would tell him where she was and what he was supposed to do. He pulled the armoire out from the wall to look behind it and found nothing. He tore the blankets off the bed, upended the mattress. Nothing was beneath it, and he flipped it over in his rage. The mattress hit the altar, overturning the candle, but he was at the dresser, pulling open all the drawers, dumping their contents onto the floor. He saw María in the doorway. She was yelling something; he couldn't tell what, but he saw that a fire had caught from the candle that had fallen onto the bedding, a small patch of flame burning the white sheets. He lifted his foot to stomp it out, but María was already on the floor, slapping out the flame with the palms of her hands.

# 22
### •••

Mazatlán. "Land of the Deer," I read in the tourist brochure.
Land of the Pacífico brewery, shrimp, and duck hunting
excursions.

I walked along the Malécon, watching the waves crash
in. It was early, the mist thick in patches over the water. I
veered away from the sea and into the quiet streets of the
old part of the city. There were the usual early morning
stirrings: women scrubbing the walks, freshly showered
people heading out for work, delivery trucks. With the help
of a woman who worked at a newsstand, I found the bus
terminal and bought a seat on a second-class bus to Mexico
City that wasn't leaving until the next morning.

I walked out of the dingy station and into the sunlight.
So much was old here—I'd almost forgotten about that.
Brightly painted colonial buildings, cobbled streets, and the
big cathedral, a real one, built in the old style, not like the

ugly tin barn we went to in Santo Niño. I knew that up the shoreline, in the Zona Dorada, there were new hotels and buildings like those at home, but here I felt like I'd gone back in time.

I had to find a place to stay the night. I ate a couple of shrimp tacos at a stand, bought a cup of coffee at another. I asked the man who poured the coffee where I could find a cheap but decent place to stay.

He put the coffee pot back on the burner and retied his stained apron. "You're just passing through then?"

I nodded, picking up the Styrofoam cup.

"Where are you headed?"

I thought that was a nosy thing to ask and not at all an answer to my question. I considered telling him it was none of his business, but I said, "I'm going to visit family in D.F."

"Ah, D.F." He raised his hands in mock exasperation. "What a terrible city!"

I had to laugh. "It's where I'm from."

"Me too!" he said. "But you couldn't drag me back there. Not for anything. Once I saw the sea, I couldn't give it up." He turned in the direction of the water and gazed out as if he could see through the buildings that blocked our view of the ocean. "I've gotten off track," he said. "You were asking about a cheap but decent place to stay." He drummed his fingers on the counter. "Not much fits that description anymore. What's your price range?"

I shrugged. "I don't know, eighty pesos?" I sat on one of the wooden stools to drink my coffee instead of taking it to go as I had intended.

"The only one I can think of is the Casablanca, but I wouldn't recommend it—"

"The Casablanca!" I blurted. "I think that's where we stayed before! When I came here with my family."

He looked skeptical. "Are you sure it was the Casablanca?"

"Well, no," I said. "But I think it was."

"Must've been a while ago."

"Six or seven years?"

A round old lady came up to the coffee stand and put down a few pesos. He poured her a cup, adding milk. "Just how you like it, Doña," he said.

"Gracias, *m'ijo*," she said, taking the cup and making her way down the street. The man told me that the old lady took her coffee to the beach every single morning and walked the Malecón. When she returned, she brought him the cup back, sometimes filled with seashells.

I glanced at the crude map the coffee man had drawn on a napkin to be sure I hadn't taken a wrong turn. The more I walked, the more lost I felt. The street had given way to rubble. I was sure this was the wrong way. When I asked a woman where I could find the hotel, she eyed me strangely, pointing in the direction I was already going.

Finally, I found it. The hotel was several storeys tall with peeling white paint. *Casablanca* was painted in faded red letters on the front of it. I remembered it—we *had* stayed here, but it was nicer back then. The walls had been perfectly smooth, the letters sharp and bright. The cobbled street had been intact. There was still the grove of date palms surrounding it, but even they looked a bit worn out.

At least I'd been here before. I told myself it would have to do; it was only for a night. As I approached, though, I saw how men milled about out front. I saw the women, the *putas*, leaning against palm trees, fanning themselves and smoking cigarettes.

The front door opened and two *turistas* walked out—two men, a Mexican and a *norteamericano*, trying to carry their heavy bags. They gave up and dragged them behind instead. "Hey, big spender," one of the women said, strutting toward them, "you change your mind?"

"No, thanks," they both said, walking straight ahead.

"Nice job," I heard the Mexican say, "you cheap bastard. Nothing but a whorehouse." Then he said something I couldn't understand, but they were arguing. That much was obvious.

As they drew closer, they noticed me. The *norteamericano* smiled when he looked at me, waving as though he knew me. "*Hola!*" he called. "You're the girl from the boat!"

They were the men whose photo I'd taken. "I remember. How are you?"

"Terrible!" the Mexican said. They both wore straw hats and shirts with tropical flower and palm tree prints. Both of their noses were red and peeling.

"You don't want to stay there," the Mexican said to me, wiping the sweat from his brow. "Come on, let's go." When I didn't immediately follow, he glanced over his shoulder and said, "Really, it's horrible."

"There you go exaggerating again!" said the other man. "It wasn't *that* bad!"

I glanced back at the hotel, wondering if it really *wasn't* all that bad. A man and a prostitute watched me, smoking, now and again leaning in to say something to one another. Finally, the man tried to wave me over. "Come on, *chiquita!*" he called. "I won't bite."

Looking ahead, I saw that the *turistas* were waiting for me, concerned looks on their faces. Deciding that they were the safer route, I caught up with them.

We introduced ourselves as we made our way down the road. James was the one I thought was Mexican, and Mark was the *norteamericano*.

I ignored as best as I could the insults the *puta* yelled after me, but James asked, "What's she yelling?"

I looked at him. "You don't speak Spanish?"

He laughed. "I know, I know. I should."

"You are Mexican?"

"Well, my dad is," he said. "So that makes me half. But it's the first time I've set foot in Mexico."

I found that strange but didn't say so. I nodded as if I understood.

We walked until the road began to repair itself. Soon it was paved, and we found ourselves walking down a fairly busy street. I walked with them, though I began to feel self-conscious, feeling like eyes were boring into me. I knew what it must've looked like, a Mexican woman walking down the street with two male tourists. It was no good. I wasn't sure which would look worse: that, or a Mexican woman travelling alone.

But I was curious about Mark and James and found it hard to pull myself away. As wary as I knew I should be, I liked listening to their banter. They made me laugh, accusing one another of being responsible for ending up in a place like the Casablanca. "Mark found it in his shoestring guidebook," James said, again wiping the sweat from his brow. "He's always so cheap."

"Listen," Mark said, "that's not my fault. It did not say in the guidebook that it was a whore-slash-crack house. It said," —and he pulled the glossy paperback from the front pocket of his bag, opening it to the page— "and I quote: 'This hotel is a little outdated, but perfect for the budget traveller.'"

"*Budget* was probably the word to look out for. Code for whore-slash-crack house. Code for *whoretel*."

I didn't know what a slash crack house was, but I took it for something that wasn't good—anything combined with *whore* was nothing but *mala*.

"Well, now we know."

Cars zoomed by us. "I stayed there before," I said. "It was better back then. I was just looking for somewhere cheap. I didn't know it was like that now."

"Cheap, indeed." James nodded. "We're staying where *I* want this time, man," he added, glancing at Mark.

"Just like the Hotel Santo Niño," I said, thinking of how the man behind the counter had told Paul it was perfect for a budget traveller.

"Oh!" James cried, rolling his eyes. "Don't get me *started* on that."

"You went there?"

"Oh, we didn't *stay* there. But genius here—well, you can probably guess how it happened."

Mark ignored him. "Where are you from?" he asked me. "I mean, here I was trying to speak to you in Spanish."

I laughed. "I'm from Santo Niño—well, I was born in Mexico City."

"How did you learn English so well?"

"From my brother Luis. And tourists." I looked at James. It might've been rude, but I had to ask. "Why don't you speak Spanish? If your dad is Mexican?"

Mark laughed. "I wish he did! He's worse than me! He's like the gringoest gringo!"

"I'm duly shamed," James said, kicking a pebble into the street. "I just didn't speak it enough. My dad spoke English to my mom, and we didn't learn much. To be honest, we didn't want to speak Spanish."

"Why?" I was really curious, not understanding at all why someone wouldn't want to know another language.

"Well," he said, not looking at me, "because it was weird to speak Spanish in my town. We just wanted to be American."

Mark put his arm around James. "Come on, babe, admit it. You just wanted to be white."

James laughed and put his arm around Mark. Then they both let go. I realized with a jolt that they were a couple.

James stopped before a brightly painted turquoise building. The sign said *Posada del Mar.* "This is it. We're staying here."

I peeked inside the lobby. It was clean and bright, with tropical plants in the corners. The woman behind the counter smiled at us.

I said goodbye to them as they walked into the lobby. "It was nice meeting you," I said.

They both looked at me, then at each other.

"But where are you going to stay?" Mark asked.

"Don't worry," I said. "I'll find somewhere."

"How about here?" Mark asked. James was already heading for the counter.

I shook my head, but I lingered on the step. I put my hands in my pockets and found the coffee man's napkin map, now in tatters.

"Quit being bullheaded," James said to me over his shoulder.

"Bullheaded?" I repeated.

"You know—*vaca de lo cabezo*," he said matter-of-factly.

"I am . . . cow of . . . head?" I said, laughing at his terrible Spanish. The woman behind the counter laughed too.

I didn't want to go back out there, searching for somewhere to stay if there was a decent place right in front of me. People passed by me without so much as a glance. I took a deep breath and walked to the counter.

The señora there greeted me kindly and chatted with me about Santo Niño and Mexico City. She herself was from Puebla. If she disapproved of me, she didn't show it. I signed a paper, paid, and she gave me the key to my own room.

After I had settled in and cleaned up, splashed water on my face and changed my shirt, Mark and James showed up at my door. "Come on!" they said. "We want to take you to lunch." I went out with them into the street in search of a restaurant that Mark had found in his guidebook.

James was skeptical. "You trust that thing?" he said. "Make sure it doesn't say *budget*."

As we walked I tried to decipher the expressions of those we passed, trying to see what they might be thinking about me. I imagined what Papá would say if he could see me walking the streets of Mazatlán with two male *turistas*.

We sat down at a little table beneath a *palapa*. I relaxed a little. Mark and James were so funny and laughed so easily it was catching. They weren't embarrassed that their Spanish was terrible, and they asked me without hesitation to translate whatever they didn't understand. They called *themselves* gringos—even James.

They kept joking about the Casablanca—*joking* about it. Nothing seemed serious to them; nothing was at stake. So I drank the beer they ordered, ate from the plates of seafood, tried to joke with them, to try and feel what it was like to be a *turista*, realizing that nobody knew me here in Mazatlán, that I knew no one. I might sometimes feel people's eyes on me, but no word was going to get back to Santo Niño. I had no past, no name to protect, no family to honour here.

The bus driver's radio was on full blast, a song by Los Tigres del Norte. He drove as fast on the tiny, winding roads toward D.F. as he did on the *autopistas*, no doubt thinking he was exempt from accidents because of how he'd transformed his dashboard into an altar. I used to believe that too. I was sure that no harm would come as long as you had a tribute to the Virgen, Jesucristo, and your patron saint, or at least San Cristóbal if you were travelling—as long as you were good and kept praying. But I saw a bus accident one day, how the bus hit the concrete barrier and flipped over on the road, and two people died, twenty more injured. I saw through the cracked windshield all the pictures of Cristo and Guadalupe, crosses and rosaries hanging from the mirror, and none of it had helped.

Or maybe it had, because what do I understand of the ways of Dios? I stared at the little shrine, the tiny portrait of the Virgen de Guadalupe affixed to the dashboard, the pile of fake roses, the glitter, the sequins, the flashy gold foil, the plastic rosaries, and the *milagros* that people had left—little tin arms, legs, breasts, and a lot of hearts—all glued down so as not to fall off at the sharp turns.

I crossed myself just as the driver laid on the horn, cursing at something up ahead. He blazed around a car, honking at another that was heading toward us because we were in the wrong lane. The car swerved onto the side of the road, knowing it was no match for a bus.

I stared out the windows, listened to people chattering around me, the bus stopping in every remote town to let people on and off so that after a while it was full. The things people brought on spilled into the aisles, everything from packages to tools to saplings to animals. Though the man with the two goats was turned away due to lack of space, another man brought on two cages with fighting roosters. They clucked and crowed the whole way to Mexico City.

There was nothing I could do but sit in my discomfort, watch the land pass by, listen to the old woman who sat beside me, and pretend to sleep. The old woman had no teeth at all, had to suck on all her food, making horrible slurping sounds as she did so. Sometimes she talked to me, but I couldn't understand much of what she said, though sometimes I nodded and said, "*Sí*, Doña" or "*Así es*, Doña." The old woman was wrapped in a dark blue *rebozo*. It covered her head and draped over her small frame. Her eyes were hard little black seeds, pushed back into her wrinkled face. The woman babbled or simply stared at everything around her, sucking on candied fruit, humming to herself. Sometimes she'd produce something that looked like a rosary out of one pocket or another. When I looked more closely, I saw it wasn't a rosary at all, but a chain laden with strange little charms and medallions. I thought for sure she was a witch woman.

When night fell, it grew cold. We climbed into the mountains, steadily upward as we moved toward the capital. I was shivering. Not even the sweatshirt I put on helped much.

I must have fallen asleep, because at dawn I found the blue *rebozo* wrapped around me, tucked under my chin. The old woman beside me was asleep in her threadbare dress, her bony arms protruding. Her head was nearly bald, with just a few tufts of white hair here and there. I wanted to keep the shawl—it kept all my heat in, and it was so cold on the bus I could see my breath. But I couldn't let the old woman freeze, so I took it off and wrapped it around her. She woke, or maybe she was already awake, peering at me with her little seed eyes.

She shook her head. "You keep it," she said. She had to say it several times before I understood her, the way she spoke.

"No," I said. "I don't need it."

The woman gathered up the *rebozo* and pushed it into my arms. "You are cold. I am not."

I tried to give it back again, but she crossed her arms defiantly across her chest. Grabbing my hand and putting it to her face, she said, "Feel me. I'm burning up."

She was indeed burning, her skin unnaturally hot. "Doña, you've got a fever. We should go back." Alarmed, I stood up. There had to be a doctor somewhere. She pulled me down by the wrist. She was surprisingly strong. She looked me in the eyes, spoke slowly so that I would understand. "We cannot go back," she said. "Only forward." And she raised her crooked hand, walking her twiggish fingers into the air, toward where the sun was rising.

# 23

...

Raúl Amador spent most of his time at El Pescado Loco as usual, but he found himself avoiding conversation, shutting himself inside his office with the paperwork. Everyone asked about Lucy, of course, and he told them that she'd gone to spend some time with family in D.F., that she had to think about how she had acted and repent. She'll be back soon enough, he told them, just like before, except she will have learned how to control her temper.

He watched their faces, seeing if there was any hint of disbelief. There was never anything out of the ordinary that he could read. Everything seemed to be as it was before. Except *he* felt different. He avoided Isabel, though she approached him often in his office. He sometimes locked the door, especially after the bar closed. She knocked and knocked, but he told her he was busy with the money and the paperwork. He rushed out when he was done.

Once he got to driving, he found he couldn't go home. He couldn't stand the thought of home. He'd drive down rough roads into the desert, or he'd take the highway to the next town, drive on the *malecón* by the sea. He often found himself heading down the road that dead-ended at the Hotel Santo Niño, pulling off to the side and cutting the engine. Staring at the hotel, the dim lights within, thinking of nothing, he felt a deep emptiness in his gut. Sometimes he'd only sit there, but other times he'd get out of his truck and go inside for a few drinks, to listen to *boleros* or whatever they were playing, and feel the hands of women. He would close his eyes and pretend he was someone else, someone younger, without responsibilities, without disappointments.

If he was lucky, the girl was there. She'd sit beside him, leaning into him, listening to him talk, indulging him with consoling looks and *pobrecitos*. Each time he saw her, he talked more and more about all the things that had gone wrong in his life. She promised to make him forget everything that pained him, leading him upstairs to one of the rooms.

Raúl wouldn't go home until morning. When he arrived, Miguel would be long gone, but his wife would be there, in the yard, hanging the clothes on the line.

With the loss of Lucy, Raúl promoted Ángel to take her place. He'd proven himself trustworthy, showing up to work on time, doing everything that was asked of him, taking out the trash, mopping, making sure all the tables were cleared, the glasses clean. He still looked a little rough on the outside, but Raúl had Isabel cut his hair and comb it back with gel.

He had given Ángel Miguel's old white shirts, long-sleeved button-downs, in an attempt to cover up the tattoos all over his arms, but the black still showed through. Through the sleeves, Raúl could still see the heart and the dagger, and the tattoo that was almost like the national flag, with the eagle and the snake—except that the snake was eating the eagle, coiled up on a *nopal* cactus. And there was nothing he could do about the tear inked at the corner of Ángel's eye.

Raúl told the boy he would still have to prove himself. He sat him down in his office, told him the tips were his but his wage would not go up until Raúl was satisfied with his work. Ángel nodded, said he wouldn't fail him. "You'll see, *patrón*," he said.

Raúl made the boy *work*. He knew he was hard on him, but he wanted to save him, wanted him to see that anything was possible if he worked hard enough—even if he had no father, even if his mother was nothing but a drunk and a *puta*. He held Ángel to the cleaning as well as serving, feeling proud of how the boy was bettering himself, of what he was becoming.

She'd slipped in behind him before he could close the office door. Raúl hadn't even noticed her following him, she'd been so quiet. She leaned against the door, closing it with the weight of her body, and turned the deadbolt.

"Isabel, listen," Raúl began, but she went to him, put her finger over his lips.

"Don't you like me anymore?" she said, wrapping her arms around him.

"Isabel."

She kissed him. He put his hands on her shoulders, pushing her away.

"Raúl, you're killing me." She tried to smile, but her mouth quivered. "What is this about? Why don't you want to see me?"

"I've got a lot of work to do," he said.

"But it's me, Raúl. Your Isabel. It's *me*." She sat on his desk, on top of the bundles of cash and receipts.

He looked at her, at her dimpled thigh where her skirt rose up, her thick waist, the breasts that were beginning to sag. The wrinkles on her neck, around her mouth. "Isabel, *por favor*," he said, "you're messing everything up. Get off my desk."

"Come get me off your desk," she said playfully.

He felt something rise up in his chest. He clenched his jaw and went to her, picking her up in his arms like she was a child and setting her down on the floor. She was not ready for it, was not balanced well on her feet, and she slipped and fell over. "*Pendejo*," she spat. "*Pinche puto—*"

"Get out." Raúl pointed to the door.

She picked herself up and sneered at him. "Don't tell me what to do."

He took a step toward her. "I'll throw you out."

Isabel grabbed a cup from his desk and threw it, then threw the glassless family picture at him. Raúl leapt for her, but she was at the shelves, hurling bottles of liquor at him, one after the other, tequila, rum, vodka, whatever she could get her hands on. They smashed all over the floor; the office reeked of alcohol.

He grabbed her, pried a bottle from her hand, unlocked and opened the office door, and shoved her out through the crowded bar and outside. She screamed the whole time: "*Ayúdame!* This man's trying to kill me!"

Raúl pointed a finger at her. "Never come back," he said in a low voice. "I don't want to see you again. *Pinche puta.*" He spat the last word at her and shut the door in her face.

Ángel stared at him. Raúl pointed to a tray of drinks that had been left on the bar. "Get to it, boy," he said. He looked out the window to see Isabel disappearing into the night.

# 24
...

Ángel took off the white shirt, folded it up, and tucked it beneath the bar. He rolled up the sleeves of his T-shirt. All the days and nights his tattoos were hidden beneath the hand-me-down sleeves. He did not want them to be white-washed. He wanted nothing to impede the snake eating the eagle, or the dagger cutting through the heart. He wanted the rose to bloom out of its thorns.

He walked across the floor he had just mopped, past the tables with the overturned chairs on top, and rapped on the office door. "*Patrón?*" he said. "You need anything else?" There was no response, so Ángel creaked open the door. The *don* looked up from the money he was counting and shook his head, frowning. Ángel studied his face, but it seemed to him that Raúl was the same man as always. Ángel's gaze moved to all those pesos and dollars, the stacks of them laid out on the desk. "You sure, *patrón?*"

"Go on, Ángel," Raúl said, waving him out of the room.

"See you tomorrow, then."

"Lock the door on your way out," Raúl said.

Ángel scuffed his way back, lit a cigarette. It was burning inside him, what Raúl had done to Lucy and Isabel. How he'd thrown Isabel out and called her a *puta*. That wasn't fair, but why did he think Raúl was fair? He underpaid his workers and kept wads of money for himself. He disposed of people as he pleased. One day, Ángel thought, it would be him. He could imagine it, Raúl shoving him out the door as easily as he had welcomed him in, calling him an *hijo de puta*.

He went behind the bar and grabbed a bottle of tequila, unscrewed the cap, and drank, feeling it burn.

He didn't understand it. How could a man who had everything throw it away? If Ángel had had a family, no matter what his daughters did, he would not throw them out on the street. Had he had *anything*, he would fight to protect it. As it was, Ángel had nothing. He hardly had a mother.

He took another drink, capped the bottle, and put it back on the shelf.

Raúl always told him that if he worked hard enough and obeyed the rules, he could make something of himself. But it hadn't turned out that way. The *don* didn't know anything—he had everything served to him, didn't have to dirty his hands.

Ángel took the last drag from his cigarette and stabbed it out on the bar. It left a tiny black mark. He grabbed a few beers before heading out the door, locking it as he was told. He stood outside a moment, one hand in his pocket wrapped around the key, the other holding the beers he would drink on the walk home, listening to the drunken shouts up and down the street. The bars and clubs were closing. He watched the drunk gringos giggling and stumbling out onto Calle Morelos. He went around the corner to sit in the shadows of the ditch and drink.

Because he didn't know if he could go home. He didn't know if he could stand it—his mamá passed out by now, some man in her bed, or maybe not; sometimes they did not stay long. Sometimes they left right away. If not, they left when Ángel came home. They only had one room, divided down the centre with serapes.

He sat in the shadows, threw the bottles into the dirt-and-cobble road. They clanked, but it wasn't enough. He got up to retrieve them, smashed them hard against the cobbles. The shards gleamed in the dim light like the curved blades of knives. He reached into his pocket for his own little knife—the one he'd stolen from the gangster, changing Ángel's life. He put the point to the back of his hand, carved a line into the skin, severing the tattooed vines. He watched the blood rise into that little canal.

As a kid, he was sent out to play whenever his mother had a client. A man would appear, and he would be sent out, his mother telling him to stay close to the house. The man would leave, and he would know to wait until his mother called to him.

As he got older he realized he didn't have to do anything. His mamá didn't give a shit anyway. He went out into town and nicked *chicle* and candy from super-minis to resell on the street. He found he was good with his hands. His small fingers could fish dollar bills out of pockets without anyone noticing.

Until he picked the pocket of the gangster. The gangster had thrown down some coins and taken a package of *chicle*, the barbed wire tattooed around his arm mesmerizing Ángel. He dipped into the gangster's pocket, came back with a knife.

The gangster threw the plastic wrapper on the ground, mauled the *chicle* between his teeth, and stared Ángel straight in the face. He took Ángel's chin in his hands and squeezed it hard. "You did okay, kid, but you missed the good stuff." He put his hand in his pocket and pulled out two gold rings, a hundred-dollar bill, and a human tooth. "You want to keep the knife? You have to earn it."

Soon Ángel was introduced to the other guys in the gang. He wanted to be one of them, go wherever they went— though he didn't really know what they did or where they went. It didn't matter. He only knew that they were tough, older, didn't take shit from anybody. Powerful. And most of all, they had money. Lots of money. More than he'd ever seen.

Now, crouched in the shadows, Ángel looked down at the knife in his hand, its simple bone-inlay handle, the blade with its diamond-shaped point. It was this knife that had earned him his first tattoos—the teardrop at his eye, the thorns around his wrists. It was this knife he had plunged into a man's throat.

He had given all that up, but now what was his life? He worked his ass off for someone he hated. His mother was still the drunk whore she'd always been. And he was still a father-less *hijo de puta*. Nothing had changed, except that he had less money than before. His life might have even gotten worse. It was as though the light that had been keeping him going, keeping him hoping, had finally gone out.

Voices and laughter drifted down the road. He moved soundlessly to the shadows of the spindly trees, crouched in the ditch. The voices were in English, a man's and a woman's. He couldn't tell what they were saying, but they were nearing him.

Then he saw them, the blond woman in a pink flowered dress, the man in shorts and a T-shirt. They kept laughing like they had nothing to worry about. He hated that easy way of the gringos, how they could just breeze in and out of this town, eat whatever they wanted, buy whatever they wanted, drink, and laugh at the backward ways of the locals. The man kept grabbing her ass. She laughed, slapping at his hand. Then he pulled her into him, and they stood there in the street, kissing. Ángel saw the gleam of the ring on her finger. It was impossible not to see it; it shone right into his eyes.

He tightened his grip on the knife.

# 25
. . .

Hadn't I just been here? Hadn't it only been a few years since I had been here with my whole family, wandering the city, eating ice cream and chilied mangoes in the Bosque? In the *museo*, looking at what was left of the Aztecs. At the *castillo*, where mad Carlotta had lived. I had been to the Zócalo and its Palacio Naciónal, the Catedral, where Tenochtitlán had been reduced to paving stones. The place where the eagle ate the snake.

Nothing was as I remembered it. I tried to walk with confidence out of the Terminal Norte, because I should know my way here—I was *from* here. I pretended I knew what I was doing, that I'd ridden the metro a million times. I remembered the rush of people, the sharp air, the peddlers on the street. Anything you could ever want you could buy on a corner. I remembered the fruit and ice cream carts, the fountains, the fire-eaters, the *mercados* and the *panaderías* and the traffic, but it all looked like a different place now. It was something I couldn't describe, as though the city's glory had worn away, revealing the grime and dirt, the crumbling buildings and the trash, the stuff it was really made of. *I am from here*, I kept thinking. Each time I thought it or muttered it to myself, it changed in meaning, hollowed out.

Below the city, I waited on the platform. When the train came, I pushed in with the others, found myself smashed against so many people. I couldn't keep track of all the people and where their hands were. I could not stop someone who wanted to rob me.

*Was this where I was from?* I'd only been on the metro a few times in my life. I'd never seen the city as I was seeing it now. I'd never been without my family around me, thick as the walls of the *castillo*.


At La Villa de Guadalupe, there were old women on their knees.

Their heads covered in *rebozos*, they walked on their knees through the Plaza de las Américas, across the hard paving stones. Some of them had cloth tied around their knees, but the most devoted had nothing but their bare skin and were bleeding by the time they reached the front doors. Blood spotted the steps before they slipped into the darkness of the Basílica de Guadalupe.

I wanted to follow them, slip inside that darkness too, light a candle and pray, see Juan Diego's cloak, the Virgen's image burned there. But it wasn't right, the way I was dressed in pants and a T-shirt, tennis shoes. Instead I knelt on the steps, said a prayer to the Virgen, a prayer for Gabi and me and

Mamá, for all of us. Hearing the sounds of the women scraping by on their knees, the *Ave Marías* they muttered under their breath, I made the sign of the cross: the Father, the Son, and the Holy Ghost. *Espíritu Santo*. Then I kissed my fingers, sending the prayer off into the blue-domed sky of Tepeyac.

I navigated up and down the streets named for jewels, looking for my Tía Margarita and Tío Refugio's house, trying to recall which street they lived on. I cursed myself for not paying more attention when I was here before. But then, I'd had my family, and they knew where to go, and I didn't need to pay attention to directions. I could look at other things. The *basílica* on the hill, stucco and corrugated iron, bars on windows, laundry drying on rooftops. I remembered seeing a lizard on the wall of a building and picking it up to study it, but Mamá made me let it go, scrubbing my hands right there on the street with bottled water and the sleeve of her jacket.

Eventually, I found their street: Calle Diamante. I remembered the little copy shop on the corner. Walking down it was like walking into my past. I looked down, nearly expecting to see my thirteen-year-old feet in my hot pink tennis shoes with the sparkly laces. I recognized a tree, the shapes of houses stuck together in rows, and there I was, standing outside of my *tía* and *tío's*. The house looked different, smaller and dingier. I'd remembered vibrant green paint, a rooftop that had a small room on one side and a garden on the other. Before me was just a house, humbled from the years, the green paint faded, with a fence on the roof looped with barbed wire to protect the laundry.

My aunt came to the gate, surprise on her face. "Guadalupe!" she cried. "What on earth are you doing here?" I had already thought about what I would say. I told her I was thinking of going to university here, that I was going to check out UNAM. Even as I said it, I sensed she didn't quite believe me. Still, she received me with kisses and *abrazos*, her two girls, Rosita and Rocío, running up behind her. They remembered me, to my astonishment. *"Prima!"* they cried. I embraced them, exclaiming that I couldn't believe how much they'd grown. Rocío in particular. She was thirteen and nearly Gabi's height. I held her out at arm's length to look at her. "You're so tall!"

Rocío blushed, and ten-year-old Rosita pulled herself up to her full height. *"I'm* tall, *prima.* I'm tall too!"

"Yes, you are," I said, picking her up and swinging her the way I used to when she was much smaller. "Oof, and heavy too."

Tía Margarita looked just like Mamá with her dark *india* skin and black eyes, her hair a deep black, but she kept it cut short. She was younger, her skin not wrinkled as Mamá's was. She showed me the couch where I could sleep, for they didn't have an extra room or an extra bed.

She reheated what was left of the midday meal, told me to sit, and placed it in front of me with a heap of tortillas.

"Thank you, Tía," I said, tearing off hunks of chicken with tortilla and shoving too much food into my mouth.

As the girls asked me a million questions about Baja, where they'd never been, my *tía* was looking at me with concern, her eyes as watchful as Mamá's. Finally, she interrupted the girls' banter and asked me a flood of the usual questions: How was the *familia*? How were all my brothers doing? When was Miguel going to get married, or Luis, for that matter—and *when* was Luis going to come home? When he was rich and could drive back in a fancy car?

"Everyone is fine," I said through a mouthful of food.

She continued on with her questions. How was my father's bar? Had Ana and Eduardo built a second storey yet? How was dear Gabriela? Was she excited about her *quince años* party? It was coming up very soon, wasn't it?

All kinds of panic went off in me. I counted the days in my head. Gabriela's birthday was in a little less than a week. How strange it was, then, for me to be here now, checking out the university this week, when I should be at home helping with the preparations. My *tía* knew something was wrong.

"Oh, yes," I babbled, "she's really excited. You should see her dress!" I went on until I felt sick to my stomach, adding that I planned to fly home to get there in time.

"I'm so glad to hear that everyone is doing well," she said. "Your mamá and I don't talk as much these days as we used to." She wiped a crumb off the plastic tablecloth. "Pity we can't come to the party, but money has been tight."

I washed the dishes, helped Rocío with her English homework, helped my *tía* prepare *la cena* for when my Tío Refugio got home, around ten o'clock that night.

He was a short, stout man with a thick moustache and wrinkled-up eyes, calling out to his family as soon as he stepped through the door. Rosita ran to him: "Papá, Papi, *prima* Guadalupe's here!" I wiped my hands on my apron and greeted him, kissing him on one cheek. "Tío," I said.

"Guadalupe? What brings you here?" He glanced at his wife.

"University," I said. "I'm looking into UNAM. Here, let me take your jacket."

I hung his jacket up in the closet, then went back to the kitchen to prepare the plates and pour soup into bowls. I heard my aunt and uncle muttering in the other room. Rocío came into the kitchen. My heart skipped—she reminded me so much of Gabriela. "*Pri-ma*," she nearly sang, "I'm so glad you're here!"

"Me too," I said. "Here, take these, will you?" I handed her plates to take out.

I opened a beer for my uncle and placed a lime slice on top, balancing it there like a boat. I took it out to him.

"Gracias, Guadalupe," he said, searching my face for an explanation.

I hadn't stopped smiling. It was beginning to hurt. If I cracked, they were going to see what was beneath.

The next few mornings I got up before anyone else. Roosters crowed in the blackness just before day began. I went to the kitchen, made coffee, prepared breakfast. I told my *tía* I wanted to earn my keep for these few days I was here. And I knew that my *tía* worked in an office when the girls were in school. I wanted to relieve some of her burden.

Each day I sent everyone off: the girls with kisses on their foreheads, my *tío* with a hearty "Have a nice day!" and eventually my *tía*, from whom I wrested the laundry basket so she could put on her polyester suit and get out the door to work. I said it was payment, but the truth was I enjoyed doing these things for everyone. It felt good to be part of a family again, a fully functioning, working family. I nearly felt happy.

But as soon as everyone was gone, the mask broke. I knew why I was here. I pored over a map of Mexico City that was so huge it hung off the sides of the table. I located myself, the street I was on, with my finger and saw how the rest of the map swallowed it up. I was so small. It was such a chaotic, intricate web of a place, like a window that had been smashed in with a fist, yet did not break. And in this web, where was Gabriela?

I began to search for addresses of family members on the map, marking the places where I knew aunts and uncles and cousins and cousins of cousins lived—or at least had lived once. That's where I began, with one family member after another. After mapping my route, I went to visit them, using the university story, telling them I was just stopping in to pass on greetings from my family. In each place I found nothing to indicate my sister was there or had been there.

One day, before setting out on yet another metro, bus, and walking journey to another cousin's apartment, I put on a pair of pants I hadn't worn yet. Something crinkled in the pocket—a piece of paper. Unfolding it, I saw it was a note:

*She might be here. I'm sorry I didn't tell you before. I didn't want you to be even angrier with me.*

Below that was an address here in Mexico City. All was written in Mamá's unsteady hand.

I *was* angry that she hadn't told me; she was right about that. But I resisted the pointless urge to crumple up the paper and hurl it against the wall, and thought about it for a moment. How could she have told me? Papá would have forbidden her to, the way he forbade us to say Gabi's name. Holding the note in my hands, I felt for my mamá defying my father, not by speaking but by quietly writing. I imagined how hard even that must've been for her to do.

I rang the bell and waited. I heard dogs barking from the inside, the rush of traffic behind me. Under my arm I had a melon, something to offer. My palms were sweating, my heart pounding. I wondered what I would do when I saw Gabi.

I studied the place, as much as I could see. Not terrible by any means. There was a tall wall topped with broken glass and a metal gate with spikes, but I could see the tops of plants and trees—there was a garden. I searched my memory for it, some recollection of this place from when I was here with my family, but I couldn't remember anything like this.

I knocked on the gate. *"Buenas tardes!"* I called. The dogs went crazy howling and barking. I put my ear to the gate, trying to hear anything. I knocked again and again, until the knocking was steady. Finally, I heard a voice on the other side.

"Who is it?" It was a woman's voice. Not Gabriela's.

"Guadalupe," I said. "Guadalupe Amador Prieto, *hija de* Raúl Amador *y* María Luisa Prieto—"

"What do you want?"

The edge in her voice caught me off guard. "I—my papá sent me—"

A smaller door within the gate opened, and I was face to face with a woman maybe fifty years old, with dark red hair reaching to her shoulders. She had hard lines around her mouth. "You're the other daughter," she said flatly. "We met once when you were a baby."

"Nice to meet you." I extended my hand, but she didn't take it.

"Did my cousin throw you out too?"

"Excuse me?" I said, not understanding.

"Your father. That's why you're here, isn't it?"

"No," I said, flustered. "That's not it at all." I told her my college story.

I looked past her shoulder, trying to see in. The dogs sniffed me, big black and tan dogs, no tails, all muscle. I tensed up. When the woman snapped her fingers, they turned back to the garden. She stepped aside and nodded so I knew it was okay to come in. The door clanged behind me.

"Right," she said, folding her arms across her chest. "And your father said, 'Oh, you must go see my favourite cousin, Magda!'"

"He sent me . . ." An uneasiness spread through my chest. "I have some things I'm supposed to give Gabriela."

Magda smiled thinly. "Is that all? What about me?"

"Oh, and you too," I said quickly, holding out the melon. I knew right away it was a stupid gesture, but I was panicking. I knew it must be true—Gabi was here.

"That?" She laughed. "Your papá sent *that*? He sent you to

bring me a *melon*?" She set her face again, looking at me suspiciously. She didn't take the offering.

"There's more," I said.

She narrowed her eyes. "What kind of *more*?"

"You'll see," I said. "But I have to see Gabriela first." I was searching the barred windows of the house, wondering if she could see me, if she was behind some curtain, watching. Maybe she would wave.

The woman shook her head. "That's not going to work." She held out her hand, her fingers like talons. "Give me what he sent."

"Take me to her," I said, trying to keep my voice strong and steady, trying not to show my fear. Something was wrong. Gabriela was here, and it was very wrong.

Her hand stretched closer to me, her finger and thumb rubbing together. I reached into my pocket, pulled out two hundred pesos. I put them in her hand. She shook her head. "That won't do, *chica*. She's cost me much more than that. Hand over the rest."

I pretended I was reaching for more money, but I bolted. I ran for the door of the house, the stupid melon still under my arm, the woman shouting, the dogs barking and running after me. I didn't know what I was doing. I ran like a *loca* through the kitchen, the dining room, the *sala*, one bedroom, another—looking for Gabriela, looking for any sign of her, looking for anything, looking for locked doors, closets, secret rooms. The woman was yelling for me to stop, the dogs snarling at my heels. One of them bit the leg of my pants and I fell to the floor.

They were going to tear me apart. I couldn't stand up before they were on me, their stinking breath in my face, their slobber all over me, my hair in their jaws. I put my hands over my face and screamed.

"*Basta!*" she yelled. The dogs stopped. I kept my hands over my face, afraid to see anything. Afraid to move. The woman nudged me with her foot. "Get up," she said. "*Hija de perra*, get up off my floor."

I lowered my hands. My yellow button-down shirt was torn at the sleeve. There was blood on the fabric from the scratches on my arms, but I was intact, and nothing was bitten, as far as I could tell.

She nudged me again. "Get up and get out of my house."

I stood up, keeping a wary eye on the dogs. They watched me rise but did not move from where they sat, ears pointing forward. I was unsure of what had just happened or what it meant.

I decided to ask politely. "Señora," I said, "can you tell me where my sister is, if she's not here?" I could feel the tears beginning in the back of my skull.

Magda spat at me, but it fell short, onto the floor. She moved toward me like a bull. I backed toward the door, finally stepping out into the garden, wanting to run but afraid to. "Such filthy *perras*, you Amadores," she said.

My back hit the gate hard. She reached past me to unlatch the door. I flinched, thinking she was going to hit me, but she shoved me out into the street. "Since you're so curious," she said, "your sister's not here anymore, and she won't be back. Go tell *that* to your papá."

She slammed the door shut. I pounded against it. "Where is she?" I yelled.

"Go tell your papá to ask around La Merced," Magda said through the metal. "Though how he'll find her again, I don't know. There are so many of them."

"Tell me where she is!" I yelled.

"You really want the truth? I'll tell you," the woman said, lowering her voice.

I leaned in to the gate to listen.

"I don't know!" she said brightly.

I slapped the gate with my palm. I heard the low growl of the dogs. "Please, tell me," I said.

"I lost her in La Merced."

"What do you mean, *lost her*?"

"Like I said, go ask around." I heard her footsteps click across the cement, away from me.

I squeezed through the boarding passengers onto the platform. There was the metro sign: a picture of a basket of apples. La Merced. I walked up the steps to the exit. As I ascended, the smells of chilies, fruit, spices, *dulces*, and rot became stronger. I remembered it from before. We'd come here, loading up on everything we couldn't get in Baja. We'd bought better shoes, *dulce de leche*, huge rounds of *tamarindo*, clothes, pots and pans, and the radio we had in the kitchen.

The light was changing; afternoon would soon settle into evening. There was the flower stall, its scent so sweet it made me dizzy. The light was an incredible gold, illuminating the stacks of *nopales*, moving through the peppers dried and hung, making them glow red like *sagrados corazones*. There was something about the light that was on the edge of going out, something strong and weak at the same time.

I tried to take in everything, the piles of spices, the rows of plastic toys, the piñatas hanging high overhead, the cut lengths of banana leaves, the empty corn husks, the steel pots and pans, the jars of dried herbs and insects. I glimpsed through the open door of the witchcraft shop, the place of *brujería* that smelled like fungus. I passed by a display of meats with a big, bloody cow's head in the middle. I searched faces, brushing by the shoppers, looking for her, sure that at any moment, *she* would appear, materialize before me in the last bit of light. I came to a great table loaded up with *dulces*, every kind of *dulce* imaginable, and I knew that if she would be anywhere, she would be here, trying to decide what she wanted: the caramels, or maybe the little packets of marzipan, the *pasta de guayaba*, or the *dulce de tamarindo*—

"Anything for you, señorita?"

She was smiling at me, the keeper of the stand, her head wrapped in a scarf. Not Gabriela.

*Why isn't she here?* The light outside was fading.

"Everything okay?" the woman asked. She was looking at my arms, the scratches, the dried blood. The tear in the sleeve of my shirt.

I nodded, pointing to the package of *tamarindo*, reaching down to pull some money out of my shoe. I gave her the pesos, and she handed me the *dulce*. "Señora," I said. "My sister. I'm looking for my sister. Maybe you've seen her?"

The woman smiled. "Tell me what she looks like, *hija*."

"Like me," I said vaguely, "but younger. Fifteen. Ears that stick out."

The woman shook her head. "I don't know . . . When did you last see her?"

I counted on my hand—December, January, February. "Two months ago. Her name's Gabriela."

The woman stopped smiling. "You mean, not today? Not at the market?"

"She said to ask around La Merced. That's what the woman told me. That she was here."

The woman shook her head and lowered her eyes. "There's another Merced," she told me, pointing through the market, toward the streets. "Maybe out there." She turned her back on me.

# 26
...

Antonio Rodríguez stayed away from the *familia* Amador. He avoided the *don*, the cross on the hill, and the barrio spread out below. He drove past the *casa de* Eduardo and Ana without stopping. He ate all his meals on the street. He'd gone to El Pescado Loco once, hoping he could smooth things over, but was so unnerved by the way Lucy stared and by the way Raúl ignored him that he left. It was probably best to wait until things settled down.

Maybe he shouldn't have talked. But he hadn't been able to help himself. He had gone to the construction site— another big hotel by the sea—at dawn with his tools, hammer hanging from his belt. He casually mentioned it to the other guys on the job as they talked about what they had done after work the day before. They whistled and pressed him for details—they wanted to know what it was like, getting with the *don*'s daughter. At first he was vague, but as the hours wore on, that was all they wanted to talk about. He gave them bits of the story as he drove one nail after the other into the wood and pried the boards off the cement that had dried.

Antonio began to enjoy telling the story, each time embellishing it with things that hadn't actually happened. He had the Amador girl doing things that only the most experienced *putas* knew about, and the guys howled and whistled, clapped him on the back.

The next thing he knew, everyone was talking, and Gabriela had been sent away.

One evening he heard a clapping outside his *lamina* shack and an unfriendly voice say, "*Buenas tardes*," a voice he recognized as his brother-in-law's. He pushed open the door and stepped out into the desert evening, prepared for a fight. He knew how it was when someone stole a sister. Eduardo had stolen his sister Ana, but they'd never come to blows because Eduardo had married her.

"*Hermano?*" Antonio said tentatively.

Eduardo twitched at the word. "Antonio," he said, "I need to talk to you."

Antonio unwound the wire from the gatepost and made an opening for Eduardo to step through, then closed it again. They stood in the yard like that, looking at each other. Eduardo stepped toward him.

Antonio stood his ground. Kept an eye on Eduardo's hands. The sun was going down over the Pacific; the last streaks of it were hitting the tallest saguaros.

"Tell me what happened," Eduardo said. "All of it. The truth."

"*Hermano*," Antonio began, watching Eduardo, trying to find the right words. "I didn't mean it to go that way. I didn't mean anything at all. It's just that your sister . . ." He trailed off, seeing Eduardo's hands turn into fists. "Your sister, I'm sorry to say, she's . . ."

"She's *what*? Say it." Eduardo's hands were still fists.

"She's . . . well . . . *advanced*. You can tell she's done it before." He kept still, watching for a sudden movement, watching Eduardo's fists, bracing himself for a fight. It was going to come. The dark was falling over them, erasing their long shadows. Soon they'd just be man to man, *hermano* to *hermano*.

"Don't you dare," Eduardo said, "say that about my sister."

"You said you wanted the truth, *hermano*. So I'm telling you." Antonio looked down at his feet, as if ashamed. "I know I'm weak."

He saw it coming in his periphery like a shadow, a lunge toward him, and he snapped his head up, raised his arms to defend himself. Eduardo's fist hit both forearms, then he grabbed Antonio's collar, slammed him against the fence post. The post loosened and leaned, but it held. Eduardo's face was in his, ugly and angry; they were nearly nose to nose.

"Listen," Antonio gasped. The collar of his shirt was tight against his throat. "Remember what you did to *my* sister?" The grip loosened. "I wanted to kill you too."

Eduardo shook his head. "It's not the same thing."

"You took advantage of Ana, *hermano*. But I forgave you."

Eduardo's breathing deepened. It seemed like he was trying to control his anger, which meant Antonio was gaining some ground. "Have you paid any attention to Gabriela?

You don't know what's going on with any of your family, do you?"

"Shut up," Eduardo said, pushing Antonio against the fence post. "I know my own sister. And I know she's not like that."

Antonio shook his head. "You don't." He told Eduardo that he had tried to ward her off, explaining to her that he had a wife and children, but that hadn't deterred her. Gabriela was a little temptress behind her girlish exterior, her school-girl uniform, her innocent facade. Gabriela had lured him, *la diablita*, and what would anyone do, when a girl did such a thing? What would any man do?

The more he talked, the looser Eduardo's grip on him became, until finally he let go.

"You know I can't marry her," Antonio said, "but tell me what to do to make it right."

Eduardo shook his head, spat on the ground. "You *are* weak," he said, grabbing Antonio's collar again, pushing him against the post, spitting the words into his face. "You are one weak little worm. She's a kid. Do you know how old she is?"

Antonio nodded. That's when it happened: Eduardo punched him in the face, the pain of it splitting his head right between his eyes. The post supporting him leaned a bit more. He'd have to fix it tomorrow.

# 27
...

There were women everywhere. There were old women, *abuelas* in their housedresses and pincurled hair, some walking with canes. There were young women in short skirts and clear platform shoes. And as the sun went down, women who wore very little clothing at all began to infiltrate the streets. I couldn't believe it was real when I saw them, how some of them walked the street in nothing but bras and underwear, or some in dresses so sheer I could see everything beneath the fabric. There were girls in school uniforms—I wanted to run after them, tell them, "Get out! Go!" But then I saw how their shirts were unbuttoned and knotted beneath their breasts, some showing off tattoos on their chests or stomachs. Street lights began to flicker on.

Some shops had pulled down their metal doors for the day. Girls leaned against them, some talking amongst themselves, others calling out to passersby. Girls would peer into the windows of open shops to pass the time, looking at *dulces* or underwear or housewares. One girl was reading a book in the dim light, one leg out in an effort to do her job. Another woman, so hugely pregnant her swollen belly stretched her dress to its limit, bit her lip at something a man was saying to her. I saw a woman dragged by two men and pushed into a car. Nobody paid them much attention, and I too looked away. I accidentally made eye contact with a man who was standing in a door frame, smoking. He called to me, whistled, waved me to him. I walked faster.

*There's another Merced*, the *dulce* lady had told me. So this is what she meant: the red-light district. A lot of good that did me—Gabi wouldn't be in a place like this. But as I walked, the words of the woman with the dogs came back to me: *Tell your papá to ask around Merced . . . there are so many of them.* I shook my head. *That can't be true. It can't be.*

But if it *were* true? She would be here. Maybe not willingly, but she'd be here. I had to consider it. If I was going to find her, I had to consider everything.

I looked into the faces of the women. There were a lot of them, and I was afraid I would miss her, the one who would be Gabi. *If this is true.* I remembered the girl at the Hotel Santo Niño, how she had painted her face. I imagined Gabi looking something like her, still recognizable beneath makeup or costume. Still able to be found. But in the crowd of women, and the men looking for women, and people just going about normal neighbourhood business, I could not see her. She was not beneath anyone's lipstick or eyeliner or rouge. She was not in any of those miniskirts or platform shoes. I wanted badly for one of them to be her and I was terrified that one *would* be her. Nothing made sense. Women spun around me. I couldn't keep up, couldn't track all the faces. I had so little time to find out who was inside.

Someone was keeping step with me, walking at my pace, stopping when I stopped. I looked down before I looked up: black, shiny shoes. A man. I jerked my head up to meet his face. He was a *moreno* with green eyes and light brown hair. He looked like a businessman in his suit and tie.

He nodded to acknowledge me. "Are you all right?" he asked.

I said nothing but kept walking, moving faster. He kept up. Finally, I stopped on a corner to face him. "Leave me alone."

"Do you need help?"

I just stared at him. Everything was beginning to catch up to me, where I was, and what that meant. My stomach ached with dread. Tears warped my vision, blurring the street, the lights of the bars, the women.

"Did something bad happen to you?" he asked.

"No," I said, shaking my head, feeling the tears leak out of my eyes.

"Listen," he said. "I can take you to someone who can help. Follow me."

He turned to walk back in the direction I had just come. Around me were so many women, their voices, their scents. Men looked me up and down, evaluating me as they passed. Evening had deepened to night.

I heard a great commotion somewhere behind me, yelling, a fight, something bad. I did not want to turn to see what it was. The man waited just ahead and I didn't know what else to do. Maybe he was telling the truth. Maybe there *was* someone who could help me. I kept my distance while trying to get away as quickly as I could from the noise behind me and whoever was screaming, "I'll kill you!"

The man did not quicken his pace. I glanced at the passing faces. After a while, he stopped in front of a bar. "In here," he said, and disappeared through the doorway. I hesitated, peering through the doorway, seeing couples dancing. It didn't seem dangerous. I stepped inside and was swallowed up by flickering fluorescent lights and *cumbias* blaring from a radio.

The man had already pulled out a chair for me at a table, a white plastic chair that said *Tecate* on the back of it. Everything about the place was cement or plastic. The floor was as cracked as the sidewalk, but the bar was festive with ceramic tiles painted with birds holding ribbons. Inside each ribbon was a woman's name: María, Cristina, Bonita, Antonia . . . I looked for the name Gabriela. I didn't find it. Criss-crossing the room was a garland of *papel picado* and paper flowers. Behind the bar were boxes of Sol and Corona, a shelf stocked with a few liquor bottles. There was a curtained doorway at the back of the room, guarded by two men built like Lucha Libre wrestlers.

Couples—rather, prostitutes and their clients—danced in the middle of the floor, arms wrapped around each other. It seemed like it had been this way forever, like it was the most natural thing in the world. Still, it disgusted me.

I sat down in the chair the man offered me. He gestured to a woman who was making drinks behind the bar, then sat across the table from me. "My name's Felix," he said. "That woman's Lupita. She's the one I was telling you about."

Lupita came to the table. She might've been as old as my mother, but it was hard to say. She looked like a movie star to me, one from a different time—a woman who would've starred in old Pedro Infante movies. Her eyebrows had been thinned dramatically, then painted back on, her skin *güera*, nearly white. She wore a polka-dotted dress, her hair tied up in a scarf like Carmen Miranda. "A new face," Lupita said. "What's your name?"

"Guadalupe," I said.

"I'm Guadalupe too," she said, "but I go by Lupita."

"I prefer Lucy."

"Does anyone go by Guadalupe anymore?" Lupita smiled a moment before wrinkling her brow. "You look a little beat up."

I examined my arms, the scratches on them rusted over. "I had a—I guess I had a fight," I said. "Dogs. I was attacked by dogs."

Lupita looked me in the eye. "Okay, *m'ija*," she said. "You're in a safe place. Go ahead and talk. Tell me what happened."

What was I supposed to say? What *had* actually happened? I didn't know this woman. I didn't know Felix. How could I trust them? What if this was all a trick to kidnap me, to force me into something? I let my gaze drift around the room, watching people come in from the street, a couple leaving the dance floor and heading toward the Lucha Libre men, the man giving each one a few bills before the couple went through the curtains. I felt sick.

Lupita reached for my hand, squeezed it in hers. I pulled away, folded my arms across my chest. No one was going to touch me. I took a deep breath and really looked at her, trying to see who was inside this woman. "I'm trying to find my sister," I said. "I was told she was—could be here. In La Merced."

The dancers swayed, clinging to each other. The fluorescent lights flickered and buzzed. "Merced's a big place," Lupita said. "There are lots of shops. Lots of places to work and be. Your sister—do you mean to say she's a sex worker, then?" Lupita's voice was kind, the words spoken as easily as if she were saying, *So it's her birthday, then?*

I shook my head. Then I nodded. "I don't know," I said.

Lupita put her hand flat on the table. "Tell me about her."

I told Lupita how Gabriela had been sent away from our home, how Papá had sent her to a strange cousin of his I'd never met, about the bad feeling I got from Magda, and how she had said to ask around Merced for Gabi.

I pictured Gabriela in my head, how she was, what she meant to me, how she looked and sounded and smelled. I did my best to describe her to Lupita. Who she had been, at least. When she was sent away, she had long, straight black hair. She looked like me. She was changing into a woman but was stuck midway. She loved easily, perhaps too easily. She was about to graduate from the sixth grade, her favourite candy was *dulce de tamarindo*, and when she laughed she truly meant it . . .

I trailed off. In the thinning crowd of dancers, I saw a familiar face. It was so out of context, so strange that it took me a moment to place him, but when he looked up and his eyes met mine, there was no mistaking that it was Tío Refugio. And he recognized me. We stared at one another for a few long seconds, then he buried his face in his dance partner's hair.

"There are some girls—" Lupita began, but I stood up.

"I have to go," I said.

She stood up as well, saying after me, "Take care, Lucy."

Felix followed me to the door. "I'll walk with you." He nodded back to Lupita, tapped his watch.

"I don't want you walking with me," I said, moving past him onto the sidewalk, walking fast.

"I just want to be sure you're safe," he said.

"I want you to leave me alone." I walked faster, bolting through the intersection without looking. He did the same, not missing a step.

"Are you looking for the metro? Because if you are," he said, "you're heading in the wrong direction."

I stopped and glared at him. He probably had a wife somewhere, and children, and none of it mattered because he was a man and free to do whatever he wanted. Women walked past us, all those women and not one of them Gabriela.

"The closest metro," he said, thumbing over his shoulder, "is that way."

I pushed past him, angry that I hadn't paid enough attention. But nothing I had just passed looked the least bit familiar—night had transformed the street. I knew I would eventually find a sign, something to indicate I was going in the right direction. The man was determined to walk with me, to keep at my side. I hated him. I hated everyone I

passed, all these *putas*, all the men who should be home like
Tío Refugio.

I broke into a run, sprinting as fast as I could, weaving
through people and intersections, running until I could see
buildings that I thought looked familiar, listening for steps
behind me. I knew I was close: there was the market. I saw
the lights, then the stairs; soon I was down them, standing
with a few others on the platform, catching my breath, waiting for the next train. I looked behind me, not seeing him.

The train approached, a beacon of light through the tunnel.
Stepping into it, I saw with a start that Felix had followed me
after all. He was standing on the platform, watching me board
the train.

# 28
...

The sheets and bedspread now had burn marks and holes where the small fire had chewed through the fabric. María Luisa washed them anyway, and hung them on the line to dry with all the other linens. They were still usable. She could tuck in the burnt edges. Or she could put them in the closet and put the old, threadbare sheets back on the bed. She didn't know if it would even matter. No one was going to sleep in that bed.

She stood between the rows of laundry, aware of the burning barrel just a few feet away from her in the yard, wondering if she should just burn the sheets, finish them off, the way they'd burned everything else.

She heard a key in the lock and the click of the gate. She wondered what Raúl was doing back so soon after he had left, and didn't particularly want to speak to him. She remained very quiet and still, hoping he would just pass by and go into the house. But she forgot her feet were visible.

"Mamá!"

She stepped out of the laundry to see her son Eduardo approaching her. He was dressed in a black suit, the one he wore for work, looking like he meant business. She smiled, called out, *"Hola, m'ijo!"* But he kept up his serious demeanour and didn't greet her back.

*"Oye,* Mamá," he said without a hello or a kiss on the cheek. "I need some answers." Like he was a lawyer putting her on trial.

"Answers?" she said.

"You know, don't you? What went on between Gabi and Antonio."

María Luisa looked up into the face of her eldest son, his stern face accusing her. Accusing and angry. *How did he get so tall?* she wondered. Nobody else in the family was very tall.

"Tell me, Mamá." His eyes drifted to the burnt sheets on the line. "What happened to the sheets?"

She shook her head. "Let's go into the kitchen, *m'ijo,*" she said. Eduardo let her lead the way, following close behind. She took the coffee pot off the stove and put her palm against it—it was still hot. She poured two cups, setting them both on the kitchen table. They sat across from each other and watched the coffee steam. María Luisa tried to find the right place to begin.

Gabriela was an hour late. María Luisa went out to the gate and opened it, looked both ways down Calle de la Cruz and saw other schoolkids, but not her daughter. Carlos was across the street, washing his papá's car.

"*Buenas tardes*, Carlos!" she called. "*Oye*—have you seen Gabriela?"

Carlos shook his head, casting his eyes down to his soapy rag. "No, Doña."

María Luisa found that slightly suspicious but didn't say anything more. She tried to remember if there were any after-school games or events she'd forgotten about, and not able to recall any, she went to the super-mini and used the phone behind it to call the school.

The secretary informed her there were no events, games, or field trips. Perhaps Gabriela had gone off with friends. "Hold on, Doña. I'll ask around."

María Luisa held her breath, counting off the seconds. The secretary returned and informed her that Gabriela's uncle had come to pick her up after school.

She almost said the first words on her lips: *Which uncle?* But the image of Antonio Rodríguez leapt to her mind and stopped her short. She saw him pressing a gift into Gabriela's hand, and Gabriela throwing her arms around him. María Luisa barely stammered out, "I'd forgotten. *Mil gracias*," and hung up the phone. She was about to dial Ana and Eduardo's number, but thought better of it. It was best she go herself.

María Luisa took a taxicab out to the little settlement in the desert, to Antonio's *lamina* shack. It was surrounded by building supplies, piles of sand, and bags of cement. His truck wasn't there, but she got out anyway, telling the driver to wait, and clapped her hands at the fence. "Antonio!" she yelled. She clapped again. The wind picked up, blowing dust into her eyes.

She didn't know where to look or who she could ask or
what to do at all. She told the driver to take her back home.

There she began to panic. She kept looking at the clock
as if it would tell her where her daughter was. Gabriela was
now nearly two hours late. The TV was off. The clock ticked
and ticked and ticked, revealing nothing.

There was a rooster crowing somewhere, the sounds of
boys playing *fútbol* down the street. But there was no voice
of Gabriela, though María Luisa listened intently, praying she
would hear her laughter from down the street. She sat at the
kitchen table, fidgeting with the plastic tablecloth.

When she heard the gate click and creak and close again,
she jumped to her feet and stood by the door.

Gabriela walked into the kitchen, obviously surprised to
see her standing there like that. "Oh! *Hola*, Mami," she said,
avoiding her eyes, heading straight for her room.

"Get over here, Gabi."

Gabriela hesitated, not looking up.

"*Now.*"

"*Sí*, Mami?" she said, moving toward her. As she approached, María Luisa saw that her clothes were dirty and
rumpled.

"Where have you been?" María Luisa said. "Look at you!
You're filthy!" She slapped at her daughter's clothes, trying to
brush off the dirt.

"The girls at school," Gabriela said. "We were playing after
school—they were chasing me in the playground and I fell."

María Luisa lifted Gabriela's face up by the chin. "I know
you were with Antonio. Don't you dare lie to me."

Gabriela tried to look at her feet, but María Luisa gripped her chin. "What have you done, *hija?*"

Tears filled Gabriela's eyes; her lips quivered.

María Luisa let go of her daughter, let Gabriela stare down at the clunky black shoes she'd always complained about. María Luisa stared at them too, watching her daughter's tears spot the leather. Gabriela's knee socks had slouched down to her ankles.

"You will not see him again," María Luisa said finally. "When he comes around, you stay away. You will not tell anyone about this—you hear me? No one can know. *No one.* Do you understand?"

"Yes, Mami." Gabriela closed her eyes, as if expecting to be slapped. That would do no good now, and María Luisa didn't even raise her hand, not even in warning.

Eduardo sat very still at the kitchen table. His untouched coffee was cold by now. "And that's all you know?" Eduardo said. "That one day? How long had it been going on? How did it happen in the first place?" She could feel his anger building. She could not look him in the face. She felt shame wash over her, and she felt defensive too, trying to anticipate what else Eduardo would say and how she would respond.

"I don't know, *hijo.*"

"You didn't notice anything between them before? Mamá?"

She shook her head. "He was . . . nice to her, but I didn't think it was like . . . like *that.*"

He raised his fist and hit the table. "That *puto!*"

María Luisa didn't say anything. She knew what he was feeling, because she felt it too: a heavy, sick feeling in her gut that climbed into her chest, which she would try to pound out at Mass with her fist and chants of *por mi culpa, por mi culpa.*

She put her hand on Eduardo's fist. "It's not your fault, *m'ijo.*"

He shook her hand off. "Yes, it is. It *is* my fault. And it's Papá's and Miguel's—all of us did this to her, not just Antonio." He looked her right in the eyes. "It's your fault too. You said nothing."

She sat stunned, as if he had slapped her hard across the face. She folded her hands in her lap and waited. For what, she wasn't exactly sure. For him to go on, or for the feeling to dissolve or to lodge in her chest like a boulder—just for something to happen.

He stood up and left. She heard the gate close behind him. Listened to the sound of the clock ticking.

"I was only trying to protect her," she said to herself, to no one.

# 29

# •••

I woke late. I felt ashamed of being so lazy—*floja*, is what Papá would have said. Tía Margarita had been up a while now, trying to get the kids ready and breakfast prepared. I got up off the couch immediately, folded up the blankets, and put them away. "Tía," I said, entering the kitchen, "*Discúlpeme*—"

She said nothing, but backed away from the pan on the stove, where scrambled eggs were frying, and went outside with a basket of wet clothes. I took over, finishing the cooking, sliding the eggs onto plates, heating up tortillas on the burners. My younger cousins sat at the table, too tired to even talk. I served them, glancing at the clock, hearing the scuffs of my *tía's* feet on the rooftop as she hung the clothes. "Hurry!" I said to them. "You only have a few minutes." They gobbled down their breakfast, and when it was time, I shoved them out the door with kisses.

I set to work preparing breakfast for my *tíos*, trying not to think about what I had seen the night before. My *tío* was still asleep in the room, maybe—I had not heard when he'd come home. I made their plates and put them in the oven to keep warm. I filled a bowl with soapy water and began to wash the dishes.

I saw Tío Refugio out of the corner of my eye. "Oh, *buenas*, Tío," I said, removing my hands from the soapy water, drying them on a towel. Tía Margarita came into the kitchen. I retrieved both their plates of breakfast from the oven and set them on the table. I poured coffee for them. Neither of them said a word to me. "I'm sorry I slept in," I said, as a way of smoothing things over.

"Late night?" Tío said.

It surprised me that he would say that. "No," I said, "not so late," thinking, *Not as late as you, Tío.* I turned back to the kitchen.

"Lucy," he said. "Come here. Sit."

I did as I was told, wondering what he could possibly say to me here, in the presence of his wife. He laid down his knife and fork, took a deep breath, and said, "Now, I know you're family." He rubbed his stubbled chin, then continued. "And family will do anything for family. You show up in the city, and we take you in. Just like that." He snapped his fingers.

I nodded, thinking how much he sounded like Papá, how he'd begin his lectures. How I had to sit and squirm through them all, nodding, pretending I agreed. I glanced at Tía Margarita. She stared down into her plate.

"We didn't ask any questions," he continued, "because you're our family. And in times of need, family helps family.

But there comes a time when knowing what you're doing becomes *our* business."

He paused to let this sink in. I nodded.

"You're living under our roof, Lucy. There are some things we can't permit."

"Tío," I said, "I don't know what you're talking about—"

"Don't play with me! Lucy, I *saw* you—"

"Tío!"

He looked at me with hard, set eyes.

"Tío, it's not like that," I said, talking fast, knowing it was likely the only chance I had to speak. "Let me explain! I'll tell you why I'm here—I'm looking for Gabriela. She ran away—"

"We can't allow that sort of woman into our house," Tía said into her plate, shaking her head.

"Someone said she was there, in La Merced—that's why I was there—"

"I know what I saw," Tío said firmly.

"Please—believe me," I said, trying my hardest not to cry. "I'm not like that. I'm *good*. I went to look for her—"

"I saw you leave with him," Tío said.

"But it wasn't like that. You have to believe me."

They continued shaking their heads, keeping their faces hard and unmoving as masks.

"Please," I pleaded.

"University, huh," my uncle scoffed.

"We can't have that here," my *tía* muttered. "We can't allow that sort of behaviour. We have two girls here. We can't have that."

"No, Lucy, we can't," Tío said. "You're going to have to leave."

For a moment I was so stunned I couldn't speak. I looked at the two of them, my uncle staring me down, my aunt looking into her plate of eggs, shaking her head.

Then I was yelling. "What if you lost your sister? What would you do? Wouldn't you do anything to find her?" I slammed my hands on the table.

"If you were looking for Gabriela in a place like that, we know what kind of girl she is," Tío said. "And now we know the kind you are—"

"I'm *no puta*!" I slammed my hands on the table again.

Tía flinched, but Tío stood up.

"I've done nothing wrong," I said quietly.

"We can't have that," Tía repeated. "Not with the girls . . ."

"I love those girls," I said.

Tío pointed to the door. "Go," he said.

I stood up from the table and went to the couch to gather my things. Morning light came in through the windows; the entire room was illuminated. I sat on the couch, regaining my composure, taking my time, organizing all of my things item by item and putting them into my bag. I took out a comb, combed through the tangles of my hair, slowly, methodically, while my *tíos* sat silently at the table, their backs to me. Who were these people? I wove my hair into a tight braid, then shook out the dark blue *rebozo* that the old witch woman had given me. I wrapped it over my head, around my shoulders, over my backpack. I walked toward the door and stopped, turning back to face them.

"You were there," I said, pointing at Tío, stabbing my finger at him. "You were there too. And you did worse." I walked out into the bright sunlight and acrid air, out into the tangled-up streets of Mexico City.

The wind whipped through the Zócalo, stirring up the dust. I stood at the centre of it, shielding my eyes. It was bigger than I remembered, so huge and empty it was almost frightening. I stood in a volcanic crater, on top of the destroyed Aztec market, the rubble of Aztec stone. The Palacío loomed on one side, the great Catedral Metropolitana on another. I stared up at the *catedral*, to the crosses gleaming atop the two bell towers, and I thought of our house in Santo Niño, the white cross on the hill—nothing compared to this, nothing but the tiniest speck on the map of the whole world. I felt as small, standing there, hearing the wind and the traffic and the voices of people all around me, the hard flap of the Mexican flag—the flag itself so big it seemed like it could cover our whole town.

My shadow stretched across the paving stones. Because of the *rebozo* wrapped around me, it was more like the shape of an old woman than of me. I unzipped my backpack and pulled out my camera, unwrapping the T-shirt from it slowly. I put it to my eye, focused until my shadow became clear. At the edge of the frame, people wandered in and out. When I felt it was time, I pressed the button.

Everything went still, everything quiet, clear—at least to me. Then the noise began to build again, the world around me resuming its pace. I was small. Yet this was where I was from, this huge, impossible place. And I could finally see it, what everyone said, how the *catedral* was sinking, sinking back into the swamp it was built upon, tilting slightly—just slightly—to one side. I wondered how they would save it, how they would hoist it back up again, find stable ground. This whole place was built on the surface of a lake—how long would it be before we all just slid under?

# 30
...

Antonio Rodríguez walked the perimeter of his property, checking that the posts were stable, that no wire had been cut. He eyed the desert suspiciously, though it wasn't the desert he had to worry about—it was Eduardo. Eduardo, who had given him his word, who had invited him here, promising him and his family a better life. He should never have trusted him—he was the same selfish *cabrón* as he always had been. Antonio kicked the ground.

As furious as he was with Eduardo, he was also furious with himself. He should've demanded the plot be put in his name, that the legal paperwork be done. As it was, his land was in Eduardo's name, and Eduardo had come by in his fancy suit, looking all high-and-mighty, with an official-looking document that said Antonio had to vacate the property.

Antonio had scratched his head under his cowboy hat and looked at the document. He didn't know much about this kind of thing, but he didn't trust that it was real. What *was* real was Eduardo's determination to make Antonio leave the property as soon as possible. "If not, we'll forcibly evict you," he said.

Forcibly evict him? What could that mean? And who did he mean by *we*? Antonio imagined a bunch of hired thugs storming his property.

Eduardo took an envelope from his suit jacket pocket. "Here are all the payments you made on the land. You were behind."

Antonio looked inside the envelope, saw crisp new bills there. He pushed it back to Eduardo. "No," he said, "I don't want the money. I want the land. You said the land was mine."

Eduardo folded his arms. "It was never yours. Use that money to get home."

"You promised me," Antonio said, holding out the envelope. "It's for my family. My kids!"

But Eduardo was already on his way out, stepping through the spooled wire that served as a gate without closing it.

Antonio, on his third or forth revolution around the property, decided he was not about to leave just because Eduardo said so. His so-called *hermano* had gone back on his word, and that was unacceptable.

The thought of going back to Mexico City to his old life, to be crammed up in that apartment—he couldn't bear it. And to think he'd be gutting it out as always. Based on what he'd been reading in the news, getting a job wasn't going to be as easy as it once had been. Unemployment went up every single day. He could be begging for work as a day labourer, and now there was one more child to feed.

A newborn girl. He could hear her cooing into the phone when he called Cristina. Cristina would coo back to her. She'd named her Anabel, though Antonio had wanted to name her Julia. But he hadn't been there to enforce the name, and so Cristina had written whatever she wanted on the birth certificate. It annoyed him, but what could he do about it? Nothing was ever up to him.

"When are you coming to see her?" Cristina asked every time he called.

"Soon, *mi cielo*," he'd always respond.

"I'm tired of this," she'd say. "You're never coming back, are you?"

He'd ignore her. "Put the phone by her ear."

Whether she did or didn't, he couldn't know, but he spoke to Anabel anyway. "*Hola, m'ija.* It's Papi." He'd tell her how he was building their future over in Baja, and soon they'd be together.

But that was now uncertain. The land would be taken away from under his feet, just as he had feared. No matter how many posts he put in or how much wire he unspooled, there was no disputing the fact that the land was not in Antonio's name.

He looked in the envelope again, counted the money. After the plane ticket, the rest of the money wouldn't keep his family going very long.

The next day, he drove slowly by his sister and brother-in-law's house and didn't see Eduardo's truck. He pulled off and parked, went through the gate, and knocked at the door. Ana answered, staring at him through her glasses without saying a word. The sun beat on his back, and he looked hopefully past her to the dark, cool living room, but she did not invite him in.

"Ana," he said, "we need to talk."

She pressed her lips together the way she did when she was upset. "There's nothing to say," she said.

"Don't be angry," he said. "I've had enough of that from your husband." He took off his hat so she could get a clear look at his two black eyes.

"*Oye, hermanita*. Eduardo wants to take my land away. You have to talk some sense into him."

He didn't like the way his sister was looking at him, examining him as if her lenses could penetrate his brain and reveal every last thing he was thinking.

"How could you have done such a thing?" she said. Beneath her glasses, he could see the glare of tears.

"*Hermana*—please—" But he knew he had already lost her. She shut the door, locked it, and didn't open it again even though he kept on knocking.

# 31

## •••

La Merced did not scare me in the daylight. It was just a neighbourhood, one of the many that made up the city. Women were scrubbing the walk outside of their stores, sweeping out shops, setting up their wares at the market or on stands in the street, or doing their shopping. Maybe some of them were the same women who transformed later in the afternoon—who knew? I could smell garlic frying in a pan, the sharp smell of chilies roasting. All of this comforted me. Things were being taken care of, even here.

As I walked, I noticed a few working prostitutes. They were masked by the other business of the neighbourhood, but they were there. I saw one at a newsstand, reading the headlines; I saw another beside a candied-fruit stand. Once I had noticed one, they were no longer hidden to me.

I thought I recognized streets from the night before,

though they looked different in the daylight. Shops had opened their metal grates, transforming the streets into ones of ordinary commerce. I was looking for Lupita's bar. I didn't know if I could trust her, but I wanted to know what she knew. "There are some girls . . . " she'd said. Maybe she knew where I could look for Gabriela.

I stopped before a familiar building. I wasn't sure at first if it was Lupita's bar because a metal grate shielded the entire front of the building, but I recognized the old, sagging structure. It listed to one side as if it were sinking, and there was a dirt-streaked awning above. It was a building that had once been beautiful, perhaps even grand. I clapped my hands. "Lupita!" When there was no reply, I knocked on the metal grate. "Lupita!" I yelled.

Someone called from above. "What is it?"

I backed away and looked up. On the second floor was Lupita, leaning out of the window. I was surprised to see she had short blond hair now that she wasn't wearing the scarf.

"Wait there," she said. "I'll be right down."

After a few minutes, the metal sheet rattled up. "Come in," she said, waving me inside and shutting the metal grate again, locking it to the ground. We went into the bar. She was in a blue nightgown, a jacket thrown over her shoulders.

"I'm sorry to bother you," I said.

"It's okay. Is it your sister?"

"Yes. Well, and no."

"Something happened last night," she said.

"Yes," I said. "But I'm here because you said something about where girls are—where my sister might be?"

"We can talk about that. But tell me what happened to *you*. We have to make sure you are safe and stable before we can look for your sister."

The words were like rocks in my mouth. I told her about seeing my *tío* here and him seeing me, about him throwing me out of the house, and how I wasn't sure where to go now. I told her how afraid I was for Gabriela. Magda had done something bad to Gabi, I was sure of it. I told Lupita what Magda had said, told her about the house, the money, the melon, everything.

"I'm going to find my sister," I said, suddenly *brava*, "and if that means searching the streets of Merced, it's worth it. If that means everyone thinking I'm a prostitute, then it's worth it." As soon as that came out of my mouth, I felt ashamed. I lowered my eyes.

Of course I wasn't, and would never be, a prostitute, I went on, but they didn't understand, my *tíos*. They didn't understand I needed Gabriela. She was vital to me; she was like my own heart.

Lupita said nothing for a moment. She pulled the jacket tighter around her shoulders. "Gabriela . . . " she said, thinking. "I don't think I've seen her. But that doesn't mean she's not here." She pressed her lips together, deciding whether or not to say something. "Some girls are hard to find. Some are hidden. But we can help look for her. For now you can stay here. There's a little room—okay, closet—at the end of my hall. It's open. It's yours for as long as you wish."

I looked down at the floor. "I don't know . . . " I said.

"Pay what you can," Lupita said. "And you can help with the cleaning."

I could feel her looking at me. She might've known what I was thinking—that I would not pay with my body.

"Whatever you're comfortable contributing," she added. "Lucy?"

"Yes?"

"You are safe here."

I nodded.

"Come on up," she said.

We walked through the red curtains that the two Lucha Libre men had been guarding the night before, heading up badly lit stairs. The smell of must and age was heavy. I followed her down a long, dark hallway. She opened a door with 201 written on the wood in thick black marker.

The room was full of light. Dust circled, illuminated, the way phosphorus illuminates the sea at night. The curtains billowed from the air of the open window. It looked like a hotel room, with two beds and a nightstand between them. A man sat on the edge of one of the beds, fully dressed, smoking a cigarette. It was Felix.

"You followed me," I said.

He nodded.

An alarm went off inside me. Why was he here? Why were *we* here? This was not the room she had described to me, the room where she said I could stay. I had my eye on the open door, ready to run.

"This is my and Felix's room. He's my husband," she said, perhaps sensing my fear. "It's a bit spartan, I'm afraid."

I scanned the framed photographs on the wall: one of Lupita and Felix and a tall teenaged boy between them;

another of somebody's parents; Lupita and Felix's wedding photo, taken in what looked like a park. Seeing those calmed me enough to allow Lupita to lead me to the flimsy card table and folding chair by the window. I sat down but did not take off my *rebozo* or my backpack.

She pointed to the picture on the wall. "That's our son, Alejandro," she said. "He's at university now in Guadalajara."

Felix stood up, tucked in his shirt. "He's the smartest of the bunch," he said, stretching lazily, the cigarette dangling from his mouth.

"I need a favour, *amor*," Lupita said to him.

"Of course," he said, putting on his suit jacket.

"If you could stop by Calle San Judas Tadeo after work," she said.

He paused, then flipped the collar of his jacket flat. He put the cigarette out in an ashtray. "For her sister?" he asked.

"Yes."

Felix nodded.

"Her name's Gabriela Amador Prieto," Lupita said. She described Gabriela as well as I had described her. When she was done, she asked me if she'd missed anything. I shook my head, amazed that she could remember so much about a girl she'd never met.

"I'll see what I can find out," he said. He leaned in to kiss Lupita on the lips. Then he was out the door, into the dark hallway. In a couple of minutes, I looked out the window and saw him on the street.

"What's Calle San Judas Tadeo?" I asked.

"It's where the new girls are," she said. "And the girls

who've been stolen." She glanced out the window. "Forced into sex work."

I felt my face go cold.

"I'm sorry. There's no nice way to say it."

"I know."

"But if she's there, we can get her back. They'll let a girl go if you put enough cash in their hands. Sometimes it's not even very much."

"You've done this before," I said.

Lupita nodded. "It's what I do. It's my work," she said carefully, trying to gauge how much she should tell me. "I used to be one of those girls. And now I'm an activist of sorts."

I swallowed hard, trying to keep the bile down. The buying and selling of human beings—my sister might just be another ware on sale at the Mercado Merced. I felt sick.

"You should get some rest," she said.

Lupita took me to the little room at the end of the hall. It had no number and was indeed more like a closet than a room. There was a narrow cot, and a tiny window I could not see out of because it was blue textured glass. The windowsill was where I would make my shrine, I thought. The glass behind where I would put my candles, my photographs, my flowers, would be like the stained glass of a cathedral—here is where I would keep my vigil.

I watched Lupita as she spoke. I wasn't even listening, just watching her, trying to see if there was anything beneath her kindness. Maybe all this was a trick to steal *me*, enslave *me*. This room might be a jail cell. The window did not open more than a crack. I kept thinking about what she'd said.

*Some girls are hidden. Girls who've been stolen. Forced into sex work.* Why would she help me? Why would anyone help anyone in a place like this? I thought of this immense city, with all its buildings and countless rooms, the labyrinth of doors, and behind them all the horrible things that were probably happening right now to so many girls even as we sat here, maybe even to Gabi. I remembered reading about it in the newspaper, long ago: girls being locked up in rooms or chained somewhere, sold, raped, and killed. Here in D.F., in Juárez, in Tijuana.

"Lucy?" She was holding out something in her hand. "The key to your room," she said, dropping it into my palm.

If I pressed my face to the blue glass, peering through one of the swells of bubbles, I could see out. I could glimpse the street, the cars, the people—all slightly distorted. If I put my eye to the camera, and the camera up against this glass, I could pretend I was not here at all, but in a place where light and darkness were the same because everything was simply blue.

Movement across the window—*palomas* flying up to roost.

The next weeks passed in constant searching; they passed in images. They passed through a lens, in pieces. It was like I was always peering through the bubbled blue glass. I found my eyes useless. I walked the streets in the afternoons, looking for her. Imagining her, reconstructing her. Deconstructing every young woman I saw. Trying to find familiarities: a trunk-like waist, ears that stuck out. The way she walked or how she laughed. Though I knew, too, that all of this could have changed in these past months. Felix had not yet found her at the place for new girls, but I did not trust him. Maybe she was there. Maybe he'd paid for her. Maybe, as a man, he couldn't help himself.

Gabriela's birthday came and went. I observed it silently, staring into the bubbles of the blue window, trying to conjure her up. I lit a special candle for her. I wished that we were both at home instead, that she were dancing at her party, that we were at least together. But that was all I could do—that and hope that somehow she knew I was thinking of her.

I looked through the lens of the camera, let it see for me. I took pictures of the streets as I searched for my sister. I took pictures of buildings, cracked sidewalks, cobbles in the road, piles of fruit, piñatas sparkling in the sun, fading in shadow. Sometimes people on the street would stop and squint in the direction I pointed my camera, trying to see what I was seeing, what could possibly be so important to photograph. One old man shook his head at me and said, "But there's nothing there but a junky old building!" More often there were confused looks as I took pictures of ordinary scenes of the street: kids fixing bikes, street shrines, the feet and legs of women—all kinds, from *abuelas* in their comfort shoes to prostitutes in high heels. But I couldn't see her in any of this. I couldn't see myself, either.

When I was too worn out to continue, I'd go back to my room and sit before my shrine. I'd bought tall candles in glass jars with the Virgen de Guadalupe on the sides. I kept them going so that when I came back to the building after a long, disheartening search, my blue window would be glowing: a beacon in the midst of the gloom. Something to return to.

Sometimes people thought I was a prostitute, no matter what I wore or how I carried myself, not least because I went to bars where women were not allowed—unless they were prostitutes. I went into bar after bar, warding off men by telling them I was already booked. I told lie after lie. I asked around for a particular young woman, but I did not find her.

Early one evening I decided to go there myself, to Calle San Judas Tadeo. I had crossed it many times without realizing it. It was just a *calle*, with nothing particular about it. The paved street was littered with *papelerías*, super-minis, appliance repair shops, clothiers, and butcher shops. People were going about their business. Bags of onions were being delivered to restaurants. A café that served *menudo* was open. An *abuela* and her grandson were buying a notebook at a *papelería*. The farther I walked, the narrower the street became; the buildings crowded in, making a tunnel.

I lowered my camera. I tucked it beneath my arm. There was something different here.

Buildings were shuttered, and some doorways were bricked in completely. One grubby shirt had been hung out to dry from a second-floor window. Up ahead, a length of blue tarp covered the whole street, and the sidewalk turned to dirt. The air went dank. I smelled smoke, like a building was on fire. Men leaned against the walls, doing nothing, silently watching me as I passed. A dead dog lay across my path like a warning.

I found myself before a shrine to Santa Muerte, the skeletal saint taking up part of the street, with offerings of dolls and sweets at her bony feet. I didn't believe in Santa Muerte, but I crossed myself anyway, because I was afraid.

Down the street, I saw a crowd. I walked toward it, thinking it might be another shrine. I tried to think of the date and which saint's day it was that would draw such a mass of people. As I neared, I saw the crowd was divided into two parts. In the middle of the street, there were perhaps fifty young girls walking in a slow circle, while even more men stood or sat at bar tables that spilled out of a building and onto the sidewalk, watching the girls. Some of the girls were very young, younger than Gabi. They wore pink vinyl, animal prints, spandex, tube tops. The men nodded to the girls they wanted, walked with them past a statue of St. Jude, where they crossed themselves, to a doorway where a grim-faced guard frisked the men.

I froze at the edge of the crowd, watching the girls. Some stared at me, stone-faced, before looking away. I wanted to talk to them, ask them questions. I wanted to see her and not see her. Did they know her? "I'm looking for a girl," I wanted to say. But so was everyone. I tried to see into their faces. The circle of girls thinned as they began to disappear, led away by one man or another.

A girl hissed at me—a sound like a rattlesnake—and tapped the medallion of La Muerte around her neck. I backed away, ducked into the doorway of the building next door.

I heard a sharp whistle.

"You!" someone yelled. "Girl in the jeans!"

Someone seized my arm. The man was very big. His meaty hand easily encircled my arm.

"Come with me," he said, trying to drag me out. I squirmed and struggled, kicked at him.

"No," I said. "I'm not—I just happened to—"

He pulled me into the street, toward the door with the guards. I dug my heels into the dirt, leaving tracks in the street. "No!" I shouted. He slapped my face and yanked my hair. I cried out, tried to pull away, but he was stronger than me.

I began to pray. I prayed to the Virgen, prayed to Jesucristo, prayed to God Himself directly, the words rising through me to finally surface at my lips. It was my voice and it was not my voice. It grew louder as we neared the door: "Santa María, Santo Niño, San Pedro . . ." He gripped my arm so hard I thought no blood would ever get to my hand—it would fall off, turn into a tin *milagro*. I called out every saint that came to mind. "San Judas! San Raúl! Santa Lucía, San Diego, San Luis!"

The man slapped his hand over my mouth. "Shut up!"

I bit the meat of his palm, hard. I tried to pull away, but I dropped my camera. It hit the ground with a crack, startling both me and the man. He let go. I grabbed my camera and ran down the street, knocking someone over, leaping over the dead dog, running and running and still calling my saints, whispering their names as I ran all the way back to the unnamed bar, to the room in which I lived.

# 32

### • • •

Raúl Amador left the bar, locking the door behind him. It was the quietest and darkest part of the morning, the palm trees dead still. Somewhere there was music, somewhere far away. He strained to hear it, wanting to hear it.

He turned the corner onto the cobble-and-dirt road, leaving Calle Morelos. His truck was parked a few blocks up by the plaza, along the row of bushes and beneath the palm trees—a cool, shaded spot during the day. He pulled up on the handle and creaked open the door.

He was shoved face down into the seat, the breath knocked from him. The keys clanked out of his hand. There was something cold at the back of his neck. He swallowed hard, said into the vinyl seat, "Please—"

"Shh," a man whispered. "Now close your eyes."

Raúl did as he was told. He closed them tight; tears squeezed through.

Then his head was yanked up by his hair, and a cloth bag was slipped over his head, easily, as if the man had done it a thousand times before. Someone else tied his hands behind his back.

They kicked Raúl to the floor of the cab, threw a blanket over him, and slammed the doors. He was curled up like a baby. A pair of feet pressed into him.

"Don't move," the man said. "I'm pointing a gun right at your head."

Raúl didn't move. Someone started the truck and drove.

Raúl tried to pay attention to the movement of the truck, tried to count the turns. Right, then left, then left again. He knew these streets well and for a while could guess where they were, but there were too many turns. The roads became rougher. Dust filled his mouth.

The truck stopped. The engine was cut and they got out, except for the one whose feet were still on him. There were voices, too soft. Raúl couldn't make out the words. They opened the doors and dragged him from the truck, shoved him to the ground, a knee in his back. "Okay, señor," someone said, "any weird moves and you die."

Raúl did not move.

He tried to count the voices, tried to count the pairs of hands. He couldn't tell how many there were. He knew it didn't really matter, but it was important to have a distraction from what was sure to come. So he counted. He let it fill his mind, the counting, all the numbers. Two voices—no, three. Five. Young voices. Male. Two pairs of hands, three, four, five—no, six—or were those the same hands, taken away, then put back? One gun pointed at his head. Five faces, and he tried to imagine them, what they might look like. He tried to imagine the car they pulled him into. They were ditching his truck somewhere, he realized. He imagined every detail of the plastic seats he was pushed across before they pressed him to the floor again. He didn't fit into that narrow space, but they made him fit, three pairs of feet stomping him into it.

They drove. The smell of gasoline and exhaust: a crappy car. Something rotten beneath the seat where Raúl's face was lodged.

Nobody spoke. He thought he heard whispering, but he wasn't sure if it was coming from them or from himself.

# 33

...

I was able to fix the camera. When it hit the ground, the impact had opened the back and dislodged the metal bottom. I had lost three screws. I imagined them in the street, rolling beneath shoes, lodging in the dirt: three tiny bits of silver gleaming in the dark.

I snapped the metal piece back on, tightened the two remaining screws. I had lost the film, but the camera seemed to work as before. I lay with it on my cot in my little room with the blue window, hugged it against my chest and cried.

I listened to the sounds around me crescendo as the night wore on. Every night, the same sounds: The *boleros* wailing from below. The shouts from the street. Voices of women in the hallway, taking men to their rooms. I wondered about Gabi, if, right at this moment, a man was taking her up a dark set of stairs to a shabby room. If so, there was nothing I could do about it. She was fading from me. I couldn't imagine her anywhere. She was beginning to flicker out, a snuffed candle. Just like Papá had wanted.

Mornings I'd wake to the rumble of traffic, truck deliveries, metal shutters opening on the shops. Women scrubbing the sidewalks. Kids playing soccer in the street on Saturdays. I'd get up, go downstairs to the little kitchen off the main room, where the bar was, and begin to make coffee and prepare breakfast. I'd hand plates of eggs and tortillas, and Styrofoam cups of coffee, to the sleepy Lucha Libre guards if they were still there. I'd hand plates to the women who were waking up or who couldn't sleep. I'd pick up a broom and a mop and clean. It was part of my payment to Lupita, the only thing I could really do that would make any difference at all.

It had taken me a while to get used to them, the prostitutes. I'd avoided them, lowered my eyes in their presence, and wouldn't say anything unless they said something to me, and even then, I kept my answers short. What could we possibly talk about? They sold their bodies to men for a living. Their lives were in another universe, far from mine.

I looked for Gabi late afternoons and evenings, taking photos as I went. Some people began to recognize me— prostitutes and shopkeepers alike—and greeted me like they knew me. I greeted them back, giving a *buenas tardes* here and there, smiles, and waves. I was becoming a part of the neighbourhood. Some people knew I was looking for my sister, and they vowed to keep their eyes open for a girl like Gabriela. Every day, though, they'd shake their heads and say they had no news.

In the blackest part of the night, which was really the earliest part of the morning, I prayed over the candles, sometimes putting my palms against the cold blue window. I don't know why. I was half pleading, half in surrender. I wanted an answer. I wanted my saints to talk to me, to send me a sign. They seemed to have left me. *Nuestra Señora, Virgencita de Guadalupe, where are you?*

The women in my building and I began talking over breakfast, or when I was cleaning the halls, or when we suddenly found ourselves with idle hands. They told me about Lupita, what she had done for them. She had worked with the government to get some of the women here out of sex slavery. I learned that a couple of the women who lived here weren't prostitutes at all, but had been thrown out of their homes and had nowhere to go. She gave them all shelter, a safe place to live, including the old prostitutes, *viejitas* who had been abandoned by their families, left to the streets to live in cardboard and newspaper. Women who were mothers and grandmothers were left on the street like that, selling themselves in exchange for a meal sometimes. Lupita got them all together—all of *us*, they said—to pool what money they could. She persuaded the city government to pitch in to buy and renovate the old building off la Plaza de la Soledad. Some of them lived there now, the old prostitutes, able to retire in peace. I saw them sometimes when I went to sit in la Plaza de la Soledad, watching them lean out their windows and look out over the street as if looking back on their lives.

The women in my building asked about my camera, which was often in my hands. A woman whom others called

Chiapas María laughed and said, "O Santa Lucía, walking around with her eyes in her hands. Santa Lucy, the virgin above the bar, living with the *putas*."

Soon they all called me Santa Lucy—even Lupita sometimes. Down in the bar, the women greeted me as *Nuestra Santísima*; even the Lucha Libre guards began saying it. "*Buenas, Santísima*," they'd say.

I was no saint, I told the women, which made them all laugh. Compared to them, they said, I had halos all over me; I was illuminated. If that had any truth to it at all, it was only because I was afraid of the dark, afraid of not being able to see. While I slept, I kept my candles lit and the lamp by my cot switched on.

One night I was returning to the building, focusing on the blue light of my window. I crossed myself when I saw it. I always did, thanking God and the Virgen for keeping me safe as I wandered the streets. A woman standing on the corner next to me crossed herself too. She whispered a prayer into the air, her gaze lifted toward my window.

I stared at her. What was she praying to? She didn't look at me. She kept walking straight ahead, past the building and down my *calle*. I thought it was strange, but over the next few days, I began to notice: It wasn't just that woman, but others too. I saw one woman kneel on the sidewalk beneath my window, the soles of her bare feet blackened. She said a prayer, kissed the medallion around her neck, and rose up.

I went straight to Lupita after I saw that. I sat at the bar and drank Fresca and told her what I'd been seeing. She smiled a little. "*Querida*," she said, "haven't you heard? There are rumours that a saint lives above this very bar, and that a blessed blue light shines from the tiny second-floor window."

I shook my head. "That's ridiculous."

"I'm only telling you what I've heard," she said, pouring more soda into my cup. "Sometimes they see the saint's palms against the glass, and they know she has heard them. Sometimes she responds in whispers." Lupita looked at me and laughed a little. "It's true, *querida*. They say the blue light carries prayers in the saddest part of the night, when sight and sound become the same thing. The saint upstairs," Lupita said, pointing up, "gives people hope. Lightens their burdens."

"No," I said. "They're wrong. It's false. I'm false. False idols."

"Let them have hope," Lupita said. She patted my hand and turned to a customer.

Offerings—candles, jars of flowers, rosewater, Barbie dolls, tamales, coins, chili powder, nail polish, medallions, *lotería* cards—all crowded against the wall in the narrow space between the door of Lupita's and the door of the bar next door. They were not quite directly under my second-floor window, but as close as you could get to it from the street.

A woman in plastic platform heels and a slip that barely covered her walked on her knees until she reached the shrine angled below the glowing blue window, blood dripping down her shins when she crossed herself and rose. I wanted to go to her, shake her, slap her, tell her to stop. I wanted to tell her there was no saint, just a girl who couldn't do anything for anyone. But she saw me, somehow recognized me, and held out her arms. "*Santísima*," she whispered, "it's you."

"No," I said. "No, you're wrong."

Tears ran down her face, black rivers of tears—smeared mascara. "*Santísima*, please. Bless me."

I didn't know what to do. I had no power to bless. I put my hands together, closed my eyes, and said a prayer for her. She smiled, wiped her eyes on the backs of her hands, and got up off her knees. "Thank you," she said. "May I touch your hair?"

"My hair?"

"*Porfa*," she said, the way Gabriela would say *porfa* when she really wanted something.

I touched my hair, which was coming out of its sloppy braid. "I guess so," I said.

She walked to me with her arms out, as if she were a blind person. When she came close enough to touch me, I closed my eyes, almost afraid. I felt her hands alight gently on the crown of my head, as if she were blessing *me*. A calm entered my body. She lifted her hands, and I felt like I was lifting with them, floating there.

Soon I found offerings of tin *milagros*—eyes, hearts, breasts, legs—outside my door. I found necklaces, crosses, a ring. There was a stuffed bear propped up outside my door, a bottle of perfume, *dulces*, a photograph of a baby. Someone stuffed a fat lock of hair beneath the door. There were also pieces of paper, notes and letters, slid beneath my door.

Estimada *Santa Lucía,*

*I heard you might be able to help me. My daughter has disappeared. Here is a lock of my hair in offering. If you find her for me, I swear I will cut off all of it for you.*

*Santa Lucía* que viene para nosotros desde Syracuse, o donde-quiera, favor *give my mamá her eyesight back. She has been a good, devout woman her entire life, always saying her* Ave Marías. *She's done nobody harm. I write this for her because she pretends she hasn't gone blind, but we all know she has.* Favor *restore her eyes, as* Dios *restored your own eyes. Have mercy on my mamá. Gracias. Alfonso A. A.*

Santísima *Lucy,*

*I make this petition so that you can help Rodolfo see how much I love him. Please convince him to marry me. I love him so much and I can't live without him.*

*Señora Lucy,*

*Please bless me with your gift of vision and sight, and tell me what I should do. I offer you this* milagro *of eyes. Please help me.*

Every morning there were more letters and notes jammed beneath my door, petition after petition, sometimes an offering of *gracias recibido*—thanks given. A woman's mother had been cured of a serious illness. Someone else had found true love. There was a paper bag stuffed full of long brown hair, a note that said, "My daughter has been found and is safely beside me. Gracias for hearing me and granting me my petition. I've done what I promised. In gratitude, Alicia P." Another note from a Margarita Salas said she would offer a Mass in my name. Outside were offerings, more objects than I knew what to do with, and every day there were more prayer candles lit. They lined the halls and pushed up against the door. The offerings began to move onto the door—people glued and taped *milagros*, photographs, prayer cards, and even petitions on the wood.

At night the mutterings of other people's prayers curled into my sleep, and sometimes I woke saying prayers too. More than once there was weeping from the other side of the door, or from the sidewalk. I couldn't see what Dios was getting at. I had prayed for help, for an answer, for guidance, and if this was His answer, I didn't understand any of it. Maybe He had a sense of humour, taking Chiapas María's joke about Santa Lucy a step further. Or maybe this was a serious matter, and He was using me for some higher purpose. But if that were true, then it was all fake—believing in God would mean nothing. Because I could do nothing to help these people. I had *done* nothing. That Alicia P. had found her daughter was not because of me.

But what did I know of the ways of Dios?

Even so, I read the petitions. I kept them. They were the pain of the human soul, the things that made us suffer, the things we were missing. I wished I could be on the other side of the door at times, offering a *milagro*, writing my own pleas, releasing them, easing the pain inside me.

• • •

I unfolded yet another petition: a piece of pink paper with a black border folded up a million times and shoved beneath my door. It smelled like roses.

Querida Santísima *Lucy,*

*I write this petition with a broken heart. I'm smearing ink with my tears. Please protect my* querida *Gabriela wherever she goes, do not let harm come to her, and please bring her back to me. Bring her back to me or let me go to her. I feel like I will die without her. In offering I bring you a* milagro *heart I painted myself and Gabriela's favourite* dulce. *I will do anything you ask if you grant my petition. I await your instruction.*

*Yours with love and respect,*
*Pilar*

I opened the door with such force that the wind from it made the candle flames shudder. There it was against the wall, beside a lit candle: the *milagro* and a large round of *dulce de tamarindo* wrapped in Cellophane.

I ran down the hall of closed doors, down the sagging steps, and through the curtains to the bar. It had just opened; not too many people were there yet. Lupita had opened a bag of plastic cups and begun stacking them on a shelf. Felix wiped down tables. I turned to the guards at the curtained door and held up the *dulce* and the heart. "Did you see who brought this?" I asked. I knew the guards were making a profit because of my sainthood, taking a small entrance fee from those who wanted to leave a petition.

"Oh, *Santísima*, you wouldn't believe it. A tall, dark woman—"

The other guard laughed. "*Woman*," he muttered.

The first guard glared and continued. "A tall, dark woman with a Spanish shawl and bejewelled fingers."

"Do you know where I can find her?"

"Not here," said the guard who'd laughed. "Those types aren't allowed around here."

"Cuauhtémoc," Felix said from across the room. "I've seen her around Tepito."

I ran out the door and into the street, running so fast the entire neighbourhood was a blur—the buildings, the people, the shops and cafés. The newsstand was a smudge. I couldn't run fast enough. A few people fell to their knees as I passed, crossing themselves. Some people I knew and some people I didn't. There was the hairdresser, the newspaper vendor, women I'd never seen before, a clerk at the *papelería*. I couldn't stop for them, couldn't do anything for them; I could only run.

Underground, the train was not fast enough. It took forever to arrive, and forever to get to the station at Tepito. Up the steps and out on the streets again, through the market stalls of the *tianguis*, I searched for Pilar. Tarps and tents lined the streets. There were tables of videotapes, CDs, jeans, and shoes. I searched for over an hour, asking around the stands and kiosks, asking the kids who sold knick-knacks on the street.

Finally, I described what I knew about Pilar to a woman who was sweeping outside of an *abarrotes* shop. The woman pointed down the street. "She's right there."

Pilar was only a few yards away, leaning against a narrow segment of chipped-up wall between the *abarrotes* and a clothing shop, smoking a cigarette. People who'd been shopping at the market, laden with bags, walked by her without a glance. But she was as magnificent as a Spanish dancer, a *flamenca*, the Virgen Morena, her fringed shawl loose around her shoulders. Her long black hair was twisted into a knot, two red roses woven into it. Moorish eyeliner jutted from the corners of her eyes. Perfect breasts rose up from her black lace blouse, her exposed belly smooth and flat. If it weren't for her broad shoulders and large hands, she would have looked more like a woman than I did.

When she saw me looking at her, she froze, either surprised or afraid. Then she smiled widely, as if we knew each other, dropped the cigarette, and ran to me. As she embraced me, the scent of rosewater, tobacco, and smoke washed over me. "*Querida!*" she said. "You came back!"

"Pilar?" I said into her shoulder.

She wouldn't let go, so I wrapped my arms around her, hugged her back.

Eventually she pulled away, held me by the shoulders. She stared into my face, her own face clouding over.

"You're not her." Her shoulders slumped, defeated. "But you look so much like her." She let go of me and wiped her eyes with the back of her hand, leaving hard, black streaks there.

I reached in my pocket for her petition, held it out to her. "I'm looking for her too," I said.

Pilar sank to her knees. "*La Santísima,*" she said.

"No, please." I put the petition in my pocket and took her hand, pulling her up. "I'm just her sister. I'm Gabriela's sister."

She kissed my hand as she stood, then held it between her own. She had long fake nails painted as red as her roses. She wore rings with fake gems, glass and plastic, like the ones Antonio had sometimes brought for Gabi.

"Come on up to my humble abode, Santa Lucía," she said, pointing to the building behind her. "I'll tell you what I know."

# 34
...

Pilar had first seen Gabriela in a *callejón* near Calle Libertad. Pilar herself had just been run out from another bar in La Merced. She swore she'd been there before and nobody had cared. Maybe she'd been mistaken, maybe the crowd had changed, but whatever the case, she'd gone into the wrong bar. It was almost like the men in the bar had planned it out, and before she could sense that anything was awry, she was surrounded. A fist caught her in the jaw—the icebreaker, so to speak, a cue for other fists to come at her. Pilar had been in many fights before, many more than any of these men, she supposed, and fought back. Seeing one another's bloody noses and mouths and swollen lips made them more infuriated—no freak *maricón* was going to best them. Once she heard "Kill the fag!" Pilar knew she had to get out immediately. She went for the balls, kicking her way out of the bar. She ran at full speed in high heels until she had lost them.

Pilar walked back to her apartment to get cleaned up. She could feel her lip swelling, and one of her eyes was closing up. She pulled a mirror out of her purse and stopped beneath a street light to check the damage—that was when she noticed the girl in the alley.

The girl pressed herself to the wall, trying to make herself invisible. She'd almost succeeded; she was half-hidden behind a pair of metal trash barrels, the rest of her easily blended into shadow, but the street light hit her face, illuminating it. They looked at each other, the girl quickly averting her eyes and crouching down, sinking behind the barrels. Pilar looked around to see if anyone was watching, then walked into the alley.

"Are you all right?"

Silence.

"It's okay. You can come with me, *hija*," she whispered. "I won't hurt you."

The girl only sank farther. Pilar could see the flash of her eyes.

"I promise you, *hija*. I swear to the Virgen de Guadalupe."

That hadn't worked either. Eventually, though, the girl's voice rose up from the garbage. "What happened to you?" she asked.

Pilar sighed. "I got beat up again," she said. "But I got them good this time. You think I look bad, you should've seen them."

The girl eased herself back up but she was shaky, her balance off. Pilar held out her hand. The girl went to take it, but drew back, startled.

"It's all right," Pilar said. "Nothing's perfect, you know."

"You're a man," the girl said.

"*Was*," Pilar corrected. "That was a long time ago."

The girl was filthy. Her dress was oily with grime and food scraps. She'd been hiding in the market trash. She stank.

"What happened to you, girl?"

She didn't answer, peering both ways down the alley.

"Is someone after you?"

She said nothing, but Pilar could tell it was true. A girl doesn't go hiding in trash for no reason.

"Don't worry—I won't let anyone come near you."

She let Pilar pull her from the trash. Pilar untied the fringed shawl from around her waist and draped it around the girl's head.

"Come on," Pilar said. "Lean on me."

She leaned on Pilar heavily, stumbling here and there.

"Steady, girl. Steady."

Gabriela stayed with Pilar for several weeks. At first she did not go out. Pilar didn't know what had happened to her exactly, but it was clear that it was something bad. The girl had fear pulsing through her veins. She kept watch at the window, crouched low. When Pilar asked what she was doing, she said, "Watching for them."

"For who, *querida*? Come away from the window. Get some sleep."

Once, Pilar woke to Gabriela sitting at the window with a pen and a piece of paper on a book, writing by street light. She seemed content sitting there, a little smile on her face.

"What are you doing, *querida*?" Pilar whispered.

Gabriela glanced over her shoulder. "I'm writing a letter to my sister," she said.

"Your sister?" It was the first time Gabriela had mentioned anything about her family.

"I miss her so much."

"Tell me about her."

Not long after that, Pilar finally convinced her to go outside to get some fresh air. At first it was only to the market to browse the countless tables of pirated goods—and only in disguise, in some of Pilar's clothes, the fringed shawl around her head so she looked like an old woman from far away.

One day, as Pilar was putting on her makeup, Gabriela said, "I don't want to be a girl anymore."

Pilar glanced at her in the mirror. "Well, come on, then. Pull up a chair." She dug through the eyeshadows and mascaras, lipsticks and rouges, and after some contemplation, picked out a few compacts and tubes. She lifted a brush to Gabriela's face to begin to transform her into a woman.

Gabriela shook her head. "I don't want to be a woman either."

"What then?"

"Make me a man."

Pilar went to her closet and sorted through the clothes at the very back, the clothes she once wore many years ago. She told Gabriela to undress, and Pilar wrapped strips of cloth from an old shirt around her breasts to flatten them. Then she dressed Gabriela in one of her old suits, pinning up the trouser legs and tucking in the waist. She pinned her hair up beneath a hat. When she was done, Pilar circled Gabriela, but something wasn't quite right.

"It's the hair, isn't it?" Gabriela said. "Just cut it."

Pilar took off the hat, unpinned Gabriela's hair, and ran her fingers through it. "Oh, *querida*, are you sure? It's so beautiful."

"I don't want beautiful," Gabriela said. "I want to be a man."

Pilar braided Gabriela's hair and sawed it off with a sharp knife. She trimmed here and there with a pair of scissors, then got out a razor to shorten the back and the sides. She combed it back with water and gel, then turned Gabriela to the mirror.

Pilar was pleased with her work. "Not quite a man," she said, smiling. "But a very nice *muchacho*."

Gabriela turned to the side, examining her new self. It seemed she liked what she saw, because she was smiling. "I don't look like me at all," she said.

They went out into the city more often; Gabriela even went out by herself. But something frightened her again. Pilar never knew what it was—Gabriela would not talk about it, no matter how Pilar prodded. Maybe she had seen the people she was hiding from, but she wouldn't say. Gabriela only said she had to leave, that there was a better place for her to live, a place where she did not have to be afraid, and she was heading to *el norte* to find it. Pilar protested, told her how dangerous it was. Gabriela told her not to worry; she had family in *el norte*. She would be safe.

"It's the getting there, girl, that's dangerous," Pilar said. "If only I was your mother. I'd forbid you to go."

"Don't worry. I have a plan." It was simple. She was going to take the bus up to the Mexico-Texas border, to the Rio Grande. She'd heard there were many parts of the river that went unguarded; all she had to do was swim across.

"Swim across! You're going to drown!" Pilar said.

"I'm a good swimmer! I used to swim all the time!"

"You don't know the Rio Grande. Promise me you won't swim across."

Gabriela frowned, then shrugged. "Fine. I'll find another way."

Pilar begged her not to go. She told her there was no promised land; one had to create it in the here and now. Gabriela asked if she wanted to come with her, but Pilar had no idea what she'd do up there. She was a *defeña*, born and raised, and her home, with all its hardships, was Mexico City. For it was a beautiful city, too, she tried to remind Gabriela. You could find beauty on every single street, every day. But no matter what Pilar said, there was no convincing Gabriela to stay.

"She promised she would write," Pilar said, tears filling her eyes again. "But nothing's come yet." She got up from the bed where we were sitting and went to the closet. From the shelf she pulled a shoebox and held it out to me. Lifting the lid, I found a thick black braid—Gabriela's hair. It was so familiar to me. I ran my fingers along it, thinking of all the times I'd brushed it and braided it like this.

"Take it," Pilar said, sitting beside me.

I shook my head. "I can't." I put the lid back on the box and set it on Pilar's lap. I couldn't stand to take one more offering.

# 35

...

Raúl sweated under the blanket, trying to talk to Dios. Or if not Dios, then at least his saints. He didn't know if any of them were listening.

They drove for what seemed like a very long time through rutted roads and dust. Then, too soon, they stopped. He wasn't ready yet for whatever was to come.

They pulled him out of the car and set him on his feet. "Walk," a voice said. Raúl took a step, then collapsed. His legs would not work. They yanked him up, dragged him until he hit the base of a tree. "Don't move." Someone tied his wrists behind his back, then spun him around and bound him to the tree.

The bag was stripped from his head. Surprised, he gasped for air. He saw the boy who'd done that. The boy had a bandana over his nose and mouth. Raúl didn't recognize him. He fed Raúl a dirty rag and taped his mouth shut. It tasted like gasoline, and he gagged; his eyes watered. He felt the others lurking in his periphery but could not see them.

The desert night was clear and silent. There was no sound at all. The saguaros were full of shadows. Raúl could see the marks in the dirt where he'd been dragged, where he'd fallen.

The boy was smiling beneath the bandana, Raúl could tell. "We're the Zapatistas," he said, laughing. Someone shushed him.

The boy put the bag back over Raúl's head.

He felt a sharp point at his chest, his shirt cut open, the night air cooling the sweat on his skin.

The envelope he'd tucked into the front of his pants was pulled from his belt. The daily deposit. There were 6,122 pesos and 2,050 U.S. dollars. He heard a whistle—the boy must've been impressed with the amount of money there.

The chain with the gold medals of his saint was snapped from his neck. His shoes and socks were removed. Someone was trying to work the wedding band off his finger.

Daylight was beginning to seep through the fabric of the bag; Raúl saw his assailants as shadows. If they were smart, they'd forget about the ring and get out of there. But they were greedy.

Raúl hadn't taken that ring off in many years, and his knuckles had swollen with age. The boy was struggling with it. "*Chinga*," he muttered.

"What?"

"I can't get the ring off."

"Cut it off, then," another voice said.

"No, I think I can get it."

"You think we have time to fuck around? Cut the finger off! We'll get the ring later!"

He heard the flick of a knife, wondered vaguely how it could possibly cut through the bone. The boy held Raúl's finger in one hand, almost gently. Raúl felt the quick cut of the blade and winced in pain. "How am I supposed to do this?" the boy asked. "We need an axe!"

"Fucking idiot! Here, use this!" His ring finger was pulled taut, pressed against the tree.

"Shut up," someone said quietly, right at his ear. "You want everyone to hear?"

That voice, Raúl thought. It belonged to someone he knew, someone he'd heard before. He turned his head sharply toward him, tried to see through the bag. Who was it?

A searing pain went through his finger and there was a benign snapping sound, like a branch underfoot; he screamed into the rag, his voice so muffled it couldn't begin to ease the pain he felt.

"Ah, *cabrón*," one of them said.

"See, you don't need an axe."

"It's all over my shirt."

*Blood*, Raúl thought, *my blood*. He screamed, but it did no good. He pulled against the ropes that bound him to the tree, trying to run, to get away from the pain at all costs, but it was like a dark curtain had pulled closed across his face—it was suddenly night. Then he was out.

# PART THREE

| | |
|---|---|
| *Para que ya no dudes* | So that you no longer doubt |
| *de mi cariño,* | my love, |
| *abre mi corazón* | open my heart |
| *—cielito lindo—* | —pretty little sky— |
| *toma el cuchillo;* | take the knife; |
| *pero con tiento,* | but with care, *niña,* |
| *niña, no te lastimes* | so that you don't hurt yourself |
| *—cielito lindo—* | —pretty little sky— |
| *que estás adentro* | who is inside |

—from "Cielito Lindo," traditional Mexican song

# 36
...

The blue *rebozo* kept me warm during the flight. Below was the clutter of Mexico City, growing smaller as we rose into the sky. It looked like so much junk—the rooftops, the shanties that swept around the city like a wall. But here and there you could see old buildings alongside shiny new ones, swatches of parks. The city was even more complicated and immense from above, running to the edges of my vision. But the city eventually did end. It butted up against a wide river—or maybe it was a canal—then stopped. One side was city; the other was dirt.

I didn't know what I would find up north. I wasn't sure what to expect, only what my brother had told me and what I had seen in pictures, on TV. But I had to go. I didn't understand what exactly God was doing, but at least He had answered me, finally, through Pilar. Gabi was not in Mexico City—she was heading to *el norte*. And if she was going to *el norte*, she would go to Luis. So would I. I thought about how Luis used to teach her dance steps, or take her on his lap and wipe away her tears, tickle her, make her laugh. I had called my brother twice, hoping to find news about Gabriela and to tell him I was coming, but both times I only got the answering machine.

From Pilar's, I had gone back to my little closet of a room. I pushed aside the candles at my door, leaving them to burn. When they had burned down to nothing, more would take their place—they needed no tending. All the offerings, I pushed them aside too. I wondered how long people would continue to leave things. Maybe this would become a holy site. I didn't know, but I didn't think it would make much difference whether I was on the other side of that door or not.

Notes of petition spread across the floor. I stacked them up in the alcove of the little blue window. I still read them, though I knew I could do nothing. It wasn't up to me. I hadn't done anything to make that woman cut off all her hair. I hadn't made a man fall in love with a woman. I was no saint, no matter what anyone wanted to believe.

The candles kept vigil outside my door. I began to sleep in the dark, turning off the light.

Of course it was Lupita who helped me with my papers so I could go across. It was Guadalupe—a real Guadalupe—who was the true saint. Maybe that's how it is: true saints go unnoticed. And perhaps that is the best way.

I gave her most of the money I had left from the kitchen jar in Santo Niño, and she was able to arrange my passport and visa in a little over a week, which is unheard of. She had connections in a few government offices due to her activist work. One of those connections led to another in the passport office. Lupita provided a statement that said I was in her care and that there'd been an emergency; I needed to go see my family up north immediately. I filled out applications and had a short interview in a stuffy office. Someone else took my picture—a man down the street with a Polaroid. He cut me out in perfect squares and showed me what I had left behind: the white screen behind me had caught the flash, sending out glowing streaks around where my image had been.

Soon I had a passport and the papers in my hands. I looked at them with a kind of wonder—I could go anywhere I wanted. I smiled at my stone-faced self in the picture.

I booked a ticket on AeroMéxico to San Diego with the last of my money. I packed my backpack, kissed Lupita adios, and handed her the stack of petitions, except for Pilar's. That one I kept with me. It was Lupita in the first place who ever had the capacity to answer these things. If anyone could grant miracles, it was her. She kissed me on the forehead. "Go with God," she said. I kissed her goodbye. I kissed nearly everyone goodbye—even Felix. They came out to the street and waved to me until I couldn't see them anymore.

Luis hadn't answered when I called him from the airport in D.F. either, but I left a message on the machine, asking him to pick me up at 9:30. It was in only a few hours' time. How quick it was to leave one world for another—almost too quick. There was no time to even imagine what it would be like. I was already there.

Luis did not look well. Off the plane, through the gate, and
into the room of chairs, I saw him before he saw me. I was
hoping, perhaps irrationally, that Gabriela would be with him,
that she would bound over to me, call out my name. But I
only saw my brother, slumped in a chair, looking straight
ahead. He wore black pants, shiny black shoes, a white button-
down shirt—the uniform of a waiter. I couldn't believe how
much he looked like Papá. He always did, but especially now
that he was older. He had the same distinctive cheekbones,
the long, hooked nose. His hair was wavy and combed back
like Papá's. If Luis had had a moustache, he would've looked
exactly like him, exactly how I imagined the younger Papá of
Mexico City, going out dancing every night, winning competitions and *chicas*, always laughing.

Except Luis looked like he hadn't laughed in a while. His
face was solemn, his brown eyes full of grief. He only saw
me when I was close enough to touch his shoulder. He
stood up, hugged me tight as though he would never release
me. It terrified me. When he let me go, he held me out at
arm's length so he could get a good look at me. It had been
a long time.

"Are you all right?" I asked him.

He opened his mouth but no sound came out. When his
voice finally came, he told me what had happened to Papá.

# 37
...

Raúl's eyelids began to move. María Luisa bent over him, wondering if he was dreaming, wondering if he would wake. She feared he wouldn't, that he would go on sleeping forever. She put her palm to his forehead even though the doctor had told her not to touch him. He was a little warm but not feverish. He had an IV in his arm to rehydrate him. His left hand was bandaged up, the place where his ring finger had been, the wound sewn closed. He'd been out in the desert for two days, they estimated, tied to a tree, unconscious when they found him.

She sat in a chair beside him, watching her husband sleep. She remembered when she had met him, and when he asked her to marry him. Down on his knees in a filthy puddle in Mexico City, he wouldn't let go of her hand, saying, "*Mi vida, siempre, mi cariño, te amo, soy tuyo, siempre . . .*" Everyone was looking. She was so embarrassed and afraid that she shook her hand from his and left him there, in the middle of the sidewalk, on his knees. *My life, forever, my darling, forever.* So much forever. "*Mi corazón es tuyo, María,*" he called after her. She was running but she still heard. And she heard it in her head after that, over and over—*My heart is yours, María*—a record that wouldn't stop skipping.

She watched his chest rise and fall, the drip of saline down the tube, filling his veins again. His eyelids twitched, his mouth, his hand. He moved his lips. María Luisa stood and leaned over him in case he was saying something important. She put her ear to him. She couldn't hear anything. Whatever he was trying to say stayed inside him, swallowed up. When she pulled away, he opened his eyes.

# 38
∴

Raúl Amador couldn't speak. His head felt shattered, his mouth dry, his tongue swollen. He could see bottles of coloured liquid on a metal cart: blue, red, orange. A glass jar of tongue depressors and another of cotton balls. Someone leaned over him, coming to him from the shadows on the edges. It was the face of his wife, her dark skin and black eyes throwing off a sort of light like the Virgen Morena—and he began to remember.

But only in slivers, rising up to the surface. What he remembered after leaving El Pescado Loco was fragmented into things that seemed odd to notice: His shoes did not give off any shine. The keys were cold in his hand. He felt strangely, deeply alone, like he was the only person left in the world. He tried to whistle, even though he was not much of a whistler. He remembered how the air felt passing through his lips, but he could not remember what song it had been, or if there'd been any sound at all.

The policeman Ortega came to visit him in the hospital. He was a stocky man, short, with a wide, flat face. He plied Raúl with questions about his assailants, but Raúl couldn't give him much. His head hurt, and what had happened was fragmented. He described the one boy he'd seen. There was nothing familiar about him; he was sure he'd never met him before. Ortega asked him to recount the entire incident as best as he could, every single detail. Anything could help them. Raúl told what he remembered, even the things that probably weren't important. Like how he could not remember what song . . .

"They cut off my finger," Raúl said. He wondered vaguely where his finger had ended up. He kept moving it, like it was still there. Sometimes he really *could* feel the finger.

Ortega waved that off like it was nothing. "What else?"

Raúl thought hard. He couldn't quite remember—but there was something trying to surface out of the murk of his brain. He just couldn't remember what it was.

# 39
· · ·

We did not go to Luis's apartment right away. We drove from the airport to the downtown area—a remarkably short distance. I could've walked to where we finally parked on the street. On the way I tried to take in this new world, to orient myself, but I was distracted, my head tight and too full. When Luis was satisfied with his parking job and cut the engine, I got out of the car. I saw a church across the street. It was a small, simple white stucco building with two bell towers on either side, both topped with white crosses. I stared at it: it glowed against the dark. I crossed myself, kissed my fingers. I wanted *in*, wanted to run across the street, up the steps, and inside the comforting silence of the place, where I could light a candle for everything wrong in my life. But the doors were shut and a chain was threaded through their handles and padlocked.

Cars honked at me. I had not shut my door and was in the way of traffic. "Come on, Lucy," my brother said from the sidewalk, staring at me like I was crazy. "It's like you've never been to a city before."

We went to a restaurant, though neither of us could really eat. I didn't know what to say. We were in a booth with red plastic seats. Low amber lights hung over our heads. I picked at my food. Luis stared into his plate. All around us was the world of *el norte*, people talking and eating, laughing and drinking. The music was soft, barely audible. People went outside to smoke cigarettes. This was how they did things in Alta California.

I thought of Papá, tied to a tree in the desert, left to the vultures. It made me sick to my stomach, but I tried to eat the french fries in front of me, shoving them into my mouth. I had terrible thoughts in my head, things I could not say to Luis. Things that scared me. Maybe Papá deserved it—maybe he deserved worse. I thought of Gabriela in the alley, covered in garbage. Papá was responsible for that. It was all because of Papá, and I couldn't let it go. I would never let it go. I kept thinking about all the women in La Merced. How many of them were there because they'd been thrown out of their homes? Lupita took in women like that—took *me* in. Pilar took in Gabi without knowing a thing about her. People who didn't even know us had taken us in and helped us. How was it, then, that family could throw out family?

Luis finally spoke. "They don't know who did it."

"They'll find out," I said, looking up from my plate to my brother, who kept his head lowered, not making eye contact. "Everyone finds out everything there, eventually." It made me wonder what the talk was about me, what rumours were circling—though now I didn't care.

Luis sighed, drank his beer. His eyes were glassy. I hoped he wasn't going to cry. I didn't know what I could do for him.

Finally, he met my eyes. "He's not a bad man, Lucy."

I said nothing.

"He never meant to hurt us."

"He beat you, Luis."

"He didn't know another way. He only wanted what was good for us, Lucy. He had a hard life. He didn't know another way."

"He threw out Gabi. Don't you tell me he wanted good for us."

"But it's true. He loves us. Everything is because he loves us."

"*Because he loves us?* What kind of love is that?" I said. I pushed my plate aside until it hit the wall of the booth. "Just like the way he loves Mamá by sleeping with other women." I threw my fork onto the table. It clanged across to the edge and clattered to the floor. I looked at Luis. "Did you *know* about Isabel?"

Luis shook his head. "I don't even know who she is."

"Isabel? At the bar? Maybe you were gone already. But he's been sleeping with her, you know, and everyone thinks that's just fine."

He looked back down at his plate. "Papá's always been like that," he said.

"See? You too. Even you. And you say it's all out of love." The waiter brought me a new fork. I picked it up and pointed it at my brother. "What about *your* love, Luis? I needed you.

I wrote and you never wrote back. I tried calling, and you were never there to answer the phone."

Luis set his jaw the way Papá did, which meant he was getting angry. "I *did* answer. And your card ran out. Remember? I *was* there."

It was true, but I shook my head, not wanting to hear it. "You weren't there when I needed you. And you weren't there to see what happened to Gabi. You don't know anything, *hermano*. Not a thing. So what can you say about it?"

"Lucy—"

"Gabi could be dead, Luis. And you're telling me it's because of love?"

"Listen to me," he said, reaching his hand across the table for mine. I folded my hands into my lap. "She's not dead," he said. "She's coming. She's on her way."

# 40
### ...

Ángel stared out the back seat window at the passing desert, the tall saguaros. Desert was all around them. They had lost the sea. They had been driving north since the robbery, which seemed like years ago, but it had only been a couple of days. They had crossed over from Baja California Sur to Baja California Norte, and once they reached Tijuana, they would be as good as free. The *frontera* was no man's land. It would be easy to disappear there.

They divided up the money as they drove. There was some argument about who would get the gold chain and the saints and the wedding band. Ángel wanted none of that, only the cash. He had it tucked into his belt. As soon as they reached Tijuana, he was going to open the car door and walk away, lose himself in the crowds, the mayhem of the city. He never wanted to see these guys again. He was going to be free of his old life, all of it, and start again. What that meant, he didn't know. Maybe he'd go under the fence to *el norte*.

"He recognized you, didn't he, *cabrón*?" one of them said. People called him *Diente*, or "Tooth," because he was missing one in the front. He had Raúl's finger, wrapped in cloth, in his pocket.

Ángel didn't respond. He watched the desert pass by, saw how the sand swept over the road, sometimes burying it completely. More than once they'd driven straight, thinking they were following the road, when really there was no road at all, only sand, all the way down.

"Man, because if he did . . . " Diente said. He seemed to be searching for the right words. "If they catch you, you don't know nothing about us. You got that?"

"Are you threatening me?" Ángel said coolly.

"I'm just saying you don't know us."

Ángel kept one hand on his knife in his pocket. "No one's getting caught," he said.

They passed by the carcass of a cow, teeming with vultures. The smell of rot permeated the air. And long after they passed it, Ángel couldn't get it out of his head: how half the cow was only gleaming bone, the flesh having been swallowed up into the bellies of the vultures. If he were to go back this way a week later, he knew the cow would be pecked down to the bone—bone that would eventually be ground to sand. But he was never coming back. He only hoped he could disappear like that, that Tijuana would carry what she could of him in her belly, and the rest of his bones would never be found.

# 41
· · ·

Raúl couldn't stop dreaming. It happened every time he closed his eyes, even after he was released from the hospital and was in his own bed. Even there, in his own house, protected by the wall and the gate, three locked doors in total, he couldn't stop dreaming. It was the same dream, over and over again. He was tied to the tree as he had been in real life, except his arms were stretched out, bound to overhanging branches. He was on top of a hill. From the hill, he could see the entire town of Santo Niño, the sea beyond it. Vultures circled above like ashes. He could see his own house down at his feet, so far away. It was in shadow, a dark little house in a valley of shadows. He tried to keep it in focus, to help him forget about the *bandidos* that surrounded him, of the terrible things that would surely come.

The house went out of focus, blurring until it was nothing but a smudge, until he couldn't distinguish it from any other shadow in the valley. They were closing in on him, so many of them, masked behind bandanas. More formed out of the wind, it seemed, and surrounded him. Behind them, thick black billows of smoke rose up from the valley. They had knives and guns. There was a knife at his throat, black eyes boring into his. He thought the boy looked familiar. Soon he realized it wasn't a boy at all, but a girl, and not just any girl— it was Gabriela. She had the knife at his throat, pushing the point into it. He wanted to talk to her, but he had no voice. He began to recognize more and more of them: Guadalupe, on the other side of him, holding a gun; Luis, Miguel, Eduardo; his cousin Magdalena; the girl from the Hotel Santo Niño; and even María, his own wife—all of them pointing knives and guns at him. All around them the entire world was burning. The vultures were lowering now, their fat, black bodies and blood-red heads whipping close around him.

It was Gabriela who killed him, plunging the knife into his throat, splitting his body in two. He fell away from himself— that was when he woke, covered in sweat, sitting up in bed and trying to peel away the layers of darkness to see what might be coming for him.

Sometimes María Luisa was beside him when he woke, her hand on his forehead. Sometimes he was alone in the room. He could hear the telenovela in the kitchen, the whispered words and dramatic fights, and through it all, he could hear the sounds of María moving about the kitchen, the sounds of dishes clattering and food frying, water running. Sounds of life. He could hear the neighbours come and go, bringing their offerings of food or sympathy, whatever they could spare. Raúl couldn't help but think how much this was like a wake, that maybe he really *had* died out there in the desert—except that there was no family weeping at his bedside. There was nobody left to weep. Sometimes Miguel came into the room. Ana had stopped by, but he'd only heard her voice from the kitchen, talking to María.

María brought him his meals, lit prayer candles by the bedside. He ate what he could, thinking of the food they brought the dead in November, laying it at their gravesides. They brought anything from the world that the dead had loved, be it chicken, mangoes, cigarettes, Modelo in cans. The dead only ever picked at their food, as he did now, even though he tried hard to eat everything she gave him. That was the only way he knew he was alive: by eating as much as he could—that and reading *La Peninsular*. Because the dead don't care what's in the news, and they certainly don't read newspapers.

As he drifted back into sleep, the dream started over again. He was going to die again, and again, and again. It wouldn't stop happening. When he died, he woke, and more than once he cried out, trying to say Gabriela's name, but it was stuck in his throat. He couldn't bring it *out*, as much as he thought that saying her name would bring him to the surface. It would not sound. It was foreign, like one of those English words he could not get his mouth around and would never be able to say, no matter how hard he tried.

Miguel was by the bed, peering down at him. Raúl shook his head. He didn't want Miguel. "Guadalupe," Raúl said.

Miguel wrinkled his forehead.

"Get Guadalupe," Raúl said, pointing to the door.

Miguel shrugged and left the room. There was light coming through the curtains, but Raúl had no idea if it was morning or afternoon.

Miguel returned carrying something rather large. As he drew closer, Raúl could see it was the portrait of the Virgen de Guadalupe that had been in the girls' room. "No, no, no!" Raúl said, shaking his head, raising himself from the pillows.

Miguel lowered the picture. "Isn't this what you wanted?" he asked.

"No!" Raúl said, remembering that Guadalupe was gone, thinking, *This is all that is left.* After everything, after working so hard so they could have better lives. None of it had mattered. This was all that was left: this portrait of the Virgen, this photo of his daughters in the Zócalo, stuck beneath the glass. They squinted up at him with wide, bright smiles. He wished he could go back to that time, that place, that moment. Before his girls had gone bad, before anyone had left him. When everything was in its place, in order, intact. He reached out to touch their faces, running his finger along the glass. Then he traced his own dark shadow, spread out across the paving stones before them.

Maybe it was time. It had been many months. He could call her. He could say her name. He might even be able to call her *hija* again.

Maybe that would help make the dreams go away. Because not even prayer would make them go away. No deal he made with Dios made them stop. Maybe this was what He was telling Raúl all along: to call the girl—his daughter—to say her name, to get it out from where it was lodged in his throat, and tell her to come home, that he'd just wanted her to think about what she'd done and to repent. Maybe it was time to give her a second chance. Because he wasn't dead, was he? He was alive. Maybe this was what he was supposed to do: to forgive as Christ might have forgiven.

Raúl got out of bed and went outside into the garden. He looked up at the cross on the hill. *Is that what I'm supposed to do?*

The neighbours were building a second storey on their house, and the neighbours on the other side of them were building their wall higher so as not to be seen from the second storey. At the moment, the wall was only grey cinder block and rebar, reaching up to the crown of the hill, right at the base of the cross. Soon the cross would not be visible from the Amador house at all.

Was there a gleam of light reflecting off the cross? A watery, glittery light? Or was it nothing at all?

He told María Luisa he was going to call his cousin Magdalena. She insisted on going with him, but he wanted to be alone. He walked out into the street and down to the super-mini, the nearest phone, and dialed her number, noticing that his hands were trembling like an old man's. How strange his hand looked with that one finger missing.

Nobody answered. He tried again. He pressed the receiver to his ear, listening to the phone ring, imagining things in the silences between the rings—footsteps, or the sound of silverware being set upon a plate, or a dog barking—and thinking that then she would answer. She would answer and say, *Yes, one moment*, and she'd pass the phone to Gabriela. And he would say . . .

What would he say? The phone kept ringing. Nobody was answering. The silences between the rings were just that: silences.

Later that evening, Raúl called again. This time, there was an answer.

He couldn't stop crying. He went back home and sat on the floor in the *sala* and cried. He'd never cried so hard in his life. He lay on the floor, his cheek to the cold tiles, and let the tears run off his face. They fell into the grooves between the tiles, darkening the cement in little spots. María Luisa tried to pull him up off the floor, but he wouldn't budge. He was made heavier with his grief. He wouldn't talk to his wife, so she left him there, alone on the cold floor. *Tan solito.* The walls he'd built were around him, the roof he'd built was above him, and there was too much space in between it all. None of it gave him any consolation.

Gabriela was gone, his cousin Magdalena had told him on the telephone. She was gone, and what had he expected? Had he really thought that she, his outcast cousin, whom he'd refused to help when she was thrown out of her house onto the streets of Mexico City, would provide a home for Raúl Amador's tossed-out daughter? His *puta* daughter? "Gabriela is gone," she said, "just like you wanted her to be."

Eventually, the light wavered from the room, then faded from the sky, and all went dark. It was night. Dogs were barking somewhere far away, off in the desert hills.

# 42
...

Gabriela had called Luis from Mexico City, he explained, asking if she could come visit him. He wired her money for the journey north and lodging. When she reached the border, she was to call again, and they would assess how much more money Luis needed to wire her. I plied him with questions that he really couldn't answer: Was she all right? What had happened to her? When would she arrive? So many questions, so many petitions. And no real answers.

I closed my eyes for a moment to imagine that phone call. To hear her voice again. "What did she sound like?"

"She sounded fine," Luis said. He thought a moment. "You know, like Gabi. But she wasn't laughing or joking or anything—you know how she was always playing with you? She wasn't like that. She was serious—more like you."

"I'm not that serious," I said, but I knew it was true: I'd

been born with a weight, a yoke around my neck. Gabriela was the one who lightened me up, gave my name meaning.

Luis lived in a newer apartment building alongside the San Diego Freeway. It was painted pink and turquoise on the outside, but inside it was a dreary place with greying carpet and marked-up walls. It was called the City Vista, but Luis's apartment had no view of the city. Its only view was of an interior courtyard and the other apartments that surrounded it. There was the noise of everyone else—TVs, yelling and clapping, and phone conversations—but noise was different in the North. I couldn't explain it. It was clearer somehow; there was more order to it. But the noise in Luis's apartment was definitely *ruido mexicano*, no matter how else Luis tried to integrate into the world of the *norteamericanos*. The TV was tuned to Univisión (a *fútbol* match was on), the stereo was blaring salsa at the same time, and boisterous conversation and laughter carried from the kitchen.

There wasn't much room for me. I was going to sleep on the couch, and when Gabriela arrived, I'd take the floor. Luis had four roommates in a two-bedroom apartment. He shared his room with Jorge, and in the other room were three mattresses on the floor for Armando, his brother Oscar, and Gustavo from Zacatecas. People in many other units of the building were *norteamericanos*—which was just like Luis, to be living with the gringos. He had made friends with many of the neighbours, and when I walked into the apartment for the first time, there must've been twenty people in that small space, *norteamericanos* and *latinos*, all shouting over the game and the music, English and Spanish all at once.

Luis wasn't in the mood for it, but he introduced me to everyone, cracked open a beer, and watched the game. I made conversation—treading water, passing the time—but in my head all along was Gabi. She was on her way.

It wasn't until three o'clock in the morning that people finally left the apartment and everyone went into their rooms to sleep. I made my bed on the couch out of sheets and rough wool blankets. It was spring now, early April, but the night was cold. I folded the blue *rebozo* into a pillow and put it beneath my head.

I couldn't sleep. I lay there, staring at my things laid out on the coffee table: my stack of clothes, my camera, Pilar's petition, her hand-painted *milagro*, the photographs I first took at the Hotel Santo Niño, Paul's letter, and spent rolls of film. This is what I had to begin a new life with up here.

# 43
...

The policeman Ortega was at their gate, rapping on it with the back of his hand. "Don," he said.

"Señor."

He handed Raúl an envelope. "We got them," he said, not without pride. "They were heading north, to Tijuana."

Raúl nodded, looking down at the envelope in his hands. He opened the flap and peered inside. There were little photos, mug shots, the boys' faces peering out of the black and white. They had hard, staring eyes. He shut the flap.

"Can you come to the station?" Ortega asked. "To identify them?"

"I didn't see them," Raúl said. "*Digo*—I only saw one."

"That's all we need."

Raúl began to feel a little dizzy, but he went with Ortega to his car, trying to listen to the story of how the police had apprehended the boys. He couldn't concentrate.

Ortega gripped Raúl's arm to help steady him as they walked from the car to the station. Before they reached the door, Raúl shook free of him. The grip made him feel accused, as though he were the one guilty of some crime.

Inside the office, he sat where he was told, in a plastic chair by the counter. The air was stuffy, sour. The fans were on, but Raúl pulled at his collar and wiped sweat from his forehead. Ortega asked another policeman to bring them in. They did it one by one, leading each boy into the front room where Raúl sat, each boy handcuffed behind the back, guarded by two young policemen with M16s.

They made each boy state his name. The first one kept his head down. Then they led in another and another, but Raúl did not recognize them and he certainly couldn't identify them. All he could think about was how they were mostly just normal-looking boys, ones he'd see anywhere without giving them a second thought. Yet one of them had cut off his finger.

They brought in the boy he'd seen. Raúl recognized his eyes. He imagined him with a bandana around his nose and mouth, and nodded.

Last, they brought in Ángel.

Ángel stated his name—it was the voice Raúl had recognized. His tattoos were fully exhibited now, vines crawling out of his T-shirt. The snake curled up on the *nopal* cactus, eating the eagle. There was a new one—or maybe it was just one Raúl had never noticed before. At the base of Ángel's neck, across his collarbone, was a jagged blue slash with a word beneath it: *Mañana*.

Raúl balled his hands into fists, wincing with the pain his stub of a finger still caused. He stood up, to do what, he wasn't sure: punch the boy in the face, beat the life out of him. After all he had done to help Ángel, after all he'd given him—

Ortega and another policeman grabbed Raúl and pushed him back into his chair, held him there while the others led Ángel out of the room.

At the kitchen table, Raúl pushed aside the bowl full of fruit, the napkin holder, the salt and pepper and pots of salsa, and dumped the mug shots out of the envelope. He lined them up in a row, looking into each boy's face, trying to see something in their eyes, but if there had been anything in real life, all was made flat by the photo. They did not smile. They did not look menacing or mean. They looked like boys who'd been caught cheating on an exam. He rearranged the photos, moving them around like game pieces, as though something could be revealed to make him understand. If he could only see things in a different way, then maybe . . .

It didn't make any sense, how Ángel had turned on him. Raúl had helped him when nobody else would. He had given him a second chance.

He arranged and rearranged the photos on the plastic tablecloth for hours, trying to find an answer, until Miguel came home and María said it was time to eat. Raúl put them back in the envelope, but he didn't let go of it. He took it with him to bed, slipping it beneath the pillow. He woke with the envelope clenched in his hand when Gabriela plunged in the knife, her name stuck in his throat, choking him.

# 44

## •••

I woke to Luis's voice—a one-sided conversation. He was on the phone. I heard my name; he was talking about me. I sat up on the couch, listening, watching the sunlight try to squeeze through the crack in the curtains. It didn't take me long to realize he was talking to Mamá. "Lucy's fine," he was saying, "just tired, asleep on the couch." He went on to say I looked healthy, that I'd eaten my dinner last night, though that wasn't exactly true. He told her not to worry, that Gabi was on her way.

Luis was quiet for a moment. I imagined my mother with her fist to her mouth, trying not to cry. "It's okay, Mami," he said, finally. "She's okay. Everyone's okay." Then he asked about Papá.

I hung in the doorway to Luis's bedroom, watching him talk to our mother. I thought of her in the kitchen, preparing breakfast, the radio on. The comforting sounds of home. How we'd talk and make jokes while pinning the laundry on

the line. It seemed so long ago. It *was* long ago. I was a different person then.

But when Luis handed me the phone and I heard her say,
"Luz? *Mi Lucita?*" I felt like that girl again, snapping out the
white sheet like a flag of surrender, pinning it on the line.
Mamá was so short, I couldn't see her over the sheet; I could
only hear her voice. Just like now.

"Mami," I said.

We hung on in silence for a while, letting our names ring
through the lines, listening to each other's breathing.

It was Luis's day off. He took me around the city, showing
me the restaurant where he worked, the naval station, the
*malecón*, where tourists and sailors in uniform strolled. I didn't
like the way some of them looked at me—maybe they were
looking for women the way men did in La Merced. Luis
didn't seem to notice; he was busy being the Tour Guide. He
pointed to Coronado Island and said we would go when it
was a little warmer. We'd pack a picnic and lounge around
on the beach like *turistas*, the way we used to do in Santo
Niño when we were kids.

All morning, airplanes flew so low over our heads I was
afraid they would crash into us. Each time, I found myself
ducking. Luis laughed at me. My heart stopped every time I
saw a Mexican girl with long black hair and stick-like legs. I
reminded myself that I didn't have to look for her, that she
was on her way. Besides, her hair was short now. I'd seen the
braid Pilar had cut. Luis nudged me. "Lucy, are you listening?
What are you staring at?"

As we wandered, I took out my camera and peered through the viewfinder, seeing the city in isolated pieces, frame by frame: the streets, the airplanes, the girls who looked like Gabriela, my brother Luis, who smiled too wide and puffed up his chest, making me laugh.

I spotted a photo place downtown and dropped off my rolls of film there. Luis looked at all those rolls lined up on the counter and asked me how I could possibly have taken so many pictures. I shrugged, unable to explain. "It's something I do now," was all I could say.

I counted out the change that was the very last of my money, and asked Luis for a dollar so I could buy film from the woman behind the counter. I opened up the back of the camera, revealing black, empty space. I unspooled the roll, tucked the tongue into the reel, and wound.

Luis laughed. "Are you crazy, Lucy?" he said. "You mean that all those pictures you just took—you knew there wasn't film?"

I laughed. "Yes."

He shook his head. "I don't get it," he said.

"You don't have to."

He took me up to Balboa Park, where the buildings were copied from Spain. He said one had actually been imported from there, bit by bit. I couldn't imagine trying to bring a building across oceans, but that was Alta California for you— nothing was impossible.

I felt good there. I was finally able to sit still. We sat on the bench in front of the reflecting ponds, looking into the blurred surface, at the lily pads floating there. Luis said that by summer, water lilies would cover the ponds in pink, white, and yellow. The water reflected blue sky and a single cloud, pushed around by the wind.

My brother was quiet, looking into the pool. He might've been thinking about Papá. I framed him in the viewfinder, took a picture. The click of the shutter drew him out of his thoughts. "Hey!" he said. "I wasn't ready!"

"I know," I said. "It's better that way."

He held out his hands. "Let me take one of you."

"Of *me*?" I had not once parted with the camera since Paul had given it to me. "What am I going to do with a picture of myself?" But I put it in my brother's hands, explaining how to use it. I stood in front of the reflecting pond and waited, feeling ridiculous. I shoved my hands in my pockets, then took them out again.

"Not so serious, Lucy," Luis said. "You look like you're dead."

I smiled. Or tried to.

"Essh—I hate to say it, but that's even worse."

"Hurry up," I said, getting irritated.

"God, when you're angry you look like . . . like a . . . God, what *do* you look like?"

I began to walk toward him, hands out. "Okay, Luis, give me the camera."

"Remember the Mad *Pollo*!" he said suddenly, his take on *Remember the Alamo!* that always made me laugh when I was a kid. And it worked now. I laughed, and he snapped the picture.

# 45
...

When María Luisa came out to the garden to tell Raúl that Gabriela was all right and was on her way to San Diego to stay with Luis, he had to sit down. He looked through the web of empty laundry lines and could just make out the top of the cross over his neighbour's wall. "Gracias, Dios, gracias," he whispered over and over. "I'll do whatever You want; just get her safely there."

But none of this eased the dreams. They were on repeat every night. He was on the hill, the town was burning, Gabriela plunged the knife into his throat, her eyes black with hate.

Raúl put the mug shots into the plastic windows of his wallet, behind the pictures of his wife and grandchildren. He looked at them often, when nobody was around, peering into each boy's face, trying to find some sort of answer.

He carried the photos everywhere he went, along with the gun he had bought from Miguel's *patrón*. It was a slightly rustic-looking revolver, but it worked just fine. He had watched Miguel's *patrón* shoot bull's eyes into the hand-drawn target outside of his house. Having the gun was like having a St. Christopher medal protecting him—except *this* protection would actually work. St. Pistol is how he thought of it. Stronger than all other saints, it was akin to Dios. Every day before leaving for work, he tucked it into his belt.

Raúl went to El Pescado Loco early; he was there long before anyone else. Sometimes he sat at the bar with a cup of coffee, but more often he sat in the office with the door locked, going through paperwork or counting the bottles of liquor, or just staring at the door, or at his hands, at the space where his ring finger should've been.

His wedding band and his necklace with the saints hadn't been returned. There had been a small gold medallion of the Virgen, with El Santo Niño de Atocha on the other side, and another of San Cristóbal for protection. They hadn't done much for him. He had been taken anyway. Or maybe they had done something, because here he was, sitting at his desk, alive. Or maybe that was his punishment.

# 46
* * *

The week after I began my job as a waitress, I heard about the container incident. I worked in a diner, not like the fancy place where Luis worked. I had checked the ads in the papers and asked around businesses for work. Some of them politely showed me the door, some not so politely—calling me wetback or *mojada*, in English and in Spanish—and I quickly learned it was not going to be so easy. My English was good, but my accent was heavy, and I couldn't pretend I was a Californian. In truth I *was* a Californian—from the Baja, sure, but it was California just the same. Luis told me to say I was a citizen and write a false Social Security number on the application. *Looking* like I was supposed to be there made all the difference.

I wasn't discouraged because I had Gabi in my head, dreams of renting an apartment of our own in Luis's building, all the things I had to do for us. At the diner, I'd told the owner a story about how my dad was Mexican but my mom was American, and I could go back and forth between countries however I pleased. I don't know if she really believed me or not, but she gave me the job. The *chicana* looked into my *morena* face, my black *india* eyes, and commented that I must take after my father more than my mother. I told her it was true.

Gabriela still hadn't called and she hadn't arrived. It had been far too long since she had called Luís from Mexico City. I prayed. I turned the coffee table into an altar, which annoyed Luis and his roommates. Where were they supposed to put their feet and their beers after a long, hard day? Even so, they couldn't help but cross themselves when they saw the Virgen, and they didn't move anything. They set their beers beside the candles and the small portrait of the Virgen I had bought at a Mexican import shop.

When I had some extra time, I would stop at the newsstand on Broadway and read what I could in various papers from around the United States and Mexico City until the clerk gave me a dirty look, saying I had to buy the papers if I was going to open them up like that.

One day I surprised him and took a newspaper up to the counter, digging out real American coins for it. It was a copy of the *San Francisco Times*, and it had an article in it about the deaths of would-be immigrants to *el norte*, and another about how the United States should expect a surge in illegal immigration and incidents like this because of the collapsing Mexican economy. Both were written by Paul O'Connell, the journalist who'd given me the camera. I read the articles right there at the newsstand, and made the clerk cringe at the haphazard way I folded up the newspapers. I took it back to the apartment to read it again.

Twenty-one illegal immigrants had died in a sealed container, a boxcar on a train, across the Texas border. There had been at least one hundred people in there, sealed into the dark in 130-degree-Fahrenheit heat. They had each paid anywhere from five hundred to fourteen hundred dollars to get across.

All I could think was that Gabi hadn't arrived. Pilar had said she was going across, and Luis had wired her money in Mexico City, but nobody knew *how* Gabi planned to get across—except that she wasn't going to swim, according to Pilar. She could have gone this route, hired a coyote, been sealed into a boxcar. She could've been there, among them, to be shipped like—and to die worse than—cattle.

Luis didn't think she was in that container, because she was going to call him when she reached the border, and he hadn't wired her enough for a coyote, but I could tell he was uneasy. Because what did he know, really? Why hadn't she called? She should have arrived at the border by now. What did any of us know? Each day, I read the papers, hoping to find the names. They must've had names. But the papers did not list the names of the dead.

At the end of the article was a contact number for Paul. One day, I decided to call him. I pulled the phone over to the table and dialed the number. He answered on the second ring, before I had time to get my thoughts together. "Paul," I said, "it's Lucy from Santo Niño."

"Lucy Amador?" he said.

"Yes," I said. "I'm calling because of your article." I went on to tell him briefly about Gabriela, giving only what I had to: that she was my sister and she might have gone that way over the border. "I read so many articles about this," I told him, "and nobody writes the names. What's wrong with you reporters? That's the most important part. Why does nobody say the names of the dead?"

"Nice to hear from you, Lucy," Paul said.

"Sorry," I said. "I'm just worried."

Paul told me all he knew, which wasn't much. Bodies were still being identified, claimed by families, and sent back over the border. There were funerals in Oaxaca, Puebla, and El Salvador. He was able to give me the names of those victims, and none were Gabriela. There were bodies that still hadn't been claimed or identified, but Paul suspected that many of the families of those left were already in the United States and too afraid of deportation to come forward. He said he would call if anyone matching Gabriela's description turned up. I prayed that would never happen.

I looked out the sliding glass door at the balcony, which was crowded with bikes, a punching bag, and cases of empty beer bottles stacked up on each other. I looked into one of the apartments across the courtyard. I imagined us in one of them. There would be clean walls, white carpet. It wouldn't matter what else, because I would have her with me. Gabi, her voice like bells. Who kindled in me . . . light. Even if that light was sometimes fire.

But an apartment without Gabriela—I didn't know. I

imagined a place without her, with only me. There would be walls to protect me like a shell. But what would fill me, give me *consuelo* and *cariño*? If only she would come back to me, I swore I would cut open my chest and give her my heart— more, I would give her the knife. I would say, *Open me. Open my heart. You deserve no less, though you may never forgive me.*

Because maybe I'd had the power to stop everything from happening to begin with, and I did not stop it. I let her go, as easily as water through my fingers. I did not fight for her. I did not put myself in front of her as I should have, to shield her, to take the blows. I did not even say a word.

I had to get out. I had to run. I had to put myself in the middle of traffic or jump from a pier into the sea. I grabbed the keys and rushed out to the street. I was burning. The sunlight hurt my eyes. Colours blurred together. I ran down the hill away from the City Vista and the San Diego Freeway. It felt like all the airplanes were out to get me, bearing down on me.

I ran toward the water. Soon I was running along the path I'd arrived on my first night in San Diego. I was running down the street to the church. I would stay there all day and night if I had to. I would stay all week. I wouldn't eat and I wouldn't drink. I would say a thousand *Ave Marías*. I would walk on my knees. I would rip through my jeans. I would bleed and bleed as I went up the steps into the church and walked on my knees all the way to the altar. I would beg forgiveness, light a million candles. Then maybe I could begin again.

I ran past familiar newsstands and diners and shops, but I couldn't find it. Perhaps I was on the wrong street. I stopped running; my heart hurt against my rib cage. People and cars rushed by. A man swept the sidewalk outside a doughnut shop. Down the street, I saw the restaurant Luis and I had gone to. I still couldn't see it, but I knew the church must be up ahead.

At the intersection I was stopped by a glowing red hand and a stream of cars. I looked up and saw it, gleaming white in the sun. The doors were open; I could see people standing inside.

The light changed. Slowly, I crossed the street, gazing up at the open doors. If I was going to do this, if I was going to walk on my knees, it would have to be now. I stopped at the steps.

I could just see the top of the life-sized statue of Cristo hanging on the cross, blood streaming down his face. On one side of him hung a portrait of the Virgen de Guadalupe, high on the wall. I could hear the Padre's voice through the microphone, speaking in Spanish. It was Spanish Mass. His voice rolled out the doors and wilted in the street. *God saw the light, that it was good, and God divided the light from the darkness.* He was saying we began in darkness. We had to spend all of our lives on our knees because of what had happened so long ago, at the beginning of the world in the Garden of Eden.

I couldn't kneel. I couldn't get myself up the steps. I could not even lift my foot to take the first step. How simple the Padre made it all seem, as if there were only black and white. But nothing is that simple. You can hope and wait and pray until the end of time, and maybe something will happen, and maybe it won't. Looking through the doors of that church, I thought that whatever happened had little to do with God, or believing, or praying, or the saints and O Nuestra Señora de Guadalupe, and more to do with our own selves. What we can do. What we're willing to do.

There is no place we can go to absolve ourselves, no place where we can begin clean. And now he was saying it, the Padre, *por mi culpa, por mi culpa*, and everyone repeated after him that it was their fault, pounding on their chests. So many times during Mass, we beat our chests with our fists like that, repeating after the priest, *por mi culpa, por mi culpa*, because we began in sin, we began all wrong, in darkness and in fault. Why couldn't we begin in light?

# 47
•••

Raúl was just going to have a drink to calm his nerves. That's what he told himself. He walked into the dismal light of the Hotel Santo Niño, through the curtains to the bar. He ordered a beer and turned to watch people dancing clumsily. *Such bad dancers*, Raúl couldn't help thinking. But then again, they weren't really there for the dancing.

Her voice was in his ear. "*Patrón*," she said, "I've been waiting for you forever." She put her arms around his neck. "Where have you been, *mi rei*?"

Raúl signalled to the bartender and laid the money down for the girl's usual phony drink. "A lot has happened, *niña*."

"Well, none of it matters," she said. "You're here now." She slipped onto the bar stool and sipped her drink in the rehearsed way that she did, playing coyly with the cross around her neck.

He pulled out some bills from his wallet, glancing at the mug shots of his assailants as he did so. He thought of telling her the whole story, but he did not. He counted out the pesos, pressed them into her hand. "Is that enough for a dance?" he asked her.

"And a kiss," she said, smiling.

He stood up, bowing slightly, trying to act like a real *caballero*—or at least a real *caballero* from the movies. The old ones, though, the good ones. The Jorge Negretes, the Pedro Infantes. "May I have this dance?" he said dramatically.

She laughed. "Of course, *mi rei.*" She took his outstretched hand.

He led her to the dance floor. A *cumbia* was playing, which was fine, just fine. He could move through a *cumbia* with ease, just like he would with a *son* and a cha-cha-cha. He was glad that it wasn't a *banda* song. This was not to be a rough, cowboy kind of dance. He held the girl at arm's length, one hand in the middle of her back, the other touching her hand, held high above their heads like the ballroom dancers do. She laughed at such airs but went along with him. He spun her around elegantly, moved her around the floor like she was something grand. People stepped aside for them and watched them dance over each other's shoulders. Raúl *moved*, like he hadn't for years, and she with him, responsive to the slightest twitch of his hand, knowing which way to turn, her feet mirroring his own. And she could take the turns, this girl—five, six, seven, even eight times, and she never got dizzy. She fell into perfect step and balance with him afterwards. He could dip her to the floor, so close her head was a breath away from it, and she wasn't afraid. In fact, she smiled, then laughed.

Something had changed in her. It was a genuine smile Raúl saw, a real laugh, not anything rehearsed. He could see something of who she really was, and it was then he understood who she had reminded him of. Gabriela. He thought of how easily she laughed, how afraid she used to be of the dark. He'd go to her, sing songs to ease her back to sleep. He'd sing her "Cielito Lindo" because that's what she was to him, his pretty little sky, and if he could never see her again, the song went, he would surely die.

The girl didn't stop smiling. He danced with her to the end of the song. He spun her at the end, catching her in his arms and dipping her. After, all he could do was bow to her, thank her for the dance, and her smile faded and her forehead wrinkled in rare, true concern because he was crying as he walked through the curtains, through the lobby, and out the door.

# 48
### ...

There was so much waiting. All I did was wait. That was all everyone told me to do. "*Espérate,* Lucy." Which, translated into English, also means "hope." So while Luis and his roommates were telling me to wait, they were also telling me to hope. *Keep hoping, Lucy. Keep waiting.*

I was also waiting at the diner: waiting tables, serving, waiting, hoping. Then cleaning up. Because there was also a lot of cleaning up to do. I cleaned up at the diner, wiping off tables with an antiseptic rag for the next customers to mess up again. How did adults manage to get so much food all over the place? How did they manage to spill all that water, salt, ketchup, rice, and all those fries? How did so much sugar and cream never make it to the coffee cups?

At the *casa* of my brother and his friends, who prided themselves on their northern ways, they were just as piggish as the customers at the restaurant, leaving dirty dishes everywhere, dirty laundry. "*Cochinos!*" I yelled at them. "*Cochinos!*" I yelled all the time, throwing their clothes into their rooms, piling dishes into the sink and washing them, mopping the floors because I couldn't stand to live in such filth.

"Well, Lucy," Luis said once—and only once—"you *are* living here rent-free. You *could* help out a bit more."

I couldn't wait for the day I could put down money on my own place. On *our* place, for me and Gabi.

I began to put all their messes in their beds, pulling the sheets over them. They came home to half-eaten plates of spaghetti under their blankets, milk-coated glasses, beer bottles with spent limes and cigarettes extinguished inside them. Anything they left lying around for me to deal with, they could find it in their beds.

I read the papers for any word, any names, following the container tragedy like a telenovela. Every day there were new developments, commentary, more people found and arrested, a few new names, but no Gabriela. Then just as suddenly as the news had come, it vanished from the papers, and there was no word about the incident at all—like it had never happened.

The phone rang. I put the plate I was washing back in the sink, dried my hands, and picked up the phone. I said hello with a question mark at the end the way they did here in America.

There was silence on the line.

I said it again, this time without the question mark. I waited. I detected a breath. Someone was there.

"All right," I said, "if you're not going to say anything . . ."

I was about ready to hang up, but the caller spoke. And she knew my name.

"Lucy? Is that you?"

The voice jolted my body like electricity. "Gabi?" I cried.

"Lucy," she said again. "Lucy! I can't believe it's you!"

"Where *are* you, Gabi?"

"What are you doing at Luis's?"

"Waiting for *you*! I've been looking for you and waiting. Where—"

"And I sent your letter to Santo Niño!" she said. Gabriela was laughing, and I was crying. Soon I was wailing, and Gabriela was the one consoling *me*. "Lucita, it's all right! I'm fine! I'm in a *pueblito* near Torreón."

"Torreón!" I cried, not knowing where that was.

"Don't worry!" she said. "I'm staying with a really nice couple, Rosa and Martín. I'm working in their garden and café—"

"And they're nice? They're good?" I said, thinking of that woman in Mexico City, that house where Papá had sent her.

"Yes," she said, "they're really nice! You'd love them."

"What happened, Gabi?"

"I was going to San Diego," she said, "but I got sick. They took care of me."

"*Sick?* What do you mean?" The phone was slick with tears, and the room fell away to nothing but shadow and light, as if I had the camera to my eye and had turned the lens as far as it would go, letting everything unravel out of focus.

"It's a long story," Gabriela said. "It's all in the letter I wrote you. Ask Mamá to send it to you. I'll explain everything when I see you. Can you come visit me—I mean, if I don't go up there?"

"Yes, *hermanita*. Of course I will—anything!"

"Tell me about you! How are you, *hermanita*? What's happened to you? I think about you all the time. I miss you so much!"

I couldn't believe her voice—to me it was the same, the same Gabriela, though I knew she could not be the same. Her voice was light, cheerful, girlish. The way she was.

"How could you miss me? How could you forgive me?" I barely choked it out.

"Lucy? Forgive *you*?"

I heard the maddening beeping on the line that indicated time on her phone card was running out.

"Please don't cry. There's nothing to forgive, Lucy. You did everything for me. I love you! I'll call back soon, okay?"

"I love you, Gabi," I said before silence took over the line. I held the phone to my chest until it began to make angry noises for being off the hook for so long.

I didn't know how to stop looking for her. I kept scanning the faces of brown girls her age, trying to find her in each one before I remembered: Gabriela had called. I'd talked to her myself. Gabriela had been found, but that had had nothing to do with me, no matter how hard I had looked.

I surprised Luis with the news—he cried with relief—and I surprised his roommates with my good humour. The light that Gabriela gave me burned bright, changing me. I was no longer the dead-serious girl yoked with sadness. I went to work at the diner with a joy I hadn't thought was possible. I saw the city of San Diego as if for the first time, appreciating the deep blue sky and water, the pastel houses. Even the hum of the freeway sounded pleasant. I sang along to songs on the radio, whether I knew the words or not.

The roommates wanted to know what was wrong with me. Why wasn't I yelling at them? "You're *always* yelling. And I haven't found any food in my bed lately," said Oscar mournfully, as if he *missed* finding his dirty dishes under his sheets.

I shrugged. "I guess I don't care anymore."

"It's like . . . " he said, trailing off.

"It's like what?"

"It's like you're happy or something."

I smiled brightly at him. It was true; I felt happiness beam through me, the way Gabriela's voice did when she called.

She called when she could, but I was out working at the diner so often that we started making a call schedule so we wouldn't keep missing each other. Rosa and Martín didn't have a phone, so Gabriela phoned from the booth outside the café. Sometimes I'd hear the wind on the line and imagine her standing there, leaning against the wall, half in shadow. I imagined her in Pilar's old trousers and dress shirt, her hair combed back with gel like Miguel's or Luis's, looking out to the edge of the land.

I savoured her voice, her laughter, the way she said each word. More than once I had to ask: "Gabi, am I awake or am I dreaming?"

"Awake."

"Gabi, are you really there?"

"Yes, I am," she'd say. "Is that really you, Lucy?"

"It is."

In between our endless catching up, we'd ask each other questions like we used to as kids, whispering to each other late at night. "What would you rather do" questions: Live in Paris or in Puerto Vallarta? Eat a bowl of cockroaches or eat a rat? Except now our questions took on true meaning, and weren't just something to do when we couldn't sleep. They were a way to ourselves.

She told me she wasn't sure about coming to San Diego, and I told her I wasn't sure about staying in San Diego. I wasn't sure where I wanted to live, but I did want to see her. We made plans for me to go visit her in the *pueblito* near Torreón in the fall, after I'd saved some money. Her voice went a pitch higher and the words came faster—how I would love Rosa and Martín, how she would show me the garden and the chickens, how we could cook for the travellers together.

I laughed. "You? Cooking?"

"I learned, Lucy!"

"Mamá's not going to believe it."

"Do you ever think about going home?" She asked me abruptly, as if she hadn't known she was going to say it before it came out of her mouth. I answered her in the same way.

"All the time," I said.

I sat in front of the coffee table altar and took stock: burning candles; Pilar's petition and *milagro*; the photographs I'd taken,

Lupita's face on top of the stack; the small, framed print of the Virgen.

"Nuestra Señora Virgen de Guadalupe," I whispered, "for whom I was named, I implore your help . . ."

But I no longer needed her help. Could she feel my happiness? I looked at the Virgen, but she did not look at me. I watched the corners of her mouth for the slightest hint of a smile, but she remained solemn. She kept her eyes down, looking into her own praying hands, hands that had to keep praying because there were so many more lost girls that needed to be found, so many petitions from desperate people, so much pain that she had no choice but to take on. So she prayed. She would never stop praying and she would never stop suffering.

The only thing I could do was thank her.

# 49
...

Someone was pounding on the outside door. Raúl, tucked away in his office, stood up from his chair and listened.

It was too early for anyone to come to work yet. He wondered if he should answer it, or if he should wait for whoever it was to go away. The knocking persisted. He felt for the revolver tucked into his belt, adjusted his vest over it. Stepping out into the bar, he tried to see who was there through the plate glass window, but all he could see was a shadow: someone wearing a cowboy hat.

Raúl opened the door. It was Antonio.

"What is it?" He hadn't seen Antonio in a long time and now here he was, at his door, with his moustache drooping over his upper lip, a greasy ring imprinted around the top of his head when he took off his ridiculous cowboy hat and held it in his two hands in a practised gesture of respect.

"I came to offer my sympathies," Antonio said, wiping the sweat from his forehead with his sleeve.

"Sympathies?"

Raúl was still holding the door open. Antonio took this as an invitation and stepped inside. "I heard about what happened." Antonio shook his head. "Those boys—a bunch of stupid punks. Think they can get away with anything."

Raúl shut the door and locked it. "*That's* what you have to say? That's why you're here?" To think Antonio had the *cojones* to come here, to show his face to Raúl. The man must be crazy.

Antonio looked at Raúl for a moment, surprised. "No, Don. I wanted to talk to you about something . . . and . . . uh . . . give you a . . . payment." He reached into his pocket for his wallet. The leather was imprinted with a naked woman's silhouette, something Raúl had seen in souvenir shops. He hadn't thought that people actually bought those things. Raúl looked at it as Antonio fished around for some wrinkly peso bills and held them out to him.

Raúl wrinkled his nose at the money. "What's that for?"

"For the loan you gave me."

"Why the hell would I give *you* a loan?" As he said it, though, Raúl realized that he really *had* given him a loan—that there was a time when he'd liked Antonio, thought he was a good man.

"For my house, señor." Confusion spread across Antonio's face.

Raúl gestured toward a table. "Have a seat."

Antonio sat down. Raúl stood across the table from him, trying to understand how he'd come to trust Antonio. He remembered sitting beneath the trees in his garden, telling this man how he reminded him of himself when he was younger. How could he have thought such a thing? What spell had Antonio cast?

"What did you want to talk to me about?" Raúl asked.

"You've been so generous to me . . . " Antonio began. He waited a moment, unsure of himself. "To my whole family. And, well, Eduardo and I had a falling-out. He wants to—"

"Take the land away." Raúl smiled. He couldn't help it.

"That's right, Don. Did he tell you?"

Raúl motioned for him to go on.

"*Bueno*—but we had an agreement. My wife and kids are supposed to come out. I have a newborn baby—"

"Ah," Raúl mused, "*your family.*" He rubbed his hand over his face. "That's right. But what about *my* family? What are you going to give me for my family? What are you going to give me for destroying my daughter?"

Antonio opened his mouth and closed it like a lizard. Finally, he found his voice and began talking. "Listen. I didn't— it wasn't like that. She—" He stopped, noticing the look that Raúl knew was on his face, the disgust brewing inside him, the anger rising. Antonio shook his head and took out his wallet again. He held it in his hands but didn't open it.

Raúl folded his arms. "Go on. She *what?*"

Antonio turned his wallet over and over. "Look, Don," he said, "what can I do to make it right?"

"You're going to what? Give me money?" He glared at the wallet. "Nothing you do will ever make it *right*," Raúl said, spitting out the last word.

Antonio pushed back from the table but did not rise from the chair.

Neither man said anything for a long time.

Outside, cars rumbled by on Calle Morelos. The sun began to angle in through the big window. Carefully, Antonio stood. "Maybe I'll come back later," he said, shoving the wallet back into his pocket. "At a better time." He took a step toward the door, but Raúl pulled the gun from his belt.

Antonio put his hands up in a weak gesture—palms out, fingers curled inward—not the hands above the head in TV shows. He did not move and did not speak. Raúl watched for any flicker of movement from Antonio, anything at all, but particularly his hands. Keeping the gun trained on Antonio's heart, he searched the man for fear, or for an explanation, or for anything at all that would make sense of how Raúl came to be standing there, holding a gun on a man. Antonio was searching for something too. Maybe it would last forever, this silent standoff.

Raúl saw his dream again: his house burning, the vultures circling. He saw the gleam of the knife and felt its point at his throat. He saw Gabriela, bandana tied around her nose and mouth as though that would disguise her—like he wouldn't know his own daughter.

Antonio pressed his lips together. "Please, señor," he said.

"You ruined her," Raúl said. "You ruined my daughter."

Antonio didn't move. "Señor—"

"Sit," Raúl commanded. But Antonio stayed where he was. "I said *sit*, you worthless *hijo de perra*."

Antonio's face reddened. "Don't you dare insult my mamá," he said.

"Sit." Raúl cocked the gun.

Antonio tried to sit but ended up in a crouch instead, as if he were just waiting for the right moment to leap at Raúl. "I didn't ruin her," he said, his words clipped and defiant. "I didn't do anything wrong!"

Antonio suddenly stood up, and Raúl saw an odd flash of white light before he realized he'd pulled the trigger. Antonio's body crumpled forward. It was only then that Raúl heard the sound of a gunshot.

Raúl's hand buzzed. Antonio did not cry out; he just fell over. There was screaming from somewhere. Raúl couldn't place it, but when he raised his free hand up to his face he found it was *he* who was screaming. He put his hand over his mouth, and when he stopped the sound from coming, time caught up to him. He had actually shot a man. Through the big window the light poured in, hurting his head. People were looking.

Raúl set the gun on the table. He went to Antonio, knelt on the floor beside him. Antonio looked up at Raúl with no expression at all. He nodded down at his arm, clutching it with his other hand. Blood seeped through his fingers. Raúl took off his own shirt, tying it tightly around Antonio's arm. He went to the phone behind the bar to call an ambulance.

# 50
### ● ● ●

When the policeman Ortega came to the gate, María Luisa was outside feeding clothes into the washer. He knocked hard, announcing himself. She dropped in the last shirt—Raúl's—filled with dread. *"Momentito,"* she called back, closing the lid and turning the dial to start the washer, trying to prepare herself for whatever it was that had brought Ortega here.

"More bad news, Doña," he said, frowning at the ground, not wanting to meet her eyes.

María Luisa did not say anything. She thought the worst: everyone was dead, her whole family, everyone she cared about—her daughters and sons, her husband—gone. She imagined herself in the graveyard on the Day of the Dead, cleaning every single one of her family's headstones. It would take her all day and well into the night.

"Your husband shot a man this morning," he said, looking at her finally. "Antonio Rodríguez."

"Is he dead?"

Ortega shook his head. "He'll be fine. The bullet hit the arm but missed the bone and anything else important. It's good your husband is such a bad shot." He cleared his throat, then continued. "Raúl will be down at the station for a while in a holding cell—until we can figure out what happened. Guilty until proven innocent," he said.

"Yes," she said, "I know."

She watched him go, then shut the gate behind him.

Maybe she would lose everyone that was left. Raúl could be charged with attempted murder, and that would be that. He'd be sent to the prison up in Mexicali for who knew how many years. Maybe forever. Only Miguel would be left, obligated to stay with her and take care of her, until he went off on his own life. She would be alone.

She locked the gate, though she didn't think it mattered. There was nothing that could keep them safe or together. Houses, walls, gates—not even the cross hoisted on the hill had done much to protect them. The outside world had its own way of moving, its own way of making itself known. It was as unpredictable as a pack of street dogs.

As María Luisa turned to go inside the house, the heel of her sandal slipped on something. She looked down and saw she was stepping on an envelope addressed to her, in familiar handwriting. She opened the envelope and saw there were two letters in there: one to Lucy, and the other to Mamá.

The one to her was only a few lines long:

Querida *Mami,*

*I am alive and well. Please don't worry about me.*
  *Please forgive me.*

Con cariño, tu hija,
*Gabriela*

At the bottom of the page was a postscript, an address where she could be found.

María Luisa pulled a clean envelope and a sheet of paper from the cabinet in the kitchen, wrote Luis's address on the outside, and sealed Gabriela's letter to Lucy inside. She sat down at the table and, taking her time, began writing a letter to her youngest daughter.

When she was done, María Luisa went to her room and pulled the dusty shoebox with Carlos's letters from beneath her bed. She cleaned it off, opened the lid to make sure the letters were still there, and took it to the kitchen, where she wrapped it up in paper, taping the flaps and edges tight. She wrote Gabriela's name and address in thick black marker, as large as the box would allow. She carried it all the way to the post office, through dusty streets and the noon heat and growling dogs, as if she were on a sort of pilgrimage. She paid no attention to anything around her—neither the looks from neighbours or shopkeepers nor the dogs—but walked deliberately down the streets, taking the better part of an hour to get to the white block of a building where she posted the box and the letters to Gabriela and Lucy. After, she made her way to the police station.

# 51

### • • •

Raúl was kept in one of the holding cells of the Santo Niño station for a number of days. How many, he was unsure—he'd given up on counting them. He let time blur and run together. When they had taken him there—he went willingly, hands up in surrender—the policemen sat him up in front of the camera and made him hold a little sign. The flashbulb went off. His image was committed to paper.

The policeman Ortega liked Raúl and let him watch TV with them some evenings, handcuffed to the chair, the young guard beside him with an M16. They'd watch telenovelas, or sometimes the news, or, if he was lucky, a *fútbol* match. But mostly it was telenovelas like *La Mala*, the one his wife watched. Ortega always put Raúl back in the cell before *Agua Prieta*, which he liked better because it was set in Revolutionary times. Men were valiant then, real *caballeros* fighting for the sake of the people and for the honour of their women.

María Luisa visited Raúl every day. She brought him the dishes he liked, even *pollo con mole*, and she always brought extra for the policemen. For that, they welcomed her with smiles and a *muy buenas tardes, Doña*, letting her sit with Raúl longer than she was supposed to.

He found that he had so much he wanted to tell her, but he didn't know how to begin. Instead, he asked her what he'd been missing in *Agua Prieta*, and they discussed what they saw on the news: skyrocketing unemployment rates; a record number of people losing their homes; the war in Chiapas; immigrants sealed into boxcars heading across the Texas border, many of them, including children, dying. All he could do was shake his head.

He didn't think about what was going to happen next. He lay on his cot in the cell and tried to sleep, reliving the visits from his wife, and the shows he saw on the evening TV. He'd banter with the guards now and again to pass the time. If he slept, he dreamed of Gabriela, the knife at his throat.

It seemed like it would go on this way forever—until Ortega came to his cell and said they would release him on certain conditions. "Rodríguez hasn't pressed charges yet," Ortega told him, "but that doesn't mean he won't. We still might have to send you up to the D.A.'s office in Mexicali." He explained that Antonio had gone back to D.F. to be with his family, to be with his newborn daughter. "The way I see it," Ortega said, rubbing his chin, "if Rodríguez forgets about it, so will we."

He went on to tell him the rules of his release. The fee had to be paid, which Ortega called "bail," but Raúl knew was more like a bribe. It didn't matter—at least he could go home. "If you skip town," Ortega was saying, "or make any more trouble, it's Mexicali for you. We'll ship you up there like we did those boys."

Raúl nodded.

"You understand you're not a free man."

"I understand, sir," Raúl said.

Ortega led him down the hall to the door of the lobby. When they opened it for him, the first thing he saw was María Luisa, rising from her chair. Raúl went to her and held her close to him, kissed her gently on the lips. At the counter, he collected all his things—all except for the revolver, which they kept. They also gave him a copy of his own mug shot, because he had asked. Raúl held the little black and white up to the light, as though trying to see something in it, something that would reveal himself. It was him, all right, but it looked like someone else. When they handed him his wallet, he slipped his own mug shot beneath the plastic, together with the others that were still there.

# 52
•••

A big, flat DHL envelope came for me. Someone set it on the coffee table altar as if it were a petition or perhaps a token of thanks. I sat on the floor before the portrait of the Virgen to open it, with her as my witness. Inside were copies of official documents—a deed and a little map—along with a letter from Eduardo, explaining that I was now a property owner. He'd sent Antonio back to D.F. and was officially dividing his land between me and Gabriela. I spread the papers across the coffee table. It took a while for me to fully understand what all of it meant.

Days later, when Gabi called, I told her about receiving the deed. "Finally!" she said. "Now we can talk about it." We compared notes. The land was in both our names, and after calling Eduardo for clarification, we learned we did not have to divide it down the middle as the map indicated, but could keep it whole if we wanted. We could do whatever we wanted with it.

What did we want to do?

We spoke quickly, trying to get in as many words and ideas per minute as we could, making good use of our phone cards.

"Would you go back?" she asked.

"I don't know. Would you?"

"No. I don't know."

"If we did go back, though . . ."

"What kinds of trees would we plant?"

"Mango, lime—"

"Orange—"

"What about the house?"

"There should be a house."

"Yes, but where should it go?"

"Set back from the road."

"How many rooms?"

"Five?"

"Me, you, shared, kitchen, bath . . ."

"A quiet place for Mamá?"

"An extra room for people who are visiting?"

"A big garden too."

"Peppers, tomatoes, onions . . ."

We'd get lost in the planning, our voices intertwining, each of us with our map out, drawing on it with our fingers, drawing anything we wished. We may have been far away from each other, but here, on this map, we came together.

I bought a blank notebook and drew plans in my spare

time, tracing the property boundaries first. If he was around, Luis would lean over me and comment on my sketches and floor plans, offering advice.

"You need a dance floor. You'd seriously build a house without a dance floor?" he said.

I laughed.

"You should have a little storefront. Maybe you should have like a super-mini."

"A super-mini?" I said, turning the page, sketching out other ideas.

"Or a bar, a bar with a dance floor. Like right here." He drew it with his finger.

"It'd be like having El Pescado Loco in my house." I started to sketch trees where Luis had drawn the dance floor.

"It'd be different. It'd be better. I could be DJ," he offered.

"I see . . ." I raised my eyebrow. "But you don't want to go back. You'd have to leave all of this." I gestured at the apartment. I was being serious, but he started laughing.

"Oh, yeah, living in the lap of luxury by the San Diego Freeway."

"But you like it here." I laughed.

"Yeah," he agreed, "I guess I do."

He watched me sketch for a while, watched another floor plan of a small house take shape across the page. He cupped his hands around his mouth and whispered, "Daaaannce flooooor."

"Fine." I drew a dance floor in the centre of the house, obliterating walls and rooms with it, like paving a *zócalo* through a small town.

Luis cheered. "Now I'll come live with you."

"I don't know if I'm going yet." I looked at the page, then flipped back through all my floor plans, wondering if that was true. Wondering if in all these drawings I was really looking for a way back home.

# PART FOUR

| | |
|---|---|
| *De domingo en domingo* | Sunday after Sunday |
| *te vengo a ver;* | I come to see you; |
| *¡cuando será domingo* | when will it be Sunday |
| *—cielito lindo—* | —pretty little sky— |
| *para volver!* | so I can return! |
| *Yo bien quisiera* | I would love |
| *que toda la semana* | all the week |
| *—cielito lindo—* | —pretty little sky— |
| *domingo fuera* | to be Sunday |

—from "Cielito Lindo," traditional Mexican song

# 53
...

Antonio Rodríguez blew into town from Mexico City and began to spend Sunday afternoons with the *familia* Amador. He was Lucy and Gabriela's brother-in-law by marriage, but they always called him Tío. He'd greet the Amador sisters with hugs in addition to the customary kiss on the cheek, handing them the little gifts he'd brought.

Gabriela knew she was the special one, and not just because he began calling her his favourite girl. He held Gabriela just a little bit longer than her sister, his cheek grazing hers. He'd breathe in her scent, saying she smelled like the sweetest flower. He called her *angelita* and *hermosita*, while he only called Lucy Guadalupe. He winked at Gabriela when no one was looking. He'd ask how it was possible that a girl like her didn't have a thousand boyfriends yet. Gabriela would blush and smile wider.

Just the way he looked at her—his sideways glances, a long look at her legs—made her walk taller, swinging her hips just a little. She stopped pining for Carlos, the neighbour boy. She began to daydream about Antonio, filling hearts in her notebook with his name. She relived his lips on her cheek, his embrace, his breath in her ear.

When Lucy found out about Gabriela's feelings for Antonio, they had a terrible fight resulting in seven days of silence that blanketed them like ash. It was Gabriela who broke the silence first, finding life unbearably lonely without her sister to talk to. And Lucy made Gabriela promise that she would stay away from Antonio.

Gabriela couldn't stay away from him, though. The attention he gave her made her feel special and wanted and loved. So instead of keeping her promise, she began to keep things from Lucy. Like how Antonio sometimes waited for her after school in his truck. He'd always have something for her, the kind of barrettes or candy she liked. Like how he'd say, "How's my favourite girl?" Like how he'd hold her hand while he drove, saying he loved her, and how when he had kissed her on the mouth for the first time, it was unlike any kiss she'd ever had.

Antonio stirred things in her that no one could. When he reached out to stroke her hair, her whole body trembled. When he looked at her, she would begin to sweat and her mouth would go dry. She was used to being looked at, but there was something different about his gaze, something that no one else could give her, not the men she passed on the street, not the señor at the corner store, not even Carlos. Antonio was a man, and he treated her like a woman.

"Gabriela, beautiful as a flower," he'd whisper, "made from heaven's light . . . Gabriela, pretty as the sea." And he'd open her hand to place one of his little gifts in her palm, a tin ring with a glass jewel, or a sheet of stickers, or a hunk of the *dulce de tamarindo* she liked.

Gabriela remembered every detail. When school had let out that day, she scanned the line of cars and found Antonio in his truck. She wanted to run to him, but she contained her excitement and walked slowly, waving goodbye to her classmates.

She got in and slammed the door. He put the truck into gear and drove off.

"Aren't you happy to see me?" He reached over and stroked her hair.

Gabriela swallowed, her skin tingling. "Yes," she said, smiling.

He drove in the opposite direction of town, turning off the main road onto a tiny rutted road she would never have noticed. Ahead she could only see the expanse of desert. He reached over and tapped the glove compartment. "There's a surprise in there for you," he said.

Gabriela opened it and found a small, velvety box. Inside was a delicate chain threaded through a gold cross. "Oh, Antonio!" she said. "I love it!" She pulled it from the box and held it up.

"An early Christmas present," he said. "It's real gold."

"Really?" She turned to look at him.

He gave her a smile. "Of course. Anything for my beautiful flower."

She put the necklace on, touching it now and again with the tips of her fingers. She sat up straight in her seat, watching the desert speeding by all around her. "Where are we going?"

"A special place," he said, pointing to a dramatic hill. "From there, *dulce*, you can see the entire town. You can see the sea and everything. It's amazing—I want to show you."

They drove up the twisty road to the top of a hill. When they finally arrived, he went around to her door, opened it for her, and helped her out. He reached behind the seat and grabbed a six pack of Modelo.

Gabriela spun around, arms out. There was the sea; there was the tiny speck of the town by the edge of the water. She felt like a princess in her high tower. "It's the most beautiful place in the world," she whispered. Overhead, the vultures soared.

Antonio opened a can of beer and handed it to her. Then he held up his own in a toast. "To us," he said, crashing his can into hers. "To the most beautiful woman in all of Mexico."

Gabriela drank the beer, looking out over the whole world. She was beaming. *The most beautiful woman—*

Antonio put his arms around her waist, squeezed her against him. She felt his breath against her neck, tickling the skin there. She couldn't stop smiling. At her feet was the city, and at her back was the man who loved her, who was going to marry her when his house was finished. They would have the biggest wedding the town had ever seen. He kissed her neck, then her ear. She thought of all the things he'd confessed to her that he'd told no one else—how his wife was leaving him, how heartbroken he had been, vowing never to love again. But then he had met her, Gabriela, and he couldn't help it, he had fallen in love with her. He reached under her shirt, his hands crawling to her breasts, squeezing them. She gasped. She told herself not to be afraid, that this was what it meant to be a woman, what it meant to be loved. He ran his hands down to her thighs, up beneath her skirt. Her body tensed; her legs locked together. His breathing was heavy in her ear. His breathing was too loud, and when he said, "Relax, Gabi, it's all right," his voice startled her. "You know I love you." He spun her around into him, pressing her against him, kissing her so hard his teeth snagged her lip and clashed against her teeth, his tongue gagging her. When she tried to pull away, he pressed her tighter. She thought she would suffocate. Tears streamed down her cheeks; soon she was sobbing into his mouth.

He stopped kissing her and looked at her. "Don't cry, my lovely flower," he breathed. "I won't hurt you." He looked deep into her eyes, and a small space opened up between them. Relieved, she tried to smile. He smiled back. "That's my girl," he said, rubbing his palm down the side of her face, wiping away her tears, then down to pull open her shirt.

"Wait," she whispered, shaking her head, "no, wait." But this time he didn't stop.

"I can't wait anymore," he whispered, his hand still moving downward, shoving her skirt up, unzipping his pants, tugging at her.

She put her hands up to push him away, but he grabbed her arms and tightened his hold on her as he pressed her down to the desert floor.

# 54
...

Each day for the rest of the week, part of her was afraid that Antonio would be waiting for her after school. But when school finally let out on Friday, and Gabriela saw he wasn't there yet again, she burst into tears, feeling even worse. She let herself cry until she turned onto Calle de la Cruz, then made herself stop.

She ran through the gate and into her bedroom, burying her face in the pillow. Her mamá must've heard her crying, but she didn't come in to check on her.

She lay on the bed until the light began to fade. She listened to her mamá in the kitchen, the clattering of pans and silverware. Then she heard the unmistakable rumble of Papá's truck, skidding to a halt outside.

She heard the slamming of the gate, the hard steps through the kitchen. Mamá saying, "Raúl, you're home early—"

Then he was in the doorway.

Papá's face. She'd never seen him look like that before. His face was contorted in anger, yet he was trying to control himself and failing. It was like a face in a carnival mirror, stretched and bizarre, almost funny if it hadn't been so terrifying. It was not the face of the papá she knew.

"Get up," he said.

"Papá—"

He had her by the wrist so fast all she could do was yelp. He pulled her to the kitchen. She stumbled and fell, but he dragged her across the floor until she stood again. *"Por favor*—Papi—"

"Raúl!" Mamá yelled. "What are you doing? She's just a child!"

"She's no child!" He gripped Gabriela's shoulders. "She's a whore!" He slapped her suddenly—his hand like a slab of wood.

Mamá grabbed his shoulder, yanked him back with all her strength. "Stop!" she yelled.

He pushed her away like she was nothing. He raised his fist at her in warning, then at Gabriela. "You know what they're saying about you? You're the Amador *puta*! I can't believe what I've been hearing!"

"Who said that?" Mamá asked, walking slowly toward Papá.

"Everyone's saying that!" he yelled. "Everyone knows what you did with Antonio—every last detail!"

"You're going to believe rumours?" Mamá tried to speak calmly, but her voice was strained. She put a hand on his shoulder; he pushed it away.

"It isn't rumour, María. It's the truth. Isn't it, Gabriela?"

Gabriela didn't move. She didn't know what to do or say. After a moment, she met her father's angry eyes.

"Answer me." He looked monstrous to her, his face so ugly. She tried to wipe her tears away, but they kept coming. "It's the truth, isn't it."

She kept looking into his face, his eyes, trying to find him, trying to find a way to him. She wanted him to remember that she was Gabrielita, his youngest, the one he used to sing songs to when she couldn't fall asleep.

She nodded. "I'm sorry, Papi," she said softly.

"I'm not your Papi," he said evenly, even quietly. "And you're not my *hija*, because I did not raise a *puta*!" His voice rose with every word. "You want to be a whore? Then get out! Go to the street!" He struck her hard on the side of her face, his ring scuffing her cheek—everything happening so quickly that it took her a moment to realize she was on the floor. Mamá had grabbed Papá, trying to pull him away, but he flailed wildly and hit her too. Sound faded from Gabriela; the room blurred. She touched her hand to her face where her papá had hit her. Movements slowed, and she had the strangest sensation, like she was watching a telenovela with the sound turned down. It was as though nothing behind the glass had anything to do with her, and that at any moment she chose, she could shut it off, make the screen go black.

# 55
...

Everything happened *to* her, as if she were a doll, able to move only when pushed and pulled about by others. She packed a bag the way Papá ordered. She was pulled by the wrist to his truck, driven by him down the highway. She heard him when he said she was going away for a little while, to think about what she'd done. She was at the gate with her boarding pass, glancing back only to see her father looking the other way. She was on the tarmac, still looking back, hoping her father would change his mind, run after her, pull her out of the line.

Then she was on the plane, and the engine revved and the propellers whirred, taking her up in the air, over the land where she was born.

The plane took her to Mexico City, to the Aeropuerto Benito Juárez, where she followed signs to the exit, not knowing what she would do when she got there. Then she saw her name, scrawled on a piece of paper. A woman with dyed red hair held it in two manicured hands, scanning the faces of girls who came through. When her eyes landed on Gabriela's face, she lowered the sign, motioned for Gabriela to come to her.

That night, and every other night there, Magda put her in her room at eleven o'clock, shut the door, and turned the key. There was no leaving the little room, not even for the bathroom, until Magda opened it in the morning. Sometimes Magda would go out during the day, locking Gabriela back in. There was not even a light in the room. Only street light during the night, when she lay awake, the fierce-looking dogs asleep right outside her window.

She wrote letters to her sister until Magda discovered them and destroyed them, taking away her notebook and pen, taking all her things away, saying she was bad and deserved no privileges. Magda read Lucy's letters aloud, laughing at the parts about herself. "You don't like me, then? You think I'm mean?"

Gabriela shook her head. Because Magda was kind to her too. She just never knew which Magda she'd get. Nice Magda would take her out to lunch or buy her a new dress, or hold her hand when they crossed the street.

On one of her kind days, she told Gabriela to put on the new dress; they were going to meet an old friend of hers. She sat Gabriela down and brushed her hair, smoothed the dress, unbuttoning its top button. "There," she said, pleased.

"You're perfect. Wait here while I get ready." Magda locked her in the room again. The afternoon grew into night, and the night was very dark.

Finally, Magda came for her. "Hurry up, dear." They crawled into a cab. "Calle San Judas Tadeo," she ordered. She consulted a notebook. "Number twenty-four."

Eventually they stopped at a shabby building, Magda leading Gabi inside a foyer so dim she could scarcely see at first. A man stepped forward and Magda greeted him, introduced him to Gabi. He looked openly at her breasts and legs and even inside her mouth. He licked his fingers before counting out the cash into Magda's outstretched hand.

But Gabriela bolted, found herself running before she knew she was going to run—running faster than she had in her life, out into the street, past a statue of San Judas, weaving through a maze of *calles* and *callejónes*, running through crowds of people and cars and bikes, darting across six-lane boulevards, not looking back, never looking back.

She ran through a *tianguis* shutting down for the night, people tearing down tarps, boxing up the cassette tapes and scarves and jeans that had been piled on the tables. She ran until she could run no more, until every muscle in her body felt like cement. She collapsed behind two metal trash barrels in an alley, burying herself beneath cardboard boxes, vegetable peels, eggshells, bones, and chicken feet. She pressed her cheek to the ground, willed herself to die. They wouldn't want her if she were dead. She prayed a crack would open in the ground and swallow her up into the dirt or whatever was below the concrete of the city. Hadn't it been built on a lake or a swamp—or was it in the crater of a volcano? Whatever it was, that was where she wanted to be.

But Gabriela would not die. Instead, she could not stop moving. Her heart would not stop beating; her entire body shook from the cold. The stink of the trash was beginning to suffocate her, so that slowly, against her will, she began to rise up from the ground. The alley was dark, save for slashes of street light. She pressed herself against the wall, trying to keep in the shadows, inching her way to the mouth of the *callejón*.

A woman was staring right at her. Gabriela slid down the wall again, but it was too late: the woman had seen her. Gabriela had also seen the woman. She had seen her face, her swollen eye, her bloody lip. Gabriela found her voice: "What happened to you?"

The first week that she stayed at Pilar's apartment, Gabriela was sick, throwing up whatever Pilar convinced her to eat.

"It could be anything," Pilar told her, "but probably it's nerves." She chewed on her finger, deep in thought. "Though it's true you could've picked up some disease in the garbage . . ."

Gabriela stopped eating. Even the thought of food made her sick. Pilar brought her a tea that the *curandera* down the street suggested. At first, she threw that up too, but Pilar kept making her drink it, and soon enough, the vomiting stopped.

But she was still afraid. It wasn't until after Pilar transformed her into a man that she felt safe enough to go out. For a time, that was wonderful, feeling protected while running errands or going to the market with Pilar. Her favourite afternoon: Wandering about the Bosque de Chapultapec as a man in a suit and tie, arm-in-arm with Pilar. Bright blue sky arching overhead, the trees swooning, the air cool and clear as the winter air of Baja. Strolling about like *turistas* from Spain, they counted the fountains, pointed at the *castillo*, and bought ice cream from the old man with the cart. They danced a clumsy waltz like she would've done at her *quince años* party, feeling like they were free.

Underlying these outings, though, was the sensation that something was deeply wrong. She tried to pinpoint where the feeling of unease was coming from, assuming at first it was the fear of seeing Magda or that man. But soon she realized it was coming from inside herself.

She was alone in Pilar's apartment, naked before the mirror, her eyes closed. Terrified to look at herself. Opening her eyes slowly, she saw it was true: her belly and breasts were pushing out in hills from the rest of her small frame, the skin tighter there.

Gabriela pulled on Pilar's old trousers and buttoned them above her belly. She wrapped the fabric so tightly around her breasts they ached. She put on a clean shirt. There was still a slight rise to her chest and belly, but with the jacket it was hardly noticeable. Besides, some young men had bellies. There was still the problem of her hands. They were small, delicate, feminine.

Dirt. Men were always dirty, weren't they? She rubbed a little of Pilar's makeup into her hands, grubbing them up a bit. She wondered how Pilar could have traded in being a man for being a woman. It made no sense to her.

As she glanced at her profile in the mirror, she counted the months on her fingers. Her belly would only get bigger, and it would soon be obvious that Gabriela was no man. They would see through her disguise, they would find her, they would take her away.

# 56
...

From the station Autobuses del Norte in Mexico City, Gabriela, dressed in Pilar's old suit, headed north toward Chihuahua with dozens of others. She scanned people's faces, wondering if any of them were planning to go across the border as she was. Most of the time she put her head to the window, looking out, watching everything pass by through the ghost in the glass, the reflection of her face.

She thought about the baby inside her, floating there, growing. It comforted her; she wouldn't be alone. It didn't matter that it had come out of pain or lies or force. She knew there was more to it than that, because a baby couldn't happen unless there was love. That's what she'd heard once: that it was love that made babies. Antonio hadn't loved her— she understood that now—but she had loved him. And Gabriela decided that she would love the baby no matter what had happened in the past. She would love it because she

couldn't bear the thought of having one more unloved creature in the world. She wouldn't cast it out because it wasn't
perfect. She would find a place for them to live, a place where
there would be love overflowing everything, where they
would never give each other up, not ever, not for anything.

She thought about the *frontera*. She thought about the Rio
Grande and wished she hadn't promised Pilar that she wouldn't
swim across—because if there was one thing she could do, it
was swim. She was from Baja California Sur, a place of two
seas. She hoped she would not have to pile into a cargo truck
or a boxcar on a train, which was what she'd heard could
happen. She tried not to think of that version, being shut into
a box, into the dark with so many others. She wanted to *see*.
She wondered what it would be like, seeing *el norte* from
across the river. Pilar had told her it was just the same on the
north side as it was on the south side, the border nothing
but a line drawn through the same shitty land.

Gabriela imagined it differently: it would be like going
from a land of black and white to a land of colour, like going
from a land of dust and death to a land of lushness and life.
She'd seen pictures of the *fútbol* fields in the United States;
she'd *seen* the green grass and white lines. Not dirt, which
was what they had to kick the ball around in back home,
choking themselves with the dust they stirred up. In her head
were images of the place, layered upon her reflection in the
window, upon the land passing by. She said a prayer, asking
for help to get her to this place of light and colour. Then she
felt a pain in her belly.

• • •

As evening settled in, the pain worsened, cramping her insides. She put a hand to her stomach, then drew it back, not wanting anyone to notice the swell there.

She turned in her seat toward the window, put her forehead against the cool glass. Her reflection was clearer now—she could see right into her own eyes—as darkness crept in over the barren landscape. If only she could see straight through her body to the baby. She wanted to put her hands on the child inside, wanted to erase the pain, wanted to calm it. *It's all right*, she thought. *Everything is all right. Be calm, just float there in your bubble. We'll get there, we will. Just hang on.*

The baby kept hurting her. *The baby must be crying*, she thought. Then she thought of La Llorona, the witch who drowned babies. *Stay away from my baby.* The cramps burned and sharpened. She wanted to claw her way to the child, hold it there, tell it to stay. Make it stay. But it kept hurting, and by the time they stopped in the little town whose name she did not know, she was flushed with fever and sweat.

The sun had just gone down. She waited for everyone to get off before her. She stepped off the bus in a desolate place. Two block structures were silhouetted by the dying light. It was a café of sorts, maybe a house, and everyone went inside to get something to eat. She walked toward the building too, but veered from the door into the darkness, following the shadows around to the back of the building. She could feel a wetness between her legs, the baby slipping. She could feel it tearing from her insides. She eased herself to the ground, pressed her hands to her stomach. She pressed them there as hard as she could, trying to stop the pain, trying to stop everything from happening. Above her was the desert sky, her only shelter, turning to night.

# 57
* * *

Someone leaned over her. Gabriela blinked several times, trying to get her eyes to focus. A hand pressed to her forehead, then a cold cloth. A woman's voice: "Rest, *hija*."

*Hija.* The word moved within her, and she wanted to hold on to it, but she was so tired. She fell into sleep again, waking when the light from the window hit her face. She was in a tiny room with only a little space left over from the bed she was in, a curtain over the doorway. A radio was playing from somewhere, a song she recognized by Los Tigres del Norte. There were sounds and scents of home, of dishes clanking together, of running water. The sharp smell of burnt chilies.

Her clothes were gone, Pilar's old trousers and dress shirt. She was now in clean floral sheets, in a T-shirt and sweatpants, a thick pad between her legs. There was a pan of water on the floor beside the bed, another of blood-soaked towels.

A woman appeared in the doorway, drying her hands. Her hair had gone grey in patches and was held back from her face with too many bobby pins. When she smiled, wrinkles sprouted around her eyes and mouth. "How are you feeling?" she asked.

Gabriela couldn't say anything. Words were stuck in her throat. She wanted to say, *Dead, señora, I'm dead.* She wanted to say, *Why did you steal my baby?* But all the words were stuck. They hurt her throat. She wanted to take a knife and cut them out. Her eyes began to water. She coughed like she was choking.

The woman sat beside her on the bed, stroking Gabriela's short hair, her forehead, wiping the tears from Gabriela's face. She put a glass of water to Gabriela's lips. "It's all right," she whispered. But it wasn't all right.

The woman kept stroking her hair the way Lucy would have done. "There will be another one," she said, "another time. When it is right. That soul—it wasn't ready to come out into the world."

Gabriela felt the warmth of the woman's hand, but it did not make her feel any better. There was all this space inside her now.

The woman introduced herself as Rosa and told Gabriela she was married to a bus driver named Martín. While he drove a bus, she ran a small café in the building next door, open when buses full of weary, hungry travellers came through. Gabriela had been one of those travellers, she remembered. But here was where she had stopped, in a place that didn't even have a name and wasn't even a dot on the map.

So many mornings Gabriela lay in the dark at the *casa de* Rosa and Martín, listening to the rooster crow. It was alone in the early morning blackness, crying for them all to get up, to join it, to keep it company. As if people got up to soothe the rooster. People got up because there was much to do, because that was life, because daylight beckoned, and the world was never going to wait.

She thought of her mother, always awake, always doing: cooking, washing, taking care of them. Her enduring strength Gabriela thought of her mother's old school books in the kitchen cabinet, wondering if she ever read them. She probably never had time.

She got up from the bed and went into Rosa's kitchen, switching on the light. She found a pan and filled it with water to boil.

Her mamá had tried to use her strength to defend her from Papá's wrath. She had tried, yet Gabriela could see how powerless she was. She was strong in the world of women, but weak in the world of men. And it was the world of men that mattered here.

By the time Rosa woke, coffee was ready and Gabriela was attempting to make breakfast. Rosa stepped in to take over before she got too far. Gabriela had never really learned to cook very well, though she could make rice pudding and *tres leches* cake—she had always been more interested in sweets.

Rosa's husband, Martín, came into the room clean-smelling and in his bus driver's uniform. "And she's up!" he said, smiling.

"*Buenas días*, señor," she said. It was the first time she'd seen Martín.

He laughed. "Call me Martín. I've never really been a señor."

Rosa put her hand on Gabriela's shoulder. "Look here," she said. "You just crack the egg, wait a few seconds, flip it, and there it is." When the eggs were done she slid them onto a plate, which her husband took out of her hands. He sat at the table and doused his eggs with pico de gallo, then sopped it all up with tortillas.

Gabriela concentrated on the frying pan, on the smooth, unbroken eggs on the counter. She picked one up and held it in her hand.

"Do you want to try?" Rosa asked.

Gabriela nodded. By the time the egg was done, Martín had kissed Rosa goodbye and had gone, so she and Rosa sat alone at the table.

"Do you want to talk about anything?" Rosa asked.

Gabriela shook her head.

"Do you want me to call anyone?"

Gabriela shook her head again.

"Do you want to see the priest?"

"No," Gabriela said firmly, imagining herself sitting in the black box, having to say, *Forgive me, Father, for I have sinned.*

"Okay." Rosa reached over and took Gabriela's hand.

"I'm okay," Gabriela said.

Rosa smiled. "All right. If you need something, tell me."

Gabriela looked at Rosa's veined hand on hers, her simple wedding band. "Actually," she said, "I do need something."

"*Díme.*"

"Do you have any envelopes and stamps? I should write to my mother," she said, "and mail a long letter I wrote to my sister."

After they washed and dried the dishes, stacking them on the open shelves, Rosa left her alone to write. Gabriela sat for a long time, trying to gather up all she wanted to tell her mother, all she wanted to understand about her, all that she was sorry for, but it was too much to write. She didn't even know how to begin. So she only wrote a few words. Maybe her mamá just knew—knew everything the way the Virgen knew—and Gabriela would have no need to explain anything to her.

A few days later, Gabriela found herself gripping the pay phone receiver in her hand, listening to the silence on the line. Warmth moved through her entire body, as well as the relief and joy and sadness she felt at hearing Lucy's voice on the phone. She had called Luis to tell him where she was so he wouldn't worry, and was astonished that Lucy answered instead. For a moment, she could not even speak.

The last words Lucy said before the phone card ran out—*I love you, Gabi*—rang so clear through her head it was almost like Lucy was still on the line. Gabriela leaned against the outside wall of Rosa and Martín's café, hardly seeing the little house, the garden beside it, or the highway in the distance. She replayed the conversation in her mind again and again, letting Lucy's voice, her tears, and her love fill the empty space inside her.

• • •

At Rosa and Martín's, Gabriela fell into a comfortable routine. Mornings she rose and let the chickens out of their roost to wander the confines of their pen, throwing them scratch and vegetable scraps. She collected the eggs and brought them into the kitchen, where she washed each one and set them in a bowl, clean and gleaming. She helped Rosa with breakfast and looked at the bus schedule to get a sense of when travellers would come through. Before it got too hot, she'd go to the garden and weed, digging her hands into the soil, liking how the dirt stuck in her cuticles and the crevices of her knuckles.

Bad thoughts and memories came and went, surfacing at any given moment—when she was in the garden, or when she was breaking eggs into a pan—but most often they surfaced when she was alone in the dark of her room. Sometimes she would think she was at Magda's house and find herself tearing through the bedsheets, trying to get out, tripping on them and falling, running through the curtained doorway, out to the kitchen, where she'd realize where she was. At Rosa and Martín's. Safe.

She tried to counter the bad memories by focusing on what she loved, and the times she had felt loved, going through them like beads on a rosary: Lucy's voice, Mamá braiding her hair, the beach, *guayabas*, roasted chilies, her friend Pilar, Rosa's hand on her forehead, Luis teaching her dance steps—*quick, quick, slow.*

She thought of the lost child, too, how easily it had dissolved and leaked from her, even though she had loved it.

She wondered if it had been a boy or a girl, what it would have been like to hold her own infant in her arms. A living, breathing creature that she had made. Where was the baby now? In Purgatory? She decided to believe it was as Rosa had said: the soul had gone back to roost in the upper branches of the tree of life, waiting to return to her when the time was right.

# 58
...

They came off the buses tired and hungry, lining up through the door of the café, a small building with plastic tables and chairs that spilled outside, half under a blue tarp for shade. Gabriela made them egg tacos and ladled soup into Styrofoam cups while Rosa ran the cash register. Rosa also sold candy, *chicle*, stamps, phone cards, paper and envelopes, bags of chips, postcards of Mexico City and Durango and burros wearing sombreros.

For a while Gabriela kept her back to the travellers, cooking on the little stove behind Rosa, scarcely turning to greet them when she handed them their paper plates of food. She was afraid she'd see someone she recognized—Magda, or the man who'd counted the money. What if Antonio came through? And she was afraid of those she didn't recognize: How could she tell if any of these strangers were bad or good?

More than once she saw a girl travelling alone. She wondered where each one was going, and why. Gabriela smiled at them, and sometimes they smiled back. She wanted to do something for them, but she wasn't sure what or how, until she saw one teenaged girl hanging back from the crowd, clutching her bag, watching people with their plates of food, then looking at her feet, as if in shame. When the line had dwindled down, Gabriela looked at the food that was left and, with Rosa's approval, took a tray of three egg tacos, a cup of soup, and a big glass of *agua de tamarindo* to the girl. "Here's your order," Gabriela said.

The girl looked around her, not wanting others to hear. "But I didn't—"

"There was extra," Gabriela whispered. "Please, sit and eat."

The girl nodded, then smiled. "*Mil gracias.*" She devoured the meal within minutes.

Gabriela and her mother began to talk via letters. Her mother's were neatly written, always fitting within the simple black border of her stationery. Together, her letters read like a book of questions, asking if she'd been eating enough—and what, for that matter—what the house was like, who were Rosa and Martín, and was Gabriela coming back home.

Her mother also sent an entire box of letters from Carlos Salvador. She sat in her room and flipped through all the envelopes, amazed, taking her time to open them. They were letters of worry, letters of heartbreak, letters of regret. He'd written to her every day for a month. She wondered what had happened that made him stop writing. Maybe he fell in love with someone. Maybe it was because she never wrote back.

She laughed as she read his letters. Sometimes she cried, she was so deeply touched. Mostly she cried for her lost self, the young, carefree Gabriela. The girl who would watch for Carlos out the window. The girl who had once sneaked into the furniture storeroom where he worked, where they'd hidden beneath a table, barricading themselves in with chairs, and kissed and held each other.

How simple her problems had been. She sometimes wished that was all she had to worry about now: loving Carlos in defiance of her mother. If only that could be the biggest of her dramas. But there was no going back. Like the day she had run faster than she'd ever run before, she knew she could not look back for a second. She was not the same Gabriela Carlos had loved.

One letter took several reads to fully understand. It was one of his regret letters, but it was not what she expected. He wrote:

*I should've done everything differently. This is all my fault. I shouldn't have obeyed your mother when she told me to stop seeing you. I shouldn't have been such a stupid little boy. I should've told her how much I loved you, explained that our love was real. I should've said no! I know you felt hurt that I quit talking to you or writing back. Your notes broke my heart so I stopped reading them. If only I could go back in time and change all that. Then you wouldn't have fallen for Antonio, and you'd still be across the street.*

Her mamá? She was the reason why Carlos had distanced himself from her? When Gabriela finally put the letter away, she sat on the bed for a long time, thinking. If she had known that, would it have changed anything? She couldn't be sure.

She thought of Antonio sitting in the garden beneath the orange tree, a shadow cast across his face by the brim of his hat. His smile, his kiss on her cheek, how special he had made her feel. Was it her mother's fault this had happened? Was it Carlos's? Was it Eduardo's for inviting Antonio there, or was it Ana's for having him as a brother in the first place? So many took on the blame; so many longed for forgiveness. Even herself.

But what about Antonio? Why wasn't it his fault? Because it was. Gabriela knew her part in the story, but he had known where he was leading her.

# 59
···

She kept the envelope that held Eduardo's letter and the deed to the plot of land in her pocket while she worked in the café, the small rectangle of possibility nearly weightless against her leg. When everyone had eaten, boarded the bus, and gone on their way, she took the envelope to a table where she sat to rest and reread the letter.

Querida *Gabriela,*

*Please accept my sincere apologies for not being a good brother to you. I did not protect you when I should have, and worse, I welcomed in the person I needed to protect you from. I do not expect you to forgive me.*

*Antonio has gone back to D.F. His land is now yours and Lucy's. It always should've been.*

*Take it. Do with it whatever you wish.*

Con cariño, tu hermano,
*Eduardo*


She spread the other pieces of paper across the table to study them. The deed to the plot of land in Eduardo and Ana's development and the map of the property were labelled with her name on one side and Lucy's on the other. She thought of all the plans and possibilities that she and Lucy had discussed on the phone. She traced the boundary of the land with her finger.

Rosa usually left her alone when she looked through the envelope, sensing it was important and that Gabriela needed to be alone. So it surprised her one afternoon when Rosa set two glasses of *agua de jamaica* on the table and sat across from her.

"Gabriela?" Rosa asked. "Is everything okay? You sit here every day with these and . . ." She glanced down at the papers, obviously curious.

Gabriela turned the deed and the map around to show Rosa. "Look, Rosa! I'm my own country!" she said. "My sister is too."

"That's wonderful." Rosa put on her reading glasses to get a better look. "That's a nice chunk of land."

"There's nothing there," Gabriela said.

Rosa slid the map back to Gabriela. "That's how we all begin," she said.

Gabriela put everything into the envelope and tapped the sticky seal closed. "It's just that . . . I don't know if I can go back." She frowned, wishing this was something she could accept, that it was that simple, that she could just return home like nothing had happened.

Rosa nodded, though Gabriela had told her very little about what had happened to her, and Rosa never plied her with too many questions. "Whether you do or you don't," Rosa said, "it'll always be there. Your sister too."

Gabriela smoothed the envelope with her palms and drew an invisible line across it with her finger, then another. *That's how we all begin.*

# EPILOGUE

### •••

It was nearly August before I made it back to Santo Niño. I had spent my months in San Diego working and saving money, sketching out floor plans and talking to the architect who had designed Eduardo and Ana's house, calling the builders he'd recommended, trying to get a sense of how much it would cost to build a house. I also spent time with my brother, going out dancing on Fridays, packing picnics and driving to Coronado Island, where we swam in the cold Pacific, screaming and laughing and feeling like kids again.

I flew from one country to another, from one life to another, in only a couple of hours. As we neared the end of the Baja peninsula and prepared to land, I was surprised by how small it was. How could I possibly fit within its borders? The plane hovered above the runway, wavering as if unsure, before touching down.

Eduardo had said he'd pick me up from the airport, but when I stepped through the green light at customs, Papá was there, waiting for me amid the people holding up signs scrawled with the names of strangers.

"Where's Eduardo?" was all I could say.

Papá pulled me in for a hug, kissing my forehead like he was trying to bless me.

We didn't say much the entire drive back. When he put his hands to the steering wheel, I was startled at the sight of his left hand, the stub where his ring finger had been. He seemed anxious, checking the rear-view mirror often, as if at any moment the police would flash their lights behind us, pull us over, and take him away. The highway rumbled beneath us; cars blazed by us. I rolled down the window all the way and breathed in the salty, fishy air of Santo Niño. I couldn't help smiling.

"Guadalupe," Papá said as we neared the turnoff to Santo Niño. I kept my gaze out the window. "Did you talk to Gabri—Gabriela?" His voice faltered on her name, like he was just learning how to say it. "About, you know, about coming home?"

"Yes."

"What did she say?"

I turned to look at him. He looked smaller, I realized. Smaller and weaker. His face was more lined than I remembered. "She doesn't know, Papá."

He set his jaw and nodded, looking straight ahead, taking the exit to Santo Niño.

We drove slowly through *el centro*, stopping often to let tourists cross the road. I glanced at El Pescado Loco, amazed to find it packed to the roof even in the off-season. Every table on the umbrella-covered patio was crowded with people and drinks. Papá barely even looked, which surprised me. It was something he would've boasted about just months before.

We went down one dusty road and another until we turned down Calle de la Cruz. All came into sharp focus: the edges of palm trees, the outlines of *casitas*, the cross on the hill gleaming like a searchlight. And there it was: my old house.

I sat in the truck, overwhelmed, not ready to get out yet. The dust of our wake caught up with us, washed over us and down the street. "Guadalupe," Papá said, opening his door, "we're here." As if I didn't know that, as if I'd forgotten the house I had grown up in.

The gate was wide open. Inside, Mamá and Miguel were waiting for me, sitting in chairs in the garden. The laundry lines were like roads in the sky, a map to somewhere. The trees offered their *papel picado* type of shade, shot through with sunlight. When Mamá saw me she stood, smoothing her shirt and adjusting the long shorts she wore, tucking loose strands of hair behind her ears. As if I needed a mamá that was in perfect order, perfectly pressed. I just needed my mamá.

We put our arms around each other and held on tight. She smelled like cinnamon and soap. "Mamá," I whispered.

"*M'ija*," she whispered back. She smoothed my hair down my back.

When she released me, Miguel swept me up in his arms, spun me around, telling me I'd lost so much weight, he could fling me into the sky like a kite.

• • •

After dinner, *bien gorda* and heavy with Mamá's cooking, I went out into the garden, leaving everyone to watch *Agua Prieta*. I went to the barrel of ashes. I picked up a stick and poked around for a while, not really sure what I was looking for, if I was looking for anything at all. I felt like an archaeologist trying to make sense of a long-lost civilization.

"What are you doing, *m'ija*?" Mamá asked. She stood in the kitchen doorway.

"Just looking," I said. I stirred the ashes with my stick like they were soup, or a pot of *mole*. I remembered cooking *mole* with Mamá over an open fire outside for Ana and Eduardo's wedding. Mamá had given me a huge wooden spoon that resembled a paddle. I stirred with everything I had so the sauce wouldn't scorch.

My stick hit the things that hadn't properly burned: shards of glass and something that felt like a bottle. I tried to feel for an opening and put my stick through to hoist it up. But what I caught was something else, something that snagged. I pressed the stick to the side of the barrel and slid it up out of the ashes. It was so blackened and warped, it took me a minute to realize it was the chain with the cross that had shown up on Gabriela's neck one day. I held it up to get a better look.

Mamá had come up beside me. Her eyes were on the cross as it swung back and forth like a pendulum.

"She's not coming back, is she?" Mamá asked.

"She might," I said. "She'll do what she needs to."

"I hope she does," Mamá said, though she hardly needed to tell me that. I knew by the way she had hugged me and by the lines on her face, by the way her hands gripped the edge of the barrel, wanting to hold on to something.

I nodded. I hoped that we could build the house together, just the way we wanted it, with rooms to share and rooms apart, with a garden and trees and laughter and light—a place where we could say anything.

I dropped the necklace into the ash, pushed it with the stick to the bottom of the barrel.

# ACKNOWLEDGEMENTS

•••

Tremendous thanks is first due to my teachers, Keith Maillard and Steven Galloway, who guided this novel through its shaky first drafts. I'm also indebted to my fellow classmates in my fiction workshops at the University of British Columbia. All encouraged me—a poet—to write a novel, and helped me get my head around the world of fiction in general.

Renée Sundaram kept me going with her daily morning phone calls. Wayne Flower made me write in all circumstances. Artist Trust awarded me a grant. John Alexander Gibson supported me and my need to write throughout all. Shauny Jaine and Tana Materi have always believed. Daniel Ryan Smith kept me alive with dinners and friendship. Betty Ledlin encouraged me from the beginning. Sean and Laura Bolan are an incredible photographic team. Lee Henderson and Kevin Chong helped me overcome writing obstacles.

Lisa Coulthard and Stephen Toban provided me with writing spaces. Luis García helped me bridge the gap between cultures. My number-one fans at Old Growth Northwest sponsored readings. All of my dear friends and family have kept me above water—and have tolerated my disappearances when I needed to write. *Mil gracias* to the many strangers, friends, and family in Mexico who shared their stories and homes with me.

Toby Tortorelli, Gloria Fraser, Sylvie, Val, and Michèle and Alec de Rham conspired to provide me with a wonderful apartment in Vancouver, British Columbia, where I wrote the first drafts of this novel. Michèle de Rham read the manuscript when she was at the end of her life. She could've read anything, and I'm honoured that my book was one of the chosen.

Thanks to Rachelle Delaney, Bren Simmers, Jana Fernandes, Claire Tacon, Conrad Evarts, Renée Shimizu, and Mike Romoth for reading and commenting on one version or another of this novel. Extra-special thanks to Nathan Fowler, who read the manuscript multiple times and offered mind-shattering suggestions that changed the shape of the book for the better.

I'm indebted to Dean Cooke, my agent, who took me on, and Jane Warren, my editor, whose brainstorming sessions and brilliance helped push this novel into new territory. Thanks to Natalie Meditsky and her copyediting team for their fine-tuning. Everyone behind the HarperCollins/UBC Prize for Best New Fiction has made a huge difference in my life. I'm grateful to you all.

Works and knowledge of others were essential to this book. Oralia Gómez let me ask even the stupidest questions about her native Mexico City. David Lida's *First Stop in the New World* showed me a Mexico City I hadn't seen in my own explorations. Richard Rodriguez writes an excellent account of the Virgen de Guadalupe appearing to Juan Diego in his essay "India." Ramón "Tianguis" Pérez's *Diario de un mojado* gave me insight into the journey of a Oaxacan villager across the US-Mexico border. Ángel's tattoos were inspired by the artwork of Dr. Lakra. Pilar could not have been created without the help of Michael Zeigler. "The Girls Next Door" by Peter Landesman investigates sex-trafficking rings and sex slavery in Mexico. Lydia Cacho's difficult but important book, *Slavery Inc.*, helped me understand how a girl could suddenly find herself trapped in the world of sex slavery. The photographic work of Maya Goded was vital to me, particularly her exhibition *Plaza de la soledad* and her accompanying book, *Good Girls*, which includes raw, stunning photographs and stories of sex workers in the Merced district of Mexico City.

Without the love and support of my family, I would be lost. More thanks than I know how to give go to my parents, Tim and Gayl Bolan, and to my brother and sister, Eli and Emmilee Bolan. They listened to me blather incessantly about the novel and the process of writing. They read everything I sent them and shared all of my woes and triumphs.

Without all of you, this book would not exist.